THE COMPLETE CASES
OF STEVE MIDNIGHT, VOLUME 1

JOHN K. BUTLER

THE COMPLETE CASES OF
STEVE MIDNIGHT
VOLUME 1

JOHN K. BUTLER

INTRODUCTION BY
JOHN WOOLEY

ILLUSTRATIONS BY
JOHN FLEMING GOULD

ALTUS
PRESS

BOSTON • 2016

EDITED AND DESIGNED BY
Matthew Moring

PUBLISHING HISTORY
"Introduction" originally appeared in *At the Stroke of Midnight: Steve Midnight Stories*. Copyright 1998 by John Wooley. All rights reserved.
"The Dead Ride Free" originally appeared in the May, 1940 issue of *Dime Detective* magazine. Copyright 1940 by Popular Publications, Inc. Copyright renewed 1967 and assigned to Steeger Properties, LLC. All rights reserved.
"The Man from Alcatraz" originally appeared in the July, 1940 issue of *Dime Detective* magazine. Copyright 1940 by Popular Publications, Inc. Copyright renewed 1967 and assigned to Steeger Properties, LLC. All rights reserved.
"Hacker's Holiday" originally appeared in the October, 1940 issue of *Dime Detective* magazine. Copyright 1940 by Popular Publications, Inc. Copyright renewed 1967 and assigned to Steeger Properties, LLC. All rights reserved.
"The Saint in Silver" originally appeared in the January, 1941 issue of *Dime Detective* magazine. Copyright 1941 by Popular Publications, Inc. Copyright renewed 1968 and assigned to Steeger Properties, LLC. All rights reserved.

THANKS TO
Rebecca Burns, Joseph Laturnau and John Wooley

TABLE OF CONTENTS

INTRODUCTION
BY JOHN WOOLEY

"Which of you guys is the hacker they call Steve Midnight—on account of he's always in a jam when the cuckoo chirps twelve?"

—from "The Hearse from Red Owl"
by John K. Butler

IN **WHAT** were probably his last words ever to appear in a pulp magazine, John K. Butler wrote almost wistfully of his plans for the tenth adventure of a Southern California cabbie named Steven Middleton Knight—Steve Midnight, for short. "Regarding Steve Midnight," he noted in a special section of the January 1943 *Dime Detective* called "Thrill Rations," "in the last month, I've been able to chart a plot and write five pages—that's all."

Naturally, you don't want a story written with both eyes closed… and frankly, I don't know how long it will take to make a good job out of "The Wrong Night for Red Owl." Can only guarantee that Yours Truly is desperately anxious to ride again with Steve, and that Steve's Red Owl cab gets the green light during every spare—and rare—moment I can find. Steve has made it clear to me, in cab-corner language, that he doesn't want to die of old age.

Butler probably never finished the story, and if he did, it never saw print. The nine adventures collected here comprise the entire career of Butler's remarkable creation Steve Midnight, a man who lived his life, saw his sights, made his choices, and fought his fights between the glossy, garish covers of *Dime Detective,* a first-rate all-fiction magazine that also provided a home in the '30s and '40s for the hard-boiled yams of Raymond Chandler, Erle Stanley Gardner, Hugh B. Cave, Norbert Davis, and W.T. Ballard, among many others. Unlike these contemporaries, however, John K. Butler never jumped from the pulps to full-length books. In fact, regardless of his obvious talent for pacing and character, eye for detail, and appealingly tough prose style, Butler disappeared from the printed-word medium altogether in 1943.

The reason? It's in the editorial preface to his "Thrill Rations" letter, which appeared almost a year after the last Steve Midnight tale, "The Corpse That Couldn't Keep Cool," had enlivened *Dime Detective's* pages. "... (Y)ou may have been wondering what's happened to JOHN K. BUTLER and Steve Midnight, the hapless hacker from Red Owl, these many moons," wrote an unnamed editor. "Steve's cab is panting outside one of the big Hollywood studios while his lord and master, Butler, gets the cinema out of his system and winds up his contract with the moguls of the silver screen."

The studio was Republic, which occupied a niche somewhere between the crank-'em-out studios of Poverty Row and the haughty big-time dream factories—a little classier than Monogram and PRC, but not quite up there with M-G-M and 20th Century Fox. And as it turned out, Steve's creator never did get movies out of his system: Butler worked more or less full time as a Republic screenwriter until the late '50s, when the studio itself had all but expired. John K. Butler jumped to television and a few assignments for other movie studios; Steve Midnight's Red Owl cab never rolled again.

BORN IN San Francisco on March 24, 1908, Butler grew up in the northern California town of Auburn, "in the Sierra Nevada mountains, the historic country of the California Gold Rush," as he put it in a biographical sketch printed in the November 1935 issue of *Dime Detective.* Later, he headed south to Los Angeles, although it's unclear whether he went with his family or by himself. As he put it in the bio, "This is always the most traitorous move a native San Franciscan can make. Frisco, forgive me; I'm still fond of the Old Town."

Although he claimed that his earliest ambition was to be a cable-car gripman, and noted that he'd worked as a mail clerk and automobile salesman, it was clear that fictioneering was in his blood:

> …Started writing stories as a kid. Enthusiastically wrote my way through, and almost out of, several schools. My university experience was largely fall attendance at football games….
>
> Once went to New York with the intention of taking magazine offices by storm; had an idea my services would be invaluable to some lucky editorial staff. But no storm darkened the Manhattan sky, no job opened, and magazines were published just as when Butler lived three thousand miles away.

It's in this sketch, also, that he mentions working for the movies, a good decade before he signed on at Republic. He writes of taking a voyage to Europe "on some Hollywood-earned gold," and continues:

> Somewhere along the line I started work in Hollywood movie

studios—not acting, though I once picked up a few bucks that way. My work in the flicker factories was with stories, both editorial and writing ends of the game, and mostly the former.

Altogether I did about an eight-year stretch at this.

In an *American Fiction Guild Bulletin,* probably published that same year, he elaborated on his early film career in a similar piece:

> Sooner or later Hollywood enters the life of every writer. The routine is that you begin by writing plays, books, criticisms, magazine stuff, poems, or obituaries, practically anything except movie scripts, and then some producer get a momentary idea he can't make a picture without you. So you trek west-ward to be disillusioned. I seem to be reversing the routine. Got my disillusioning first. Started story work in a flicker-factory some years ago. Was on the editorial staff of several studios. Had my fling at penning scenarios—which is the one experience I can't crowd into this thumbnail. Get me tight some night and learn why. I'm rather new—hope not too green—at magazine writing. But, after about 8 hectic years of Hollywood battle, I find contact with editors, an agent and fellow scribes very normal and pleasant. You would, too.

Although Butler probably worked in silent pictures, and was undoubtedly around the business in the early days of the talkies, little is known of his first run at picture-making. In his essential pulp-detective study *The Dime Detectives* (Mysterious Press, 1988), author Ron Goulart indicates that Butler broke into films "in the late 1920s, after getting hired as a reader for Universal"; a search of pre-1935 film credits hasn't turned up any bearing his name.

Butler's son Mark, born in 1945, believes that his mother, Florence, worked in the film business—and may have met his father during this period. "If I had to guess, I would say they met at a studio," he says. "I have no idea what my mother did there, or when she was there, or where she was. She never talked about it. The only thing I know about her is that she had a degree in math from Columbia in New York."

In the early '40s, when Butler began his second tenure in the movie biz, most of America still had the romantic notion that working for a Tinsletown dream factory was just about the swellest job a person could have. In his "Thrill Rations" letter for the January '43 *Dime Detective,* however, he pointed up the downside of his new job in a couple of paragraphs enlivened with typical Butler hyperbole:

> Whoever once shot his mouth off to the effect that Hollywood was a soft touch for writers… that guy had it all wrong. Minimum hours are from nine to six—and I haven't met a writer yet who can get his work done in those hours.
>
> I drive forty miles per day to be present at the studio, driving carefully on tires that can't be replaced [because of wartime rationing], most of the mileage over a twisting mountain road. I find I need an average of an hour and a half to two hours for the daily trip. I also need breakfast, but often have to skip it in order to spring out of the corner at the bell for the first round. By dinner time—often as late as 10 p.m.—I'm usually such a nervous wreck my wife has to put me to bed and feed me hot soup through a glass straw. (We gave up glass straws after chattering teeth accidentally ate a few.)

In those years, Republic Studios was a humming movie machine. Although the company released an occasional prestige picture—Orson Welles' version of *Macbeth* in 1948, Lewis Milestone's take on Steinbeck's book *The Red Pony* in 1949, and a number of big-dollar pictures from the cranky but brilliant John Ford—it kept the gears greased and the rural movie screens lit with more modest fare, primarily westerns and serials, written by solid craftsmen who knew the conventions of their genres and could crank out a screenplay quickly and on order, like building a cabinet.

Butler jumped into the westerns immediately. In 1943, the year after his last story appeared in the pulps, he got story and screenplay credit on four Republic oaters, including a Roy Rogers vehicle *(Silver Spurs)*, a Three Mesquiteers feature *(The Blocked Trail)*, the debut entry in Republic's "John Paul Revere" series *(Beyond the Last Frontier)* and an intriguing little Eddie Dean starrer featuring a group of cowgirls called the Women's Army of the Plains, hired by the government as law-enforcement agents because of the World War II manpower shortage *(Raiders of Sunset Pass)*. In his 15-year affiliation with Republic, Butler would knock out as many as seven screenplays a year, working in a potpourri of genres—mostly westerns, but also crime *(Post Office Investigator, Streets of San Francisco, I Cover the Underworld)*, horror *(Vampire's Ghost, The Phantom Speaks)*, drama *(G.I. War Brides, Pride of Maryland)* and comedy *(Tell It to a Star, The Main Street Kid)*. In 1953, he even helped adapt a couple of stories by his old *Dime Detective* compadre W.T. Ballard into a John Derek western called *The Outcast*. (For a fuller treatment of Butler's movie career, see Popular Press' *Hardboiled in Hollywood* by David Wilt, which features a whole chapter on Butler and his films.)

Like his first, his last screen credit was for a western, 1958's *Ambush at Cimarron Pass*, a 20th Century Fox picture with a young up-and-comer named Clint Eastwood third-billed. By that time, Butler was also finding plenty of work in television; he continued doing teleplays for major-studio series until his death, on September 18,1964. Not surprisingly, a lot of his small-screen work was in the western genre, although his best-known teleplay was probably a 1962 episode of *The Defenders* called "The Legend of Jim Riva." Written with Boyd Correll, it was nominated for an Edgar by the Mystery Writers of America, coming in as runner-up to a *Kraft Mystery Theater.*

Of course, the western-fiction image of the strong tough cowboy taking it upon himself to make things right against big odds has much in common with the hard-boiled pulp detective, so maybe it's natural that Butler made such an easy transition from writing one to writing the other. According to Butler's sons, the transition was personal as well.

"He had a horse in those days, named Prince, a big black horse, and he would take me riding," says Butler's younger son Rod, a Texas-based writer, musician, minister, and creator of *Funlight Radio,* a kids' show heard on nearly 200 stations worldwide. "And, you know, that was *him.* The whole cowboy thing was not just a career for him—it was his career, but it wasn't nine to five. It was what he did. In the pictures I have of him, that's how he dressed. He'd get into his jeans and his cowboy hat and his boots."

"This horse… if you looked in the dictionary under 'swayback,' you'd see his picture," adds Mark Butler, a Colorado-based computer expert, with a laugh. "It was lovable, but dilapidated. When I came down to live with him in '61, he had it, and he got along wonderfully with it. He rode all over Griffith Park with this horse. In fact, he broke his back riding that horse.

"He used to love riding up there, because everyone knew him. With all the mounted police, it was, 'Hi, John. Howya doin'?' And he got his thinking time, his alone time, by doing that.

"So he was on a trail up in Griffith Park, coming down, and there was a piece of hose on the trail. The horse thought it was a snake, stopped on a dime, and my dad went right over its head and landed flat on his back. He didn't know that he had done anything to his back, and he got up and dusted himself off. I forget whether he rode back or walked back, but he went back, took the saddle off, the whole bit. Drove back home. He was divorced then, and he had a girlfriend, and they were going out someplace. So he took a shower, got dressed, and called her and said, 'Okay. I'm ready to go when you are.' And he sat down in his big leather chair and waited. She came over and said, 'Okay. Let's go.' And he said, 'Um… I don't think I can.'

"She asked why not, and he said, 'Because I don't think I can get up.' They ended up hauling him out on a stretcher and taking him to the hospital. He was in traction for a couple of days, and he had to take it easy for a long time, wear a brace and all that stuff."

Butler was living the bachelor life in a Studio City apartment at the time, and he was there when he died. But in the early '50s, after he had divorced Mark's mother and remarried, he was living in the L.A. suburb of Sherman Oaks.

"He and my mother got a divorce when I was about three, so that'd be '47 or '48," recalls Mark. "I lived with my mother and went over and saw him whenever she'd let me. I really looked forward to those times.

"He was remarried then, and they had a little house that was a perfect writer's house. It was a one-bedroom two-story, and his writing studio was over the garage."

Mark visited his father regularly until 1955, when he left the home of his troubled mother and went to live with her sister in Seattle. But in those pre-1955 days, he met a couple of his dad's friends who have stuck in his memory to this day.

"John Tucker Battle and Ron Davidson," he says. "I've never forgotten their names, and I don't know why. I know that Ron Davidson had a sailboat—I think it was down at the Balboa Bay Club—and one of the times I was visiting, my dad took me down there and we went on this sailboat. We didn't go out on it, but they sat around and talked, and had a couple of highballs or something, and I got to look around the boat.

"I remember almost exactly where the Battles lived," he adds. "We went up there once or twice while I was visiting. But being that little then, 10 or 11 or less, I don't really have any idea what he did."

What he did, as you might imagine, was what Mark's father and Ronald Davidson did, which was write for the movies. All three had ties to Republic: Davidson was one of the lot's busiest writers, singlehandedly scripting each episode of such later Republic serials as *Jungle Drums of Africa* (1953) and *Panther Girl of the Congo* (1955) as well as B-features like *Daredevils of the Clouds* (1948) and *Range Justice* (1949). Battle's work includes *A Man Alone,* the 1955 Ray Milland starrer for Republic that also marked Milland's directorial debut.

Rod Butler recalls that his dad also palled around with the character actor Eddy Waller, veteran of many a Republic B-western. "Doris Waller was my godmother, and Eddy was her husband," notes Rod. "When I started knowing him, he was already older and retired. He was always just Uncle Eddy."

Butler and Waller undoubtedly met through Republic, perhaps on the set of the 1943 Roy Rogers western *Silver Spurs*, which Butler co-wrote with J. Benton Cheney. Certainly, Butler met his second wife, Rod's mother, during the course of his work at the studio. "My mom, Marguerite, was Czechoslovakian, a skinny, wiry, woman with an accent and blonde hair," says Rod. "She was a script editor, or at least a reader, when they met. That seems humorous to me, that English would be her second language and that she would be employed as a script reader. But she was good. She was very grammatical and all.

"My mom was unsentimental. I mean, she did not keep a scrapbook. She did not keep photographs. She would throw everything away. And she was extremely talkative. I might say compulsively talkative." He laughs. "It's funny to me that the two of them got together. I don't know how long they were married, but for a man who needed solitude to work and a woman who was incapable of not talking, I think it's amazing how they got along."

When John and Marguerite Butler lived in Sherman Oaks, the Wallers were their neighbors. Later, after John and Marguerite were divorced, Rod still spent time with the Wallers. "In 1960, when I came down to visit over the summer, my dad introduced me to Rod," says Mark with a chuckle. "He'd never mentioned him before that, and I'd never asked. I never knew! So we drove out to the Wallers' house over in Sherman Oaks, Rod comes out, and my dad says, 'That's your brother.'" Mark laughs. "I said, 'Oh. Okay.' It was an interesting family."

When Mark came to stay with his dad for good in '61, he began sharing the Studio City apartment. Says Rod Butler, who joined them on weekends, "It was on Moore Park, in a little grouping of bungalow apartments. I can see in my mind this little front room—a dinky little apartment with two bedrooms, or maybe three. I'd go there every other weekend, and part of the deal was get there and be quiet."

"He was very particular, having not had kids living around him for a long time," adds Mark, "and he wasn't sure how to handle that. We had things divided up into his and mine. When I started working, I started buying my own food, so he labeled the shelves in the refrigerator, 'John's Shelf and 'Mark's Shelf.'"

Mark laughs again. "There was a little open area about two-thirds of the way up the wall as you went from the kitchen into the living room, and that's where his desk was, where he worked. I was working second shift out at Rockadyne in Canoga Park, and one day I was having my favorite breakfast, bacon and eggs, before I went in. I put the bacon on, and went into the shower, and when I came out I heard him say, 'Mark I think the bacon's done! I came out into the living room, and there's smoke filling the entire room! But he wasn't about to go into the kitchen and touch it, you know. He just sat in that smoke bank, yelling at me that it was done.

"Once, in winter, the pilot went out on the heater. And he had absolutely no idea of how to get it back on. He was going to call the gas company. I said, 'I can light it. It's okay.' I was, I think, 18.

So he says, 'Well, that's good.' And with that he goes into the hallway, closes the hall door, goes into his bedroom, closes the bedroom door, gets down on the floor on the far side of the bed and says, Okay! Go ahead and light it!' I was laughing so hard I could hardly light the thing."

At the time, their father owned a 1955 Thunderbird convertible. Mark remembers its color as turquoise, Rod as light green; both believe that he bought it new. "He had a peculiar way of driving and thinking at the same time," notes Rod. "He'd have his right hand kind of straight-armed on the wheel of the T-Bird, at 12 o'clock, and he'd have his other hand on his chin. I didn't know if he was driving or creating. Or doing both, simultaneously."

"He was one of the world's most aggravating drivers," adds Mark with a laugh. "He'd drive down Ventura Boulevard, he'd be on the gas, and off the gas, on the gas, and off the gas, well under the speed limit. God help us if we got on a freeway. We'd go through Malibu Canyon, and we'd have a line behind us—it was amusing, but a little aggravating, too.

"Sometime in late '63 or early '64, I bought a new car. I was working, and had all kinds of money—or so I thought—and I got this nasty Dodge Polara that had all kinds of horsepower. Then, in August of '64, I had to go toddling off to boot camp. And I told him, 'Gee, I really screwed up. I got this thing, and I've got no way to pay for it while I'm in the Army.' He'd gotten the engine replaced in the Thunderbird a year or two earlier; the cylinders were falling off because they never got blown out.

"He came to my rescue. He told me he'd take over the Dodge and pay for it, and I could take the T-Bird until I went into the Army, which wasn't all that long. And one day I was on the Ventura Freeway, tooling along in the Thunderbird past the on-ramp at Laurel Canyon—and here comes my dad up the ramp like Stirling Moss. He's going to Burbank to ride, and he's got his ten-gallon cowboy hat on, so he's slouched down in the seat because it's hitting the roof. And he's coming off that ramp like the cops are chasing him! I thought, 'He's gonna *kill* himself!'"

Mark laughs again. "Not long after that, he'd gone somewhere, and he wasn't supposed to be gone that long, but he was gone forever. I guess there'd been an accident on the freeway. Finally, he comes in, takes his hat off, whaps it against his leg like John Wayne, and says, 'Boy, they're really slammin' around out there today!'" I thought, '*They are?*'"

Both Mark and Rod share other memories of their father, of his love of the sea, reflected in their outings and the seafood restaurants he took them to; of the three of them watching *Twilight Zone* and *The Outer Limits* on a television Rod describes as "one of those classic TVs, where the tube is unboxed and upright, like a big eyeball looking at you." And, of course, they both remember how he worked.

"I think of my dad there at the typewriter—typing, typing, typing," says Rod. "I remember, too, that he didn't type in the traditional technique. He was a hunt-and-peck typer, and when you add that into how many words he must've pumped out...."

"While I was living with him, he was collaborating with another writer named Lou Houston," adds Mark. "I'd be in the other room watching TV, and they'd be working, and I'd hear them *laughing* out there—they'd get off on some tangent, and go off from the sublime to the ridiculous. They'd just laugh until they hurt."

By the early '60s, Butler had left Republic and was freelancing for various television shows; Mark believes he was happier then, working at home, than he'd been in his office at Republic. He certainly wasn't the type to flaunt his show-biz connections, staying out of the Hollywood scene and never even taking his kids to visit the sets of his pictures. "I remember when I was little, in the early '50s, we'd go down to the Studio City Theater, and you could see Republic from there," Mark says. "I just remember him saying 'that's where I work' or something. But he never took me in there."

Butler was only 56 when he died, suddenly and unexpectedly. Perhaps it's ironic that his love of horses, undoubtedly fueled by the cowboy pictures that provided a good part of his living for two decades, probably ended up killing him. "The guess is that it was a side effect of his breaking his back when the horse threw him," says Mark. "When that happened, I remember him mumbling and grumbling and grousing because the doctor told him, 'You really screwed up your back, John. Don't ride anymore. It's not good.' Well, he kept the horse, and started riding again. He waited quite a while, but he really wanted to get back and ride.

"I was at basic training up at Fort Ord in Monterey when it happened. They flew me out, I got down to L.A., and I found out that he'd passed away. He had been out riding, and he came back and just collapsed. Wham. Over. The guess is that there was still a blood clot there and the riding shook it loose. It went to his head and gave him an aneurysm, and he keeled right over."

At the time, Mark adds, his father had been, for years, active in Alcoholics Anonymous. "Somewhere along the line, he'd had difficulty with alcohol, but how bad it was and whether it affected his work I really don't know," he says. "He was going to meetings and everything, but he seemed to handle it really well. It didn't seem like it was really, really hard for him, and if it was, you wouldn't have known it. He was more concerned about helping other people. We'd be sitting around watching TV or something, and he'd get a phone call. Someone would be upset about something and about to go off the wagon, and he'd go driving off into the night, pick 'em up, and go down to the AA place where they'd have coffee and talk. He did a lot of that, and it was really nice. That was kind of a neat side I saw of him."

The same side surely that Rod, ten years Mark's junior and a weekend visitor to the Sherman Oaks apartment, saw as well. "I would come over to these little apartments, and he would type, and then he would take me out. He'd take me riding or to the seafood places—I remember looking at the tanks with the fish swimming in them—or to Pacific Ocean Park. He wasn't talkative, but he was very loving, and we had a great relationship. He called me Rod-Pal, and that's stuck with me ever since."

AND THEN there was the middle of John K. Butler's life, between the movies and before either child. The years 1935–41 were his pulp years, and they began, fittingly enough, in Popular Publications' *Dime Detective,* the magazine that would become his biggest showcase. The April 1 issue (the book was so popular at the time that it came out twice-monthly) of *Dime Detective* carried a tale called "Murder Alley," which the editors later said was Butler's first published piece of fiction. It was also the introduction of Rex Lonergan, a hard-boiled dick based in Butler's hometown and known as "Lonergan of Frisco."

A little less than a year later, he'd begin another series for the magazine, this one featuring a character named Tricky Enright, an ostensible crook who's actually an undercover op for the governor of California. Both characters alternated in stories for *Dime Detective* until 1940, when the May issue debuted his new creation, cabbie Steve Midnight, in the wonderfully titled "The Dead Ride Free."

Meanwhile, Butler was also knocking out some terrific work for other pulp magazines, including *Double Detective, Detective Fiction Weekly,* and *Black Mask.* The latter magazine, for which Butler wrote four tales about General Pacific Telephone troubleshooter Rod Case along with creating several one-off characters, had been responsible for kicking off the whole hard-boiled genre a few years earlier; it was *Dime Detective's* biggest rival up until the time Popular Publications bought it and it became a sister publication. In most of these magazines, Butler's writing not only adheres to the conventions of the "tough" school of crime fiction, but also gives us some indication of the poet's eye brought into the genre by Raymond Chandler, Butler's neighbor and friend. David Geherin, in his book *The American Private Eye: The Image in Fiction* (Frederick Unger, 1985) points out two "notable qualities" that infuse Butler's writing—his plot development and attention to detail—and also recognizes his skill with characters and pacing.

In addition to all that, there is in Butler's work an appealing mixture of sentimentality and toughness. The old saying about scratching a cynic and finding a romantic underneath plays itself out again and again in his stories; certainly, every one of the Steve Midnight tales has two approaches running through them. In a tough, hardscrabble world, eking out a living by driving a cab at odd hours for odd people, forever besieged by criminals, crooks, and come-on artists and harassed by a heartless dispatcher named Pat Regan, Steve Midnight still finds himself pulled along by big-R romantic notions of how things ought to be, and what he can do to make them so, even if he knows his efforts will probably never be appreciated, much less rewarded.

This hard-edged sentimentality runs through all of his work, stories and scripts alike. In addition to the Midnight stories, two great examples are the short story "The Cop From Yesterday," which appeared in the September 28, 1940, issue of the pulp *Detective Fiction Weekly*, and the 1949 Republic B-movie *Streets of San Francisco*, which he scripted from a story by Tinsletown vets Gordon Kahn and Adele Buffington.

"The Cop From Yesterday" is set in Sacramento (not far from where Butler grew up) during a festival called the Days of the Forty-Nine, celebrating California's gold-rush era. The narrator is a deputy sheriff from Montana, taking in the celebration from a barber's chair, who frames the tale by speculating aloud about an old guy in a touring car, riding along in the parade with the Sacramento police.

> He was probably the oldest, weariest man I've seen in my life, with a thin stem face, deeply lined, and snow-white hair. He wasn't wearing any kind of uniform, just a plain gray suit, and I wondered what he was doing in the police unit of the parade.
>
> "That's Bill Bogard," the barber told me.
>
> "Honorary Lieutenant of Detectives."
>
> "Local hero?" I asked.
>
> "In a way, I guess."
>
> "Too old to walk?"
>
> "Him?" The barber eyed me sharply. "Not too old. And he wouldn't like to hear you say that, either. He'd like to walk with the rest of the cops, I guess. I bet he'd like to be on his feet right now, marching with 'em. But he can't. He hasn't got any legs."

From there, Butler deftly weaves the tale of Bogard, forced to retire from the police department he loves and instead take a dull job as watchman at a riverfront ware-house. He eventually becomes pals with a steamboat pilot, another old fellow at the end of his career, and they begin sharing twice-weekly nips from the pilot's flask. But when two crooks drug the pilot's liquor and take a blackjack to Bogard, the latter gets fired for drinking on the job and threatened with arrest by the warehouse owner. After the police captain rebuffs his request to become a special deputy, Bogard tracks down the hoods and outsmarts them—but not before he gets his legs blasted away in a bloody melee. The story ends at the same point as the beginning, with old Bogard, having at least temporarily cheated both age and infirmity, riding proudly past.

> I heard some cheering at the corner, and when I glanced down that way I saw a gang of kids yelling enthusiastically from the curb. They seemed to be cheering the victor of a World War, but the old man just made faces at them and thumbed his nose.
>
> "Who are those kids?" I asked.
>
> "Those are his grandchildren," the barber said.

An oldster—along with a kid—also lies at the heart of *Streets of San Francisco,* in which hard-boiled Frisco cop Willard Logan (Robert Armstrong) takes in crook's kid Frankie Fraser (Gary Gray) after killing his old man. The cop doesn't care anything about the kid, but he hopes the little delinquent will be able to lead him to the rest of the gang and some stolen cash.

Meanwhile, Logan's childless wife, Hazel (Mae Clark) and her father, kindly old Pop Lockhart (J. Farrell Mc-Donald), befriend the young tough. Not knowing her husband's real motive in bringing Frankie home, Hazel starts pushing for adoption. But just about the time the straight life starts looking okay to Frankie, he discovers Logan's true motives, and ankles the Logan setup, searching out the remnants of his dad's gang—none of whom are exactly finalists for Surrogate Father of the Year, either. They even whack old Pop around, despite Frankie's protests. In a windup that deftly manipulates emotions both hard and soft, Logan takes on the crooks, who've made a hostage of the kid, as the little wise guy shouts words of encouragement—"Come on, copper! Come on!"—to his old nemesis.

Granted, exposing the soft center under the hard shell was a common melodramatic device in the films and other popular literature of the period, but it's still fun to watch a master like John K. Butler reinvent the idea that, underneath it all, maybe we're not so bad at that. It's a message that could use a Butler to deliver it right now, when so much entertainment and so many stories seem irredeemably brutal and coarse, absent of the leavening of humanity once taken for granted but now awfully hard to find. And the world could use a few more cabbies like Steve Midnight. Although the riders he picked up during those fog-enshrouded nights in a long-gone California usually turned out to be sinister, or on the lam, or even dead, everyone—even the corpses—got a fair shake. Maybe you'd expect nothing less from a former rich boy who'd straightened himself up with no whining after years spent blowing his dead pop's fortune, taking a job as a cabdriver to support his mother and plunging into a world that often seemed to be lined up solidly against him, from his remarkably cranky dispatcher to the pairs of detectives from Malibu or L.A. who were forever hauling him in for rubber-hose facials.

But Steve Midnight persevered. And there was never any question that he'd do what he knew to be right, even if he thought and talked cynically about it while he was doing it, even if his life seemed always to be stuffed with psychotic no-goods and beautiful women who'd lie to you just for practice. In Butler's Steve Midnight stories, we find the shining heart of the hard-boiled detective, shimmering inside a good guy in an often-crummy world—a man who's a source of hope to the hopeless, a shot at redemption for all who dare to trust. Steve Midnight is the essence of the hard-boiled crusader, distilled beautifully by John K. Butler into stories that still crackle with excitement and resonate with images rich enough to taste.

And now, after all these years, the Red Owl cab's back on the road, its underpaid and under-appreciated good guy once again at the wheel, ferrying big-band musicians and old vaudevillians, suspicious blondes and worried little wives, war heroes and thorough heels, crackpot religionists and grim-faced killers, through an evocative, almost dream-like, place and time.

Finally, Steve Midnight's back… and wherever we are, we've got him for good.

John Wooley
Foyil, Oklahoma
March 29, 1998

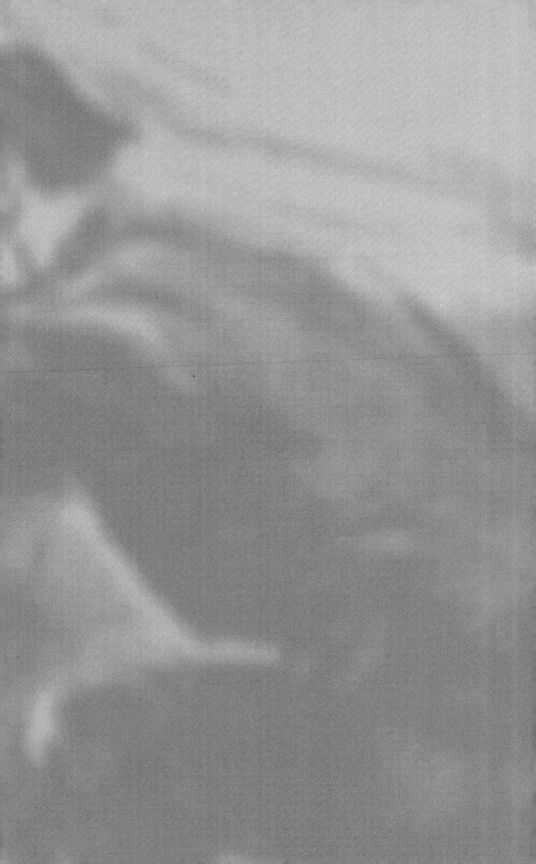

THE DEAD RIDE FREE

INTRODUCING STEVE MIDNIGHT, HACKER EXTRAORDINARY FOR THE RED OWL CAB COMPANY, AND HIS AMAZING FARE, ZOHAR THE GREAT. STEVE HAD SEEN ZOHAR WORK HIS MAGIC ON THE THREE-A-DAY VAUDEVILLE CIRCUITS, BUT THE TURBANED MYSTIC HAD NEVER BAMBOOZLED HIM SO THOROUGHLY FROM THE STAGE AS HE DID THE NIGHT HE PRODUCED A BLOND CORPSE INSTEAD OF THE CUSTOMARY RABBITS FROM HIS GIMMICK COFFIN—RIGHT IN THE BACK SEAT OF STEVE'S OWN HACK.

CHAPTER ONE
ZOHAR THE GREAT

IT WAS one of those chill nights you so often get on the Coast in the winter—too cold to rain, never cold enough to snow. The sky was cloudless and you could see every star in it, millions of them, all standing out with the sparkle of diamonds and the color of bright gold.

I sat at my cab station on the coldest corner this side of the Finnish front, and wished I was off duty, or that I had a fare. I also wished I had a drink.

That last wish was just as futile as the others—even more so—because I used to have a pretty large reputation for drinking and the Red Owl Cab Company would can me in a minute if they thought I took a snifter while on duty.

So there was nothing I could do but just sit there and slowly freeze to death. I was making a pretty good job of it, too, with my coat collar turned up to my chin, hands sunk deep in pockets, when a lone man came briskly along the sidewalk. I thought he was going right by and I didn't pay much attention until he stopped at the cab and spoke.

"Are you engaged?" he asked.

"Not at the moment."

I touched the visor of my cap and opened the rear door for him.

"Topanga Canyon," he said. "What's the fare?"

"About a dollar sixty. Depends on how far up the canyon you want to go."

"All right," he said.

I heaved the mummy at him.

HE WAS a queer-looking duck—too tall, too lean. I'll bet he stood over six-foot-four in his socks, and right now he wore trim black patent-leather shoes with lifts in the heels that gave him extra inches. He was thin as a skeleton and wore a silk turban wrapped around his head that added another six inches to his height. There was a sparkling ornament on the front of it, bright as the shield on a cop's cap. His face was dark and thin and negroid. His eyes were set deep under shaggy brows and a barbered little beard graced the tip of his chin.

I tried to remember where I'd seen him before. It seemed like a hundred years ago. Then memory pictures came back from the past, and I said: "You're Zohar the Great."

"Thank you, young man." His smile exposed a brief flash of gleaming white teeth against the leathery dark of his face. "Your recognition is the acme of flattery, young man. Have you visited my Temple on the amusement pier?"

"No," I said. "The last time I saw you was up in San Francisco at the old Alcazar Theater. I was about ten years old at the time. You put a woman in a coffin and sawed her in half."

He chuckled reminiscently. "Really? You remember that?"

"Sure. And I saw you a couple of times on the old Orpheum Circuit. You sawed a blond woman in two, and told fortunes from a crystal ball. You could even tell what a person in the audience had in his pockets. I was a kid then, and it used to drive me nuts trying to figure out how you did it."

He rolled gaunt mysterious eyes to the roof of the cab. "Lord, how time passes! You say you were a child of ten? Good Lord!"

I'd stuck my foot in it, all right. I hadn't intended to insult him about his age, yet I knew it must've been nearly twenty years ago when I first saw him do his stuff. Besides the business with the blonde and the coffin he'd take live rabbits out of silk hats, and coins from the atmosphere—

enough to tinkle in a bucket. He used to be the biggest box-office attraction in vaudeville. A top-notcher even in the days of Harry Houdini, or Thurston, and all those other old-time headliners.

And now I had him in my cab, a hero from my kid days.

I said: "I'm pleased to see you again, Mr. Zohar."

"Thank you, my dear boy. Thank you very much."

His voice was deep and somber and theatrical, and a little bored. He said he wanted to go to Topanga Canyon, but first he wanted to know if I made an extra charge for baggage.

"No," I told him.

"The baggage I have in mind," he said, "is a few small cases and a box. The box is rather a large item. Weighs about a hundred and fifty pounds. If you're unable to take it, I'll get an express company."

I told him I'd take the box for no extra charge. After all, I had a fare at last and I was glad to accommodate him. Maybe the tip would be good, and certainly I didn't want any tips slipping through my fingers.

"Can you drive out on the pier?" he asked.

"At this time of night? Sure."

OUR TOWN, Pacific Park, is a suburb of Los Angeles and located on the beach. Our main street is rather honkey-tonk, crowded with beer parlors and night clubs and cheap restaurants and cheaper hotels, and it leads straight down to the pier. This—built out half a mile over the water—is sort of a western Coney Island, with shooting-galleries, roller-coasters, merry-go-rounds, a penny dance pavilion, and lots of ways for spending nickels and dimes. In the summer time they do a big business, and even in winter most of the concessions stay open to catch the tourist trade. But in the winter they don't stay open past midnight.

It was well past midnight now when I drove my cab out on the pier.

There was no sign of activity. The colored lights had gone out on all the concessions. The hot-dog and peanut stands had closed, and there was just a lone hungry alley cat on the prowl.

I drove slowly along the midway till my passenger tapped me delicately on the shoulder with a long thin hand. "Here we are," he said. "You'll have to help me with the box."

We got out in front of another dark concession which had its ticket office covered with canvas. In the frail light from the headlamps of the cab a poster showed up an oil portrait of my passenger. He wore the silk turban, the ornament gleaming in it, and he was in the act of gazing ponderously into a crystal. The poster said: "SEE HIM IN PERSON! ZOHAR THE GREAT! FACE YOUR FUTURE UNDER THE GUIDANCE OF THIS MYSTIC OF THE UNKNOWN! COME ONE, COME ALL. ZOHAR THE GREAT. LIMITED EN-GAGEMENT!"

Zohar the Great—in person—now unlocked the door and took me inside. He flipped a switch and dim yellow lights came on. We were in a square room draped with a cyclorama of black curtains which contained only a ped-estal bearing a ponderous crystal ball the size of a giant honey-dew melon. He slipped the ball into a canvas bag with leather grips like keglers use to carry their pet bowl-ing-balls, and led me into another room draped with more black curtains.

Here a few packed bags and suitcases stood neatly in a corner, and there was a flat coffin placed on a black platform.

"This is the box," he said. "Snap the padlocks."

The coffin was slim and long, and engraved with ancient Egyptian hieroglyphics. It didn't look heavy. On the side of it were steel fasteners and padlocks. The padlocks had already been snapped.

"It's locked," I said.

"Fine," he said. "Mr. Martini must've locked it."

I carried the light luggage out to the cab, and then came back for the box. He had to help me with that, because it seemed to weigh at least the hundred and fifty pounds he ascribed to it, and more.

As we labored out to the cab with it, I said: "Feels like there's a body in this thing."

"There is," he told me somberly.

"Really?" I missed a step.

"Yes. A body three thousand years old…."

TO GET to Topanga Canyon from Pacific Park you drive through Santa Monica and take the Roosevelt Highway. That's a wide paved road, sometimes four and six lanes, following the coastline to San Francisco. We followed it for only a few miles and then turned up the canyon off of it, and up a narrow twisting road into the hills.

My meter ticked off two dollars, two-ten, two-twenty, and then, following directions, I drove up another steep dirt road past a gas station.

The station, lighted, with the attendant sitting inside the glass enclosure reading a magazine, was our last contact with the sleepless world. We went straight up a mountain in the cab, and the house of Zohar squatted on the lonely crest. There was no sound but the song of crickets and distantly the wash of the surf on the beach. All the crests of the mountains stood up lonely and black against the cold star-studded sky.

We got the luggage out of the cab, carried it into the house, and Zohar the Great lit some lights.

He lived in a crazy kind of shack, decorated in a way which could easily give you the delirium tremens without benefit of alcohol. The pine walls were painted dark and plastered everywhere with theatrical photographs of himself. Publicity poses of him on the stage, sawing a woman in half—shots of him shackled in torture chains, sweat beading his narrow brow—poses of him, half-naked, nailed to a wall, while snakes coiled about his legs. It was the damndest place I'd ever seen in my life. The ash trays were imitation human skulls, the tops sawed off, and a wax hand, bloody at the wrist, was the magician's quaint idea of a neat little gag for holding a humidor of cigarettes.

"Care for a drink?" he invited.

I told him it was against the rules, but that I might take just a light one. He served imported brandy, and it was so good that I accepted another, because it was convenient to forget, temporarily, the rules of the Red Owl Cab Company.

"I've had good fortune tonight," he said. "Just came from a conference with my theatrical agent. He's scheduled an important engagement for me in San Francisco, so I'm closing at the pier."

He tossed down a deep slug of brandy, poured himself another, and smacked his lips over that one. He was certainly no piker when it came to drinking.

"Well," he said, "let's get that box in."

We lugged in the coffin and placed it on a studio couch wide enough for a dozen Roman orgies, and somberly draped in black velvet.

I tapped the top of the coffin and said: "You mean it's some kind of a mummy in here?"

"Exactly, young man. But it's not just *some kind*. I purchased it five years ago. Cost me plenty, but I've found it an aid to my performance. A decided advantage as a museum piece. And a beautiful representation of the historic art of Egyptian mummification. This particular corpse, as near as can be judged, was embalmed and wrapped sometime during the Age of Rameses II, or about 1300 B.C. Are you interested?"

Naturally I was interested. There was this bottle of brandy on the table, and maybe if I stuck around and showed interest in his mummy, he might crack out another light snifter. I told myself that it wasn't that I was getting the habit again. It was just that it was a chilly night and I needed another one for warmth.

He said: "Let me give you a treat, young man."

I thought he meant another brandy, and it was a great disappointment to me when he just got out a ring of keys and unlocked the mummy case to "treat me to a view of a three-thousand year-old corpse." He opened the cover of the case, and then he shuddered, and for a flashing moment I thought he might be sick. He stared gauntly into the coffin.

"God.... It's Anna.... It's Anna.... Good Lord!"

I looked down into the case, and it wasn't any mummy. It hadn't been dead three thousand years, either. It probably hadn't been dead more than three hours.

SHE LAY flat on her back, arms at her sides. She was young, not much over twenty, and she had a small body that maybe didn't weigh a hundred pounds. She had the lithe curves of a professional dancer, and her hair was honey blond, and her features were small and smooth and perfect. She wore a green silk dress that fit her body snugly, and the hilt of a dagger protruded from between her breasts, leaving a stain with the effect of a corsage of red roses. Her eyes were blue and wide-open and dead.

I said something dumb then. I said: "Do you know her?"

"Yes… of course…."

For an instant I thought it might be some of his magic, like sawing the lady in half, like any other of his trick specialties, but that was only a fleeting thought. There couldn't be any trick about this. The worried strain of his face proved that. So did my own eyes.

"She's dead," he said. "Good God!"

His eyes glanced away from her and stayed away, lost in thought. Then, shrugging off whatever shock he felt, he became again the calm self-assured showman, unruffled by this sharpest of realism. He took a drink of brandy, without hand-tremble, and picked up his overcoat and his silver-headed cane.

"We'll have to call the police," he said.

I glanced around the room. "Phone?"

"I haven't one," he said. "But that gas station, possibly, is still open."

IT WAS still open. I drove us down there in less than two minutes, running in low gear over the narrow twisting mountain road, blowing the horn full blast. I applied brakes outside the station and barged inside.

"Where's the phone?"

The attendant pointed to one hanging on the wall, and I put a dime in the slot. "Operator, I'm in Topanga Canyon and want some police. Who shall I call—Santa Monica, or Los Angeles?"

She said briskly: "I'll connect you with the nearest sheriff's sub-station."

And a moment later a tired voice said: "Hello. Sheriff's office. Malibu Beach."

I said: "I'm calling from Topanga Canyon. I'm a cab-driver for the Red Owl Company. Just took a fare up to 936 Mountain Road, and there's trouble. A young woman stabbed with a dagger. Will you come up here?"

"Yeah. What's that address again?"

I gave it to him and could imagine him calmly writing it on a pad while he puffed the soggy stub of a cigar in a small overheated office.

"We'll be there in a few minutes," he said.

When I rang off, the gas-station attendant was eyeing me curiously. He'd put down his magazine.

"Did something happen up there?"

"Just a corpse in an Egyptian mummy case. Only instead of being dead three thousand years, it's only been dead three hours."

I returned to the cab, and Zohar the Great was still sitting in the back seat, in shadow. I told him we'd better go back to the house and wait for the officers, and I skidded the car around in loose gravel and climbed the hill again, roaring in low gear, tooting the horn on each tight curve.

Zohar the Great said nothing, not even when I braked the cab down in front of his house and opened the rear door for him.

He made no move to leave the cab, but suddenly he crouched and made a lightning movement of his right arm, and the cane with the silver head on it swung down in a swift driving arc.

The first chopping blow knocked my cap off, and the second one rapped down the hand which I'd raised for instinctive protection. There were more fast hard swings of the cane after that, and my skull exploded, and Zohar the Great became a dozen mystic men beating me with canes through deep green water. Then I fell into the road beside the cab with the whole dozen of them still slugging me. The dark water closed in, with sparkling phosphorescent flashes in it, and then the cane came down hard, and my teeth bit my own tongue, and I floated down, through darkening water, into oblivion.

CHAPTER TWO

THE CLINK'S NO OPTICAL ILLUSION

WHEN I opened my eyes to reason again there was a police car parked beside the cab. It had twin red lights as well as bright headlamps, and a yellow fog-lamp over the bumper. It also had a long range spotlight adjusted to shine straight down into my eyes.

I lay sprawled on the ground beside the cab, my head propped up against the running-board, and three men were bending over me as I came out of the deep water of unconsciousness.

"Give him some more coffee," somebody said.

They poured hot coffee into my mouth and I had to either swallow it or choke. I tried to compromise, and my stomach flopped over and I was sick on the ground.

"He's drunk as hell," one of the cops said.

I tried to sit up. "Listen…. I'm not drunk…. He hit me with the cane…."

Two of them laughed, and one said: "Not with a cane, buddy. It was Johnny Walker, and the Wilkens Family, and Mr. Three Star Hennessey. They all ganged up on you and hit you with bottles."

"I'm not drunk," I insisted thickly.

"Then you're giving a swell imitation, buddy, and I'd hate to have your hangover tomorrow."

I tried to get to my feet to show them I wasn't drunk, but my legs wobbled, and all of a sudden I realized I was drunk. I didn't know how the hell that could have happened. Zohar the Great had only given me a couple of light brandies, but now I was cockeyed, with the taste of liquor so strong in my stomach that I felt somebody had poured it down me from a spigot.

I tried to, stand up, and the two cops caught me under the arms to prevent my falling.

"All right, buddy. Take it easy. Hold him, Chadwick."

I recognized them, then. They were Chadwick and Carnes, from the Malibu sub-station. I'd always thought of them as a pair of square-shooting cops, and if they said I was drunk, I must've been. Chadwick reached into the cab and took out a couple of empty whiskey bottles, and an empty bottle of brandy.

He said: "Sorry we have to pinch you, fella. But a cab-driver has no business drinking on duty."

His partner asked me: "What did you call us for?"

"About a dead blonde in a mummy case." My own voice sounded thick, and my words stammered. "Zohar the Great opened the case to show me a mummy, but there was a dead girl in it. If you don't believe me, you can go look."

"We'll do just that, buddy. Give me a hand here, Chad."

They held me under the arms and boosted me up the stairs into the shack.

It was just like before, the same screwy place, except the bottle of brandy had vanished. The flat slim mummy case was still on the couch, and I pointed to it, and said: "Take a look in that."

Chadwick grinned and patted me gently on the shoulder. "We've already looked, buddy. But we're about a hundred drinks behind you."

I stared down blearily into the coffin, and there was nothing in it. It was just an empty mummy case which had been lined with satin for show purposes. I could hardly believe my own eyes.

I said to them: "I saw a corpse in there!"

"You probably did, fella," Chadwick admitted. "And you probably saw four pink elephants and a bunch of little green goblins. Come on, let's take a little ride."

Zohar the Great smiled sympathetically and looked at the cops. "As I explained to you already, he was so drunk he fell from the taxi on his head. I'm sorry you must arrest him. I hope it won't cost him his job. He's a nice young chap. Used to be an admirer of my magic performances." Zohar chuckled. "Perhaps he saw too many of them. They must have gone to his head."

Chadwick said: "We know what went to his head, Mr. Zohar. Too much refreshment from the inside of bottles."

"I'm sorry if this caused you officers any inconvenience."

"It's all right, Mr. Zohar. We get these cases ten times a night. We just slap them in the clink to sober up and think it over." Chadwick got big hands under my arms and danced me down the stairs to the police car. "Let's take that ride, fella, and we can tell a judge about all these elephants and corpses and goblins. Come on. *Oopsa-daisy!*

SO I got pinched on a drunk charge. And the funny part of it was that I really felt drunk when they took me in, and I couldn't walk the chalk line, nor read the alphabet chart, nor answer questions in the sobriety test.

They took me into the police court where Judge Folger Vaughan presided.

He barked sternly: "What's your name?"

"Steve Knight."

"Ever been arrested before?"

"Twice. Both times in this court. You must remember it, Your Honor."

"Yes." He nodded angrily. "I regret that I do remember it. Your full name is Steven Middleton Knight. They call you Steve Midnight. Your father was a friend of mine, before he died, a victim of the Wall Street crash in '29. You were born with the proverbial silver spoon in your mouth, but you grew up a drunken playboy in night clubs, a complete damned fool."

"I admit to those charges, Your Honor. I used to be a heel, but I've been trying to live it down."

"Live it down?" He gave a mirthless laugh. "Listen young man, I'm glad your father can't see you now standing before this court on another drunk charge. This is the third time you've been brought into my court, and it's the end of my patience. I gave you the benefit of every doubt when you abandoned your life as a social butterfly, as a bar-fly, and took the bit in your teeth and secured a job as a cab-driver to support your mother and your sister. I thought you had the blood of the Knights in you then. But you've turned out just a bum, a disgrace to your late father, and to your family, and this court now sentences you to sixty days in the county jail, or a fine of sixty dollars!" And to the bailiff, "Next case, please!"

So that was that. I didn't have the sixty bucks, of course, and he dismissed me with a shrug, and when I woke up in the morning it was past nine o'clock and I was lying in a bunk in the drunk-tank.

I felt like hell. My head ached to splitting and my stomach had a taste in it that crawled clear up into my mouth. I'd experienced hangovers many times in the past, but this was the first time I woke up from one without even the faintest remembrance of alcoholic indulgence.

I swung out of the bunk, and a dozen seedy-looking guys in the same tank, on the same charge, grinned at me sadly, "How do you feel, pal? You missed breakfast. Guess you don't care much, huh?"

I didn't care.

I drank four cups of cold water and sat down gingerly, hoping that I could hold it down.

And one of the bums in the tank handed be a morning paper which was folded back to the sixth page.

"Wanna read about yourself?"

I glanced at the paper, and there was a notice about me.

CAB DRIVER HAS THRILLING EXPERIENCE—
SEES DEAD BODY IN MUMMY CASE

Pacific Park, Dec. 20th:—Nothing can be more adventurous in this modern day and age than driving a taxi. Ask Mr. Steve Knight, known more familiarly as Steve "Midnight," who last night in the wee cold hours before dawn, picked up a fare who turned out to be Zohar the Great, famous magician currently performing on the local amusement pier.

Steve took his fare home to an address in Topanga Canyon,

THE DEAD RIDE FREE 17

and he also took a mummy case in which he thought he saw
the body of a beautiful blonde—mysteriously dead.

It was all an optical illusion, of course, and it was not caused
by the magic of Zohar the Great, but by too many drinks out
of too many bottles.

And Steve Knight, cab-driver, now resides in the county jail.

He was booked last night on a drunk charge by officers
Chadwick and Carnes, and he has sixty days in which to think
over beautiful dead blondes in mummy cases, pink elephants,
and little green goblins.

I was sore of course. Burned up. If my dad had been
still living, and if we had anything left of the Knight millions, I'd put that damned paper on the wrong end of a
libel suit.

For once in my life I hadn't been drunk—or anyway not
at the time I saw that blonde in the casket. But there didn't
seem anybody in the world who would believe me. My
past reputation as a toper had caught up with me once
again, and nobody would believe I'd reformed, and nobody
wanted to give me the benefit of the doubt.

I rattled my tin water-cup against the bars of the cell
and called: "Guard! Guard!"

A man in blue uniform came along the corridor. "Pipe
down, fella."

"I want to phone," I said.

"You got the nickel?"

"I had a pocketful when pinched," I said. "It's probably
still at the booking-desk—if some of your sneak-thief cops
haven't chiseled it."

"Don't get tough," he warned. "Do you want your ears
knocked down?"

But in the end they let me phone, and first I called my mother and told her I was all right, and then I called the Red Owl Cab Company and spoke to Pat Regan, the Chief Dispatcher.

"Look," I said, "I'm in the clink, Pat."

His voice just about tore up the mechanism of the phone receiver. "In the clink? You're telling *me*? Listen, you no no-good son-of-a-flat-tire, you put the whole Red Owl Cab Company in the doghouse! Did you see the morning papers? What'll our customers think? Our drivers— drunken bums!"

"The papers didn't name the company," I suggested lamely.

"No? Well, the hell with that! Everybody in town knows what company you drive for. You've given a bad name to the entire personnel of the Red Owl Cab Company! Furthermore, you're a stinker, and I regret the day I ever gave you a job! You came to me with a sob-sister story and told me you used to be a bum, and that you wanted to reform, and I fell for it. And look what I get! You ruin the reputation of the company, and we have to shell out fifteen bucks on your cab. The police impounded it, and we had to pay towing-service this morning. The only time I want to see you again is when you turn in your meter receipts for last night!"

"You mean I'm fired, Pat?"

"Fired? Don't make me laugh!" He gave a short imitation of the rasp of an electric saw. "Listen, you dopey-excuse-for-a-heel, I wish you had ten jobs with Red Owl, so I could fire you ten times! I wish I could fire you ten times a day, seven days a week, including Sundays! Fired? I wish you'd come around to the office sometime, so I can nail you to the floor and spit in your puss! Fired? Geez…!"

When he rang off, snapping the phone connection, it just about pulled down the wires between the county jail and the offices of the Red Owl Cab Company.

FOR LUNCH in the jail they gave us stew in tin plates, and bread, and coffee. I traded in my stew and bread with some of the guys in the tank, and after five cups of black coffee I wished I'd kept the stew. I'd begun to feel good again and even have a little appetite.

Along about one o'clock in the afternoon, with sixty days of jail still ahead of me, I heard a guard shout dismally: "Steven M. Knight?"

"Here," I said.

He unlocked the steel gate and beckoned me into the corridor.

"You're released," he said.

I couldn't understand that. Pat Regan and the Red Owl Company were much too sore to go bail for me, and my mother and kid sister certainly didn't have enough money to meet bail. Not unless some phony bondsman got hold of them.

"Who's my Santa Claus?" I asked.

"Your girl-friend."

"Don't own any such animal."

"Then you've sure as hell been overlooking something," he said, smirking.

We went downstairs and I got all my stuff back at the booking-desk and signed the release. I noticed on the release-card that a woman named Joan Lindsey had paid my fine. The name didn't mean anything.

They opened another steel gate for me, and I stepped out into the waiting-room and got a jolt to remember.

The blonde in the mummy case was alive again, and there was no dagger in her breast. She didn't wear that same slinky green dress, but the honey color of her hair, hung long to her shoulders, no hat to spoil it. Her hair was something you didn't forget. And eyes blue as the water in the Catalina Channel, just as liquid, were other things you didn't forget.

She came toward me and said: "Are you Mr. Knight?"

"Probably," I said. "I can't guarantee it. I'm not sure of anything any more. Are you the lady who went bail for me?"

"Yes."

"Why did you do it?"

She looked embarrassed and glanced around the waiting-room of the jail. "Can't we go somewhere to talk?"

"Sure."

I took her by the arm and led her away from there, while a couple of cops behind the booking-desk gave us the eye. You couldn't blame them. She was only about five-foot-two, and cute as Sonja Henie, even without ice skates and the short skirt with fur on it. She wore slacks, and a tight-fitting turtle-neck sweater, and a corduroy jacket belted in tight at the waist. The jacket, dark tobacco-brown, matched the slacks, and the sweater was brilliant yellow. None of the outfit was expensive and didn't have to be. It wasn't the way she was dressed that really counted.

We crossed the street to a little cafe next to the Bail Bond Office, and for a little while I couldn't escape the thought that maybe I *had* been drunk last night, and that the girl in the mummy case had been the result of a combination of Zohar's brandy and his magic. Because here was the same girl with honey hair, and she was alive again.

I said: "I hope your real name isn't Anna."

"Anna? Why do you ask that?"

"Just trying to check up on my own *delirium tremens,*" I said. "Do they ever call you Anna?"

"No." I felt her shiver against me. "But that's the name of my sister."

"You have a sister?"

"Yes. We're twins."

"Thanks," I said. You just saved me from taking another rest cure in an alcoholic sanatorium."

IN JOE'S PLACE we took a booth where we could talk, and I ordered, progressively, a bromide, tomato juice doctored with Worcestershire and a cup of black coffee. That combination finally licked the headache and reduced the hangover.

The blonde didn't order anything. She said: "I'm going to have to ask you a lot of questions, Mr. Knight. I hope you'll answer me truthfully."

"Sure. But can I ask one first? Just why did you buy me out of the clink?"

"Because I had to talk to you."

"Sixty dollars' worth?"

"Yes. And don't think money comes easy to me, Mr. Knight. I'm a working girl—when I can find a job."

I had the feeling the spending of that sixty bucks had cut deep into her resources so I told her: "You can consider it in the nature of a loan. I'll pay it back—someday. I've been a lot of things in my life, including every kind of heel, but nobody's caught me welching on a debt." She reached a timid hand across the table and touched my wrist briefly, and retreated into the corner of the booth again. "I guess we should get to the point. I saw in the paper this morning...."

I nodded, and added for her: "Drunken cab-driver sees pink elephants and green goblins. Is that what you saw?"

She didn't smile. "Yes. I saw it in the *Daily News,* and the *Examiner,* and I'm terribly worried, Mr. Knight. You can't fully understand how worried I am. And you just gave me an awful scare when you used that name—*Anna.* Why did you use it?"

I started to say, "I heard Zohar the Great use it when…" and I broke off and sipped my coffee. "I get it now. You saw that business in the papers and you can't be sure I was really drunk. You're the one person in the world who thinks maybe I wasn't. Is that it?"

"Yes."

"Why do you think so?"

"I'm Joan Lindsey," she said. "My sister and I used to be in theatricals together, and for six years we worked with Zohar's act."

"Zohar the Great?"

"Yes, that's his professional name. His real name is Louie Fryberger, and he's from Brooklyn, New York. He never saw India, or Egypt, in his life, but he's a clever showman, and in the old days of vaudeville he was a headliner. In recent years he's been on the skids. We played cheaper and cheaper theaters. Finally we wound up in carnivals and circuses. I quit the act two years ago."

"Why?"

She blushed a little. "Personal reasons."

"Meaning what?"

"Well, he has thin, sticky hands, and lots of the girls had to quit. I quit along with the rest of them. But my sister, Anna, kept on. She was in love with him, I guess, but I know she wasn't happy. And when she didn't come

THE DEAD RIDE FREE 23

home last night I got worried. And then this morning I saw in the papers about how a taxi-driver was arrested for intoxication. The taxi-driver saw a girl at Zohar's house—dead."

"That meant something to you."

"Yes. Anna wore a green dress last night. And one of the papers said this girl you saw at Zohar's place wore a green dress." Tears filmed her eyes but she wasn't crying. "Don't you understand why I have to know about it?"

I drained my cup of black coffee. "If you think something really happened to your sister, why don't you file a report with the police?"

"I can't," she said. "Not till I'm sure." She shook her head at the cigarette I offered and sipped part of a glass of water. Her lips left a mark of vermilion lipstick on the clean rim of the glass. "Will you come home with me, Mr. Knight?"

"Of course," I said.

CHAPTER THREE

MR. ANONYMOUS AND THE BLONDE

SHE LIVED in a small old-fashioned bungalow in a district of identical old-fashioned bungalows. Big pepper trees covered the narrow street with shade, and the small houses stood back from the sidewalk in tiny neglected gardens. There were kids playing ball in the street, and weary old men puttering in the gardens, and tired women taking down wash from the lines in back yards.

Joan Lindsey brought me there in a battered Ford road-ster, and we got out of it and walked through a creaky picket gate into a garden where an old lady sat idly in a wheel chair.

"Mother," Joan said, "this is a friend of mine in show business. His name is Mr. Knight."

The old lady stared at an obscure point just over my left shoulder and said in a kindly smiling voice: "I'm pleased to make your acquaintance, Mr. Knight." She put her hand out and missed my own by several inches, and blushed, and kept looking empty-eyed at something obscure over my shoulder.

Joan said: "I'm going to show Mr. Knight some of my press-clippings, Mother. He might be able to get me a job."

The old lady beamed pleasantly. "She's a clever girl in the acting business, Mr. Knight. I'm proud of them both. They're twins, you know. Have you met Anna?"

"Not yet, but I certainly hope to, Mrs. Lindsey."

And then Joan and I went into the house while the old lady remained outside in the wheel-chair staring vacantly at the pepper trees and at the children who were playing touch football along the street.

"Mother's blind," Joan Lindsey whispered.

"I know," I said. "That's why you hesitate to talk to the police about Anna, isn't it?"

"Yes. Mother's health isn't good. I have to spare her shocks—when I can. But of course if something really happened to Anna, then I'll have to go to the police. Do you think something did, Mr. Knight?"

That was a hell of a question to have to answer. I knew for sure, of course—and could swear it on a stack of Gideon Bibles—that the body of the girl in green, in Zohar's casket, had been a real body. It hadn't been an optical illusion, and I hadn't been drunk. I was positive the body had been Anna, because of the green silk dress, and because Zohar had used the name Anna in an involuntary exclamation when he unlocked the case. But it was hard as the devil to present that conviction to a swell girl like Joan Lindsey, and to her mother who was blind.

Yet at the same time I was out on a limb myself. I had to prove I hadn't been drunk last night—prove it to the satisfaction of the Red Owl Cab Company. I had to find a real body if I ever wanted my job back.

So I said to Joan Lindsey, my way of compromise: "Let's investigate this a little bit more. Let's not jump to conclusions."

She took me into a bedroom—her sister Anna's.

It was small and square, its one window giving an outlook on the neighbor's chicken-yard, and it possessed all the feminine frills of a young woman who wanted a better home and didn't know how to get it. The bed was narrow and inexpensive, but it had a flounced spread on it that tried to suggest a movie star's boudoir.

The curtains at the bleak window were fussy and frilly. A dressing-table was cluttered with perfume bottles from Woolworth's, and fancy cosmetic jars from the corner drugstore, and framed photos, most of them autographed, of Zohar the Great.

The walls had more photos—of Anna herself in theatrical poses—and Joan Lindsey pointed to them and said: "That's my sister."

"She looks just like you," I remarked.

"Is she the girl you saw in the mummy case—like the papers said?"

"Might me. Might be. It's a little hard to tell."

HOW CAN you tell a girl that her twin sister is dead when you don't have any proof of it except your own hazy knowledge? How can you throw a bombshell of shock and worry into a blind old lady who sits in a garden in a wheelchair and stares empty-eyed at the street?

"I can't be sure," I lied. "Do you think anybody would want to harm your sister?"

"I don't know, Mr. Knight. But like I've told you, Anna's been in love with Zohar—or Fryberger, or whatever you want to call him. And I know she wasn't happy. Maybe he jilted her. She never told me that—not directly—but I heard her crying in here at night. And she was worried about something and wouldn't eat much, and she got pale and thin through the last year. I knew she was in some kind of trouble, and last night I came into this room and found a letter in her desk. Would you care to see it?"

I told her I would, and she handed me a letter in a plain envelope, addressed to her sister in longhand and postmarked day before yesterday. While the envelope had the address in longhand, the neatly folded letter inside was typewritten on business stationery.

PACIFIC INVESTIGATIONS, INC.
515 Ocean Avenue
Pacific Park
California

Dear Miss Lindsey:

In accordance with your instructions of December 1st, our operatives have had the party in question under surveillance, and we herewith submit the following report.

We have been able to verify your suspicions and can inform you that the party in question is in the habit of holding rendezvous with a woman answering the description you gave us.

Our investigation discloses that her name is Mrs. Arthur J. Breckenridge, formerly Gertrude Hamilton, born and raised in New York. Present age: 46. Married to Arthur Breckenridge, prominent western oil financier, on March 4th, 1920.

Our last report covering the investigation in your behalf discloses that Mrs. Breckenridge and the party in question met at the Union Depot at 2:15 P.M. yesterday afternoon. They then went to the Elite Jewelry Company, where they made a secret bargain for the sale of a valuable pearl necklace and at the same time arranged to have Elite Jewelry supply an imitation of same for a sum only ten percent of the value. Sale price of the matched pearl necklace was twenty thousand dollars.

We regret being unable to supply you with further information at this time, and we suggest that you retain our services in the future for the same fee.

Yours truly:

J.J. Mawson

Pacific Investigations

I read the letter over again, and Joan Lindsey watched my face anxiously while I read.

"It's a puzzling letter isn't it?"

"In a way."

"Do you think we should go see these people at Pacific Investigations and find out what it means?"

"No," I said. "They're a private detective agency and they won't violate the confidence of a client. Anna Lindsey was a client."

"But she's my sister."

"Makes no difference," I said. "They wouldn't tell you anything."

"But suppose something happened to Anna?"

"We have to prove that first."

I folded the letter, slipped it back into the plain envelope, and tucked that into my coat pocket.

"Are you going to keep it?" she asked.

"Yes. It might come in handy when we see the police."

That gave her a jolt I hadn't intended. "Then you think something did happen to Anna?"

"Well, it's possible, of course. And we can't overlook anything."

She gave me a slight nervous nod that passed her entire problem into my hands. She needed a confidante and had elected *me* I could tell by the nod. I don't know why she passed that obligation on to me, unless it was just that maybe I have an honest, truthworthy face. Maybe she had nobody else to put trust in and merely thought I'd be better than nobody. Probably it was that.

I said: "Is there a phone around here?"

"Yes, in the hall."

"Phone book?"

"Yes, by the phone."

WE WENT into the hall of the old house and I thumbed through the telephone directory under the "B" listings, but there was no number recorded under the name of Arthur J. Breckenridge. That was understandable. He probably lived in a swank house that had an unlisted private phone. I'd only looked into the directory on an off chance.

I knew I could reach him through the Consolidated Western Oil Company, down in Los Angeles, because I'd heard his name before in connection with the oil business, and I knew he was president of the company, and general manager, and chairman of the Board of Directors. But I didn't want to get in touch with him at all. I only wanted to get in touch with his wife.

I wondered how I could do that. The telephone company wouldn't give out information on an unlisted number. His office wouldn't give out his home number without consulting him. Not unless the excuse was good....

I sat there by the telephone trying to think up a good excuse, and my eyes caught a calendar on the phone table. The date was December 20th. That gave me an idea.

I called the main office of the Consolidated Western Oil Company and asked to speak to Mr. Breckenridge's personal secretary. I had to speak to three other people first, but finally they connected me with a sharp old-maid's voice which announced briskly: "This is the office of Mr. Arthur J. Breckenridge. Miss Cook speaking." She made the announcement mechanically, like a train caller in the Union Depot.

I said: "This is the Southern California Furniture Company, Miss Cook. We regret having to bother you—"

"If you're a salesman," she snapped, "you can get off the line!"

"Please," I said, and went on smoothly, "we must ask your help in the matter of a Christmas present which was ordered yesterday by Mrs. Breckenridge in our main store. Mrs. Breckenridge placed on order with us for a leather chair for her husband's den at home. A surprise Christmas gift, of course. She selected the chair from our floor sample and wanted it in green leather upholstery. However, we find we can't supply the same chair in anything but red or brown leather, unless it's made to order, and in that case we can't deliver by Christmas. We'd like to get in touch with her at once."

"Yes?" the secretary said.

"Our records," I went on, "show Mrs. Breckenridge's home address, since she's had a charge account with our store for a number of years, but we find no phone number listed, and we can't get this number from the phone company. If you'd be so kind as to give us the number—"

I thought I'd pulled a smart stunt then, and that she'd give me the number without question. But the secretary probably had had stunts pulled before. She wouldn't take chances.

"I can't give you the private home phone," she said, "But I'll ring Mrs. Breckenridge and deliver the message and she can call you."

That left me in a hell of a spot. I didn't want Mrs. Breckenridge calling the Southern California Furniture Company, where she hadn't—I was sure—bought any chair for her husband.

I did some fast thinking and said: "Just a moment, Miss Cook. I wish you'd give her another message for me at the same time."

"Yes?"

"Tell her that I want to help her with that selection at the Elite Jewelry Company about the twenty-thousand-dollar pearl necklace and the substitute. Tell her it's very important for her to call me back at once. She'll understand." I glanced at the number in the center of the Lindsey phone's dial. "My number is Pacific Park, 59-79. No name is necessary."

"Thank you," the secretary said briskly, and rang off.

I rang off too, and grinned at Joan Lindsey, and winked. "Not bad if it works…. Huh?"

IT WORKED fine, bringing results in less than five minutes. I picked up the phone when it rang, and the voice was a woman's and had worry in it. "Is this Pacific Park 59-79?"

"Yes," I said.

"Is there someone there who wanted to get in touch with Mrs. Arthur J. Breckenridge?"

"There is. Speaking."

The voice faltered with a nervous little choke. "... Well, I didn't order any leather chair from the Southern California Furniture Company...."

"Of course not," I admitted. "I didn't call you about a chair. The furniture business was just a stall to get in touch with you. No doubt you've already guessed that."

The voice dropped into a husky whisper hardly audible over the phone. "Was it something about a pearl necklace?"

"Exactly."

"Are you the Elite Jewelry Company?"

"No," I said.

"But how... how did you know...?" Then she became demanding. "Who *are* you?"

"Somebody who wants a little information on that pearl necklace transaction, Mrs. Breckenridge."

She said haughtily: "I don't know what you're talking about! I've a notion to slam down this telephone!"

I gave the laugh to that. "You won't ring off, Mrs. Breckenridge. You can't afford to. For the same reason you were forced to phone me at this number."

"Who are you?"

"You can call me *Mr. Anonymous.* I'm just somebody interested in that necklace. I know you sold a certain string of pearls, and had an imitation made by Elite. It arouses my curiosity. I've got a notion to go to the Consolidated Oil Company and ask your husband about it."

"Wait!" Her voice was almost a cry, desperate. Then it calmed down, under effort, and she whispered tensely:

"Can't I meet you somewhere? I don't like to carry on this discussion over the phone. You can meet me inside half an hour at Barney's Bar in Pacific Park."

"Listen," I told her, "if I ever want to meet you at all, I'll name the place and the time. Where can I reach you in a hurry? Through your husband?"

Her voice became pleading. "Please don't call Arthur! I mean about this necklace matter. You can reach me at the private home phone number. Beverly Hills—Four hundred. Or you can get in touch with me through a certain actor—"

"Zohar the Great?"

"Yes, of course! But please let's get together now, the two of us, and talk this over! I can make it worth your while in the matter of money—"

I said: "Good-bye, Mrs. Breckenridge. And pleasant nightmares!"

I hung up, and the phone rang again, almost immediately, so I took the receiver off the hook and left it face down, like an inverted glass, useless.

I said to Joan Lindsey: "Let's go out on the amusement pier. Let's try to find out if your sister went there last night."

CHAPTER FOUR

THE MUMMY
WAS A WITNESS

JOAN AND I drove down Ocean Avenue in the battered Ford and left it in the parking lot near the pier. It was a cold windy afternoon, with dirty thrown-away papers blowing along the pier planks at your feet, and most of the concessions closed. Wind flapped the canvas covers over closed business, and there was practically nobody out on the pier in the late afternoon.

Joan had said: "There's one other man besides Zohar the Great who might tell us if Anna went to the pier last night."

"Who's that?"

"Nick Martini. He's been with the act for three years. Ticket-seller and barker."

"Think you can get any information out of him?"

"I'm not sure. He's always been quite a friend of Zohar."

"We'll try him," I said. "We'll try anything and every-thing."

And as we walked the length of the deserted pier, that on-shore breeze blew cool against our faces and carried the scent of the sea. The breeze got into Joan Lindsey's blond hair and skittered it and made it fluffy. The breeze tugged at her slacks and shaped them against her legs.

I tried to light a cigarette while we walked, but each time the wind whipped the match out, and I wasted about five matches and gave up.

"Here we are," Joan said.

The concession of Zohar the Great was the same as when I had seen it in the dark last night. Same advertising banners, same canvas over the ticket office, only now a man stood on a tall step-ladder, busy taking down the banners.

"Hello, Nick," Joan said.

He looked down at us from the top of the ladder, a stocky-built man with dark hair and an oily complexion. He seemed more like a gangster than a ticket-seller or a barker. He was chewing a mouthful of tobacco, and he spit a brief brown stream, and then climbed lazily down the ladder.

"You want to see Zohar?"

"Is he around?"

"Not today," Nick Martini said. "We're folding up the act. Moving it to Frisco."

"Oh," said Joan. She made no attempt to introduce me to the man, just ignored me completely while she talked to him. "Better engagement up there, Nick?"

"More money," he said. "Zohar's agent lined us up for it. We heard about it last night."

"That's swell," Joan told him. "How about my sister? Is she going with the act?"

Nick Martini's eyes narrowed a little and he spat tobacco juice at the pier planks and shrugged. "Suppose so."

"Was she out here last night, Nick?"

He didn't answer right away. He looked at her thoughtfully and his jaws worked over the mouthful of tobacco with the rhythm of a cow chewing a cud. His eyes looked her up and down, then glanced sideways at me, and traveled down to my shoes and up again.

Then he wiped his lips on the back of his hand, and said to Joan Lindsey: "I don't know. Why?"

I didn't like the guy on sight and wouldn't have trusted him with a bag of empty beer bottles on which there were two-cent deposits. I didn't like his caution, or the sultry smolder of his black eyes, or the bulge under his left armpit that suggested a gun.

Joan Lindsey said: "Wasn't Anna working in the act last night?"

He regarded her thoughtfully, mouthing his tobacco. "Yeah. Guess she was. But she left early. Why?"

There was no chance of getting information out of him, I decided, so it was time to pull a gag.

I said: "Anna came home late last night. A little bit under the alcoholic weather. She didn't bring her purse home with her. We figure she left it here. We'd like to go inside and hunt for it."

He gave me the once-over again, from head to foot, like a jockey appraising a horse, and all the time his jaws worked in rhythm on his cud of tobacco.

"You a friend of Joan's?"

When I nodded he just shrugged and spat on the pier planks. "The act's closed, pal. Nothing inside. If there was a purse, I'd-a found it."

"I'm sure you would," I said.

His eyes darkened suspiciously. "Is that a crack?"

"Look," I told him. "Joan and I want to go inside and hunt for Anna's purse. It boils down to this. Will you let us in, or do we have to call some men in blue uniforms with brass buttons? Do you get me?"

"Yeah, but you don't have to get so damn tough about it." He glared at us from under dark shaggy brows and then fished a ring of keys from his pocket. He went behind the canvas-covered ticket-office and unlocked the door into the concession.

"Help yourself," he invited nastily.

He held the heavy wooden door open for us while we went in, then shut it. That left Joan and me in the complete darkness of the little theater, and when I reached back and tried the door it was locked.

"Looks like we let ourselves into some trouble," I said.

IN THE dark I groped for the light-switch. I tried to remember where Zohar had found it when he brought me here last night to help him pick up his stuff, but my hands only felt the heavy curtains along the walls at each side of the door. Finally, striking a match, I groped through a slit in the curtains and felt the switch and flipped it.

Frail greenish light seeped from a mysterious globe in the ceiling, but it was enough to see by, and I saw the fright written on Joan Lindsey's features.

"Keep your chin up," I said. "We'll get out of this."

But I wondered how we would.

The room was the same as when I'd seen it before. Black drapes shrouding the walls and drawn up tent-like to the ceiling globe. I pawed at the drapes, found openings in them here and there, but behind them was just blank wall and no windows.

I went into the next room and found another electric switch. More frail light glowed greenishly from a center globe, and this room was like the first—empty. Just an ornate table-like pedestal that held a mummy case during show times. The case wasn't there, of course.

Joan Lindsey asked tensely: "Are you really looking for Anna's purse?"

"No. Right now I'm looking for a way out of here. There probably isn't one."

"Do you think my sister really left a purse here last night?"

"No," I said. "That was just a gag."

"Then what did we come in here to hunt for?"

"An Egyptian mummy," I said.

I kept parting the black drapes and only finding blank walls behind them, but finally, in a corner, I found the mummy.

It stood stiffly behind the drapes, propped in the corner wrapped in faded brown linen. When you touched it, the ancient cloth powdered under your finger, and you could brush it away like dust. Even the head was wrapped but the face was exposed. A dried face, shriveled, hollow eyes with closed lids over them, the mouth tight and brown. It looked like a corpse which had been too many thousand years out of its tomb.

I dropped the black drapes over it and wondered how the hell Joan Lindsey and I could get out of here. No windows in the place, but it stood to reason there must be some opening, somewhere, for ventilation. The City Health Department would demand that.

I examined every inch of the room, hunting for a ventilator, and I was just thinking about standing up on the pedestal and trying behind the ceiling canopy, when the outer door opened abruptly and slammed again at once. Quick footsteps came across the bare floor in the other room, and Joan Lindsey and were in the presence of Zohar the Great, in person. It had only taken him about twenty minutes to get here.

"Well, well," he greeted, and not pleasantly. "Well, well, the cab-driver again. You seem to be making a good deal of trouble for me."

I didn't say anything to that, but Joan asked him suddenly: "Where's Anna, Mr. Zohar?"

He gave her a sidelong glance. "I'm sure I wouldn't know. I'm not in the least concerned with where my employees are, except during performances."

"She didn't come home last night, Mr. Zohar. I'm worried about her."

"Really?" His lean face remained impassive and his whole bearing took on a haughty dignity. The silk turban helped him get it across. "I'm sorry if you've been having trouble keeping track of her. But I must admit your sister always struck me as rather a wild impetuous girl. Perhaps she ran away with some man."

"You know that's ridiculous!" Joan snapped. "You know she was in love with you and that she wouldn't just run away from you."

"In love with me?" His eyes were untouched by any emotion. "Quite flattering—if true. But I assure you I'm not in the least interested in your sister."

"Not even in what happened to her last night?" I asked.

He flashed me a sharp glance. "What do you mean by that?"

"You know exactly what I mean," I said. "I mean about that girl in the mummy case. The case I took to your house up in Topanga Canyon. Can't you remember that far back?"

He chuckled scoffingly. "You were drunk last night."

"Is that why you slugged me with the cane?"

"I didn't slug you. I don't know what you're talking about. You were drunk."

"The hell I was," I said. "Not that drunk. Something happened to Anna Lindsey last night and I think I know what."

"Yes?" He cocked one black eyebrow with bitter politeness.

"She was killed last night," I said.

JOAN GAVE a little cry deep in her throat, but there wasn't too much surprise in it. Tears filmed her eyes and she became pleading. "Please, Mr. Zohar. It's not fair for you not to tell us...."

"Tell what?"

"What happened to Anna."

He twirled his cane lightly in a thin dextrous hand, like a drum major with a baton. His dark eyes got bored.

"I really don't know what you're talking about," he said.

"Really?" I leaned against the pedestal and imitated his imitation of boredom. "You're not fooling us a bit, and you can save the Zohar-the-Great stuff for your customers. Right now you can tell us why Nick Martini locked us in here and then chased out and phoned you, and why you raced here in such a hurry."

Nick Martini came quickly from the other room. His right hand hovered about his coat lapel, where the bulge was, under his armpit. "You call me, boss? Is this guy shooting off his mouth too much?"

"No." Zohar gave him a level penetrating stare. "But you're about to shoot yours off, Nick, and I don't like it."

"O.K., Louie." Martini retreated reluctantly, and leaned heavily against the drapes and eyed me like he thought he might have fun taking me apart.

I said to Zohar: "You still haven't answered the question. Why did Martini lock us in here?"

"Nick was afraid you were drunk and might cause a disturbance."

"Then why didn't he call the police? Why pull this stunt of locking us in? I'll tell you why. He figured Joan and I were getting too warm on what really happened to Anna last night. He got himself worked into a panic. He's dumb. So he barged out and sent you an S.O.S. And now you're trying to talk yourself out of a jam."

Zohar stopped twirling the cane and allowed a little emotion to creep over sharp features. But the emotion was phony. "You force me," he said shruggingly, "to tell you where Anna went. I'd hoped to be able to spare Joan and her mother the truth. But now I'll have to go back, partly, on my word to Anna." He tried to appear embarrassed, saying: "Anna got into some trouble when we were playing the act last year. Another state. Under an assumed name, she swindled one of our customers out of seven thousand dollars. She worked it through the fortune-telling act. But last night the police arrested her—still under the assumed name—and she's been extradited out of the state. She'll probably receive a two-year prison term for fraud."

"You're a liar," I said.

"Really?"

"Yes. What state was Anna extradited to?"

"I refuse to tell you that." He gave Joan a kindly smile. "I'm sure you'll allow me to keep the rest of my promise to Anna. She didn't want you to know. She didn't want your mother to know—to bear the disgrace. And as long as no issue is made of this—if we keep it among ourselves—Anna can serve her term under the assumed name. It's better that way for Anna. And when she's finally released, she'll be able to take up life again under her own name, with no smirch against it."

HE WAS the smoothest liar I'd ever encountered in my life, and I had no intention of letting him get away with it. "That story won't go, Zohar," I said.

He went over and took Joan's arm. "Please, Miss Lindsey, you must understand I'm only trying to keep my promise to Anna, to help her rehabilitate herself in the years to come. Please tell this cab-driver friend of yours that we need his silence. If you can't influence him through friendship, then perhaps I can assist with a little money. I might pay him as much as five hundred dollars to keep Anna's secret. I'm more than glad to do that—for Anna's sake."

Joan Lindsey studied his face for several seconds, lips tight, eyes narrowed. I noticed that her slim hands were clenched when she told him firmly: "Mr. Zohar, I don't believe you."

"Atta-girl," I said. "Neither do I, and we won't let him get away with it." I parted the drapes behind me and lifted out the Egyptian mummy and stood it beside me. "This man was an eye-witness to a murder last night, only he's too dead himself to tell us about it. This man saw it and he was even a sort of victim of it. He got taken out of his casket and pushed behind the drapes, and his casket was used for another body—you know what I mean."

That threw a bombshell into both Zohar and Martini. The magician managed to get control of himself, even while his hand trembled with the cane, but Nick Martini had the kind of mind which could be touched off as easily as a match against black powder. I saw his hand snap up to his lapel, and I heaved the mummy at him.

That started a nightmarish struggle which raced so fast, was over so soon, that I don't think I was wholly aware of all of it. I was just aware of Joan Lindsey's husky stifled cry, of Martini staggering back off balance as the mummy hit him, of Zohar the Great—all his phony Far Eastern dignity suddenly gone from him—raising his cane to strike me.

I grabbed hold of the wooden pedestal which had always held the mummy case in the act, and I tipped it hard against his legs—hard enough to knock him down—and I turned to see Nick Martini shoulder the mummy aside. To see it flop stiffly to the floor with a faint rising powder of ancient dust. Martini's right hand now jerked out from under his coat with an Army automatic in it, and I clutched his wrist desperately, forced the gun downward, without a split second to spare.

It fired in a continuous hot blast, and I could tell by the twist of Martini's features that all the slugs weren't hammering harmlessly into the floor. Two of them smashed bones in his right foot, another damaged his left kneecap. The last took the fight out of him, and he crumpled suddenly, hugging his leg, and his shriek of agony was something you couldn't ever forget.

At the instant he fell I was lucky enough to glimpse Zohar coming at me around the tipped-over mummy pedestal. He had the cane raised, ready to fracture my skull, but somehow I managed to duck under it and crack him flush on the jaw with the butt of Martini's gun. It must've been a beaut of a blow because my whole arm tingled with the impact. My hand holding the gun went abruptly numb, and Zohar the Great threw both arms over his head and fell straight backwards the way Indians used to get shot in Wild West movies.

"Come on," I said to Joan Lindsey. "We've still got a job left."

CHAPTER FIVE

NEVER AGAIN

WE WENT outside, Joan and I, and locked the door to Zohar's concession. I saw a light burning in a hot dog stand across the way and a guy behind steamy glass windows busy cleaning up the griddle. I went over and spoke to him.

"Listen, bud, I just locked the door on a couple of guys in the Zohar concession. Here's the key. Give it to the cops when they come."

"Cops?" He eyed me blankly. "Are cops headed here?"

"They'll be headed here when you phone them for me."

I left him at the telephone, with the key, and took Joan Lindsey by the hand and led her briskly along the pier. "You've got to keep your chin up, kid. Your sister is dead."

"I've suspected it, Mr. Knight. And you said so a little while ago...." She blinked tears and tilted her head with courage. "You know that for sure, don't you?"

"For sure," I said. "And you've seen enough excitement for one day. You'd better go home."

She shook her head at that. She wanted to stick with me, so together we walked up the windy avenue to Barney's Bar and crowded into a phone booth.

I dialed the unlisted number, Beverly Hills 400, and talked to a maid and then to Mrs. Arthur Breckenridge. I said to her: "This is the party who called before about the pearl necklace. You said you wanted to meet me secretly at Barney's Bar in Pacific Park. I'm there now. I'll wait fifteen minutes in the private dining room. Can you make it?"

Her voice had hysteria in it. "Please wait there! I'll come right away...."

Barney himself showed us upstairs and into a small cozy room in which, under other circumstances, I might enjoy dining privately with a girl like Joan Lindsey. Soft lights, an intimate table for two, and Barney lit candles on the sideboard.

"The regular dinner, Mr. Knight?"

"Not tonight, Barney. Send up a couple of Bacardi cocktails—make it three. We're expecting another party."

THE COCKTAILS came, and about ten minutes later, Mrs. Arthur J. Breckenridge. She was a tall woman, not too young, wearing a black seal coat around a full Mae West body. Her hat was tiny and modern and ridiculous, set fastidiously slantwise on beauty-parlor blondness. Her eyes, framed in mascara-laden lashes, were sultry and at the same time ruthless.

She closed the door carefully behind her and leaned against it, a little out of breath from rushing here. She said in a low-toned nervous voice: "Are you the persons who phoned me?"

I nodded and gestured toward the third cocktail. She shook her head, glaring at me impatiently. "What do you know about that pearl necklace?"

"Plenty," I told her. "Your husband gave it to you for a present. You like your husband all right, and you like the wealthy setting he lets you live in, but a tall dark man came into your life. He probably announced his own importance when he told your fortune in a crystal. He's a chiseler, and frankly liked your money, but you had such a crush on him you didn't care."

She eyed me steadily. "You refer to Mr. Zohar, of course."

"Of course," I said. "To give him cash you sold the necklace. Got twenty grand from Elite Jewelry. But you didn't want your husband to miss the necklace, so you had a cheap substitute made by the same firm. That was to fool the Old Boy at home. Because no matter how hot your crush is on Zohar the Great, you still love the soft rich life your husband gives you, wouldn't ditch it for a has-been actor."

I let those words sink in, and watched her open her black bag and take out a lipstick and a small mirror. Her fine white hands trembled a bit, in rage, as she applied new crimson to full lips. "You want hush-money, of course," she said.

I shook my head slowly. "It's too late for anything like that. This thing is a lot worse than just cheating on your husband and peddling that necklace. There's murder in it now."

The lipstick cylinder and the mirror slipped suddenly from trembling fingers. The mirror cracked in half as it struck the floor. She clutched the black bag desperately against the seal coat. "Murder? Please explain what you mean!"

I didn't feel in any hurry about that. "Anna Lindsey," I said, "was also in love with Zohar—or Fryberger, or whatever you want to call him. Anna was hurt when he began to ignore her, and she hired a private detective agency to find out why he grew cool. The agency discovered about you and Zohar. About the necklace. Do you follow me?"

All this time Joan Lindsay said nothing, just toyed with her cocktail glass and studied Mrs. Breckenridge.

"Late last night," I went on, "Anna was out on the pier doing her bit in the Zohar act. Zohar had to leave, go to town to see his theatrical agent. That left Anna and Nick Martini in charge of the concession. And I guess Nick went out for a drink, or whatever lugs go out for when they can. That left Anna alone.

"Then you went out there. Anna told you what she knew about you and Zohar and the necklace. She tried to use that information as a lever to break up the romance. Because she loved Zohar herself. Maybe she even threatened blackmail—"

"She did," Mrs. Breckenridge snapped involuntarily.

"That's what I guessed," I said. "And so the two of you, alone in the concession, staged a fight over a man. You've got a mean temper and in the heat of battle you snatched an Oriental show dagger off the table and stabbed Anna."

Joan Lindsey let out her breath in a gasp. Mrs. Breckenridge smiled hatefully.

I said: "When you realized you'd killed a woman, you were scared plenty. You didn't want to lose your husband, your wealth, your social position. You didn't want to spend the rest of your life in prison, or end it in a State gas chamber. So you were in a panic. Somehow you had to hide the crime. And the first step was to conceal the body.

"That's where you had an inspiration. You took the mummy from the coffin, placed it behind the curtain and then lifted Anna's body into the basket. You snapped the padlocks. That prevented anyone from making an immediate discovery of the body, and you figured it would be an easy task, with Zohar's help, to smuggle the body off the pier as long as it was in the mummy case. After that Zohar would help you get rid of it. You knew your money could buy him.

"In the meantime," I went on, "while you were out hunting for Zohar, Nick Martini locked up the concession. He must've assumed Anna went home. And in the meantime, too, Zohar had concluded his interview with his agent, and hired a cab to go home in—mine. You still hadn't located him and he didn't know what had happened when we went out on the pier and picked up the mummy case and took it up to his house in Topanga Canyon. And when he opened the case to show me the prize display of his act—the mummy—there was Anna inside. He guessed it was you who'd killed her."

The voice of Mrs. Breckenridge was a high-pitched cry. "I didn't! I didn't!"

"You did," I insisted. "And Zohar the Great tried to cover you. He slugged me to sleep with his cane—forced liquor down my gullet—told the cops I was drunk, that I hadn't really seen a body—and that was all to cover you. And why not? Zohar and Nick Martini could live in easy street, on blackmail, if they covered you for murder."

The Breckenridge temper exploded then. She snatched a carving-knife off the sideboard and came at me. It must have been just like the time she snatched up the Oriental dagger and killed Anna.

I was sitting at the table, holding a cocktail glass, and I stuck out my foot and tripped her. The point of the carving-knife jabbed an inch deep into the table. I pushed her in the face—hard.

I said to Joan: "Call the cops, kid. We just caught a killer."

THE POLICE kept me all night at headquarters in a small bare room that had only a table, a wood chair, a cuspidor, and strong white lights—asking questions.

Then about dawn, after I'd told the story a hundred times, they eased off the pressure, and Chadwick and Carnes, the cops who'd arrested me on the drunk charge, got very friendly.

"You did a nice job, Steve. We're sorry about that drunk rap."

"It's all right," I said.

The papers came out on the streets that day, making me a kind of hero, and I spent the rest of the day at the inquest.

They'd grilled Zohar the Great, and found where he'd buried the body of Anna Lindsey in the Topanga hills.

I testified at the inquest, and early in the evening phoned the Red Owl Company and talked to Pat Regan.

"I want my job back, Pat. I wasn't drunk after all."

"Be here at eight!" he barked.

"You mean *tonight?*"

"You heard me, Steve."

"Geez!" I said. "It's seven thirty now. I haven't had any sleep!"

"You heard me," Pat said. "You be here at eight—or you're fired again."

So there was nothing else to do but hustle out there and get my cab from the garage and brood over nasty Christmas presents I'd like to mail to a certain hard-boiled Irish cab dispatcher named Regan.

I only had a single fare that night.

She was a doddering old lady I'd picked up on a call at the Oceanside Hotel. She had seven pieces of luggage, wanted to go to the Union Depot, and after I got the luggage into the cab, she said hesitantly: "I've got a wooden box, too. It's only about five feet long and—"

"No, Madam," I said firmly. "You'd better call the express company. It's not the policy of this cab to carry boxes...."

THE MAN FROM ALCATRAZ

WHEN THE RED OWL CAB CO.'S HARD-LUCK HACKER GOT A MIDNIGHT CALL TO PICK UP A TALL BLONDE ON THE BEACH, AND FOUND THAT THE SKELETON IN HER CLOSET WAS A TROMBONE-TOOTING STIFF, IT LOOKED LIKE HE WAS IN THE SOUP FOR FAIR. HE MANAGED O.K. BEFORE THE NIGHT WAS OVER, HOWEVER. ANY HACKER WHO CAN SELL A ROD FOR $300,000 IS BETTER OFF THAN IF HE JUST LETS HIS METER TICK OFF THE TOTAL AND TAKES HIS CHANCES ON A TIP.

CHAPTER ONE
THE BLONDE IN BLACK

NORTH OF Santa Monica the Roosevelt Highway continued in broad sweeping curves following the coastline through the wet night. Traffic moved fast, and I bowled the hack along at a good clip until after Castle Rock when the beach houses began again. Then I slowed and tipped the spotlight beam across the road and hunted for house numbers.

The one I wanted proved to be a one-story stucco cottage built precariously on the left bank of the road. It had stilt-like underpilings standing knee deep in the high tide, and I risked my life and my cab swinging in a U-turn and coming back on the other side of the pavement.

I parked, then walked through the rain to the covered stoop of the cottage and pressed a button beside the door. I couldn't hear a bell ring—not with the sound of the surf and the roar of highway traffic. I didn't think anybody inside could hear a bell either, but somebody did, and when the door opened I removed my cap.

"Red Owl Cab Company," I said.

"Will you step inside a moment?"

I stepped in past the tall blonde and waited while she closed the door, and tried not to stare at her too boldly. That wasn't easy, because she had a striking, metallic kind of beauty. She was tall and full-bodied in a trimly cut suit of black oxford.

She wore shoes of soft-grained black leather and silk stockings the tone of Florida sun-tan and a simple Robin Hood hat that didn't look silly on her. Under the brim of the hat her hair was as blonde as hair ever is—maybe a little blonder—and she had sultry blue eyes which could decide quickly whether she like you or not.

She waved a gloved hand toward an archway. "I'm packing in a hurry. Have to catch a train at Union Depot. I'll be ready in a few minutes," she said.

THE LIVING-ROOM of the cottage had a row of windows on the seaward side. The glass was steamy, and the rain beat hard against it, and you couldn't see out. There were comfortable chintz-covered chairs, a wide divan. There was a piano, a radio, a phonograph, a silver-plated trombone on a table. It seemed to be a very musical room, but I didn't think it was the blonde who played the trombone. She had several suitcases and grips and a small steamer trunk. The divan was piled high with dresses and coats, and one of the chairs had a clutter of fragile, high-heeled little shoes on it.

"I'll help," I offered, and began to pack shoes no bigger than my hand into one of the grips. She thanked me for that, and I've never seen a woman do a faster job of packing. She flung things into suitcases without bothering to fold them. She packed the cases tight, and stepped on them to cinch the straps. All this time her gloved hands trembled.

I said: "What time's your train?"

"It's... What time is it now?"

"Ten after eleven."

"Well, my train…. Well, as a matter of fact I don't have a ticket yet. It doesn't matter as long as I catch the next one possible. My mother is very ill in the East."

"Here's a couple of hundred grand," the Duke said, and fired twice.

All of which sounded like she'd made it up on the spur of the moment.

But it didn't matter to me, of course. A cab-driver gets used to things, and I helped her pack the bags and cinch them, and then we went to work on the steamer trunk. We put things into it any old way. We put in at least a dozen evening gowns of the kind that cost money, the kind that make girls leave home. There were satin ones and velvet ones and lace ones. They reminded me of my former days as a nightclub play-boy and of all the lovely ladies I used to see across a table by candlelight, with soft music and champagne. The days before my dad lost his shirt in the depression, the days when I used to ride on the back-seat cushions of cabs—not up front under a steering wheel, listening to the click of the meter.

I found myself becoming sentimental as I handled those feminine frills and remembering the past. I found myself dreaming over a white organdie gown which had a slim waist, puffy shoulders like wings, a long full skirt, a narrow belt of entwined gold leaves. Altogether the gown looked about as delicate as something butterflies might spin for an angel.

The tall blonde snatched it from my hands and crammed it into the trunk. She grabbed up the remainder of the gowns, packed them carelessly, ruthlessly, closed the lid. "Guess that's all. Can you take all this luggage?"

"Certainly."

"Then let's hurry."

I carried the trunk out to the cab and placed it up front. It took two more trips to carry out the bags and cases. When I came back for the third time I found the blonde having a quick straight rye in the kitchen. She put down

the glass so suddenly it broke against the tile of the drainboard. Her cheeks flushed.

"Are we ready to go now?"

"All set," I said. "Sure you haven't forgotten anything?"

"I'll take a last look."

She went through a door into a bedroom, and to assist
her in a last minute checkup I opened another door into
a blue-tile bath. There was a man's shaving stuff—brush,
razor, tube of soap, lotions, all in the medicine cabinet. I
decided not to mention them.

I tried a closet door in the living-room but found it
locked. Then I happened to glance down to the carpet and
see a stain which might be mud from outdoors. A trail of
ants came to it, swarmed over it, and marched away under
a crack in the molding. Ants which had come in from the
rain. But not ants which would be drawn to mud....

I stooped over and touched the tip of a finger to the
stain. It was damp and cold. It didn't actually leave a mark
on my finger, but it somehow telegraphed a hunch that
sent a shudder up my spine.

THE BLONDE returned from the bedroom pulling a
black Oxford swagger coat over her shoulders. She saw
me tampering with the lock on the closet door and she
stopped in her tracks as if someone had struck her. I noticed
that her cheeks flushed even deeper, that abruptly all
natural coloring fled from them and left just two bright
spots of rouge at her cheekbones.

"This closet," I said. "Thought you might've forgotten
something. It's locked."

She swayed a little, and nervously tapped a gloved hand
against a black suede bag. "I've.... I took everything from

the closet." Her voice was throaty and lacked conviction. "I'm in a hurry to get to the depot," she told me.

"All right," I said, and hastily snicked off lights... but I managed to forget one in the kitchen—intentionally, of course.

Outside, the rain came down in hard gusts, blowing across the dark highway. An oil truck and trailer, blinking red and green lights, went speeding north with a clank of chains and a drifting odor of diesel. A night bus raced behind it, trying to pass, heading for San Francisco.

The blonde said: "I think we left a light burning...."

I didn't give her a chance to turn back through the open front door of the cottage. I helped her over the muddy road shoulder and into the back of the cab out of the rain. "I'll put the light out and lock up," I said.

I intended to do a lot more than that. As soon as I stepped back into the cottage I closed the front door and switched on the living-room lamps. I went straight to that closet door and examined the lock. It was the stock kind.

Any other interior key in the house would turn it over.

I got the key from the bedroom door and brought it back to the living-room and tried it in the lock. Rain beat harder now on the cottage roof, wind rattled the seaward windows, and the surf smashed with gusto against the underpinning of the floor. I eased open the closet door, felt pressure behind it, and a man in a gray tweed suit slumped gently to the floor in front of me, a pile of coats and hats tumbling on top of him.

I stooped and put a palm against his heart. His chest, under its tailored tweed vest, was utterly without warmth. There was a gun in a tan imitation leather holster under his left armpit. I didn't touch it, but the butt of it looked like a foreign-made automatic—maybe a German pocket

Mauser of light caliber—the kind of gun somebody gives somebody else for Christmas. It wasn't the kind of gun a regular rodman would carry, and the under-arm holster was something a kid might buy in the Woolworth toy department.

He was a youngish man, perhaps in the early thirties, with dark straight hair pomaded to a shoe-polish glisten and combed flat to the shape of his head. He had a delicately handsome face, and it seemed to me I'd seen it somewhere in the past. I frisked his pockets.

There was a tan leather wallet bulging with currency, driver's license and club cards which made him Kim Patrick, "The Prince of Swing."

Five years ago I'd danced to Patrick's music at the Mark Hopkins Hotel in Frisco. Now I knew why his face brought me memory pictures. He'd been playing currently at the Sunset Club.

I found a flat silver cigarette case bearing his initials and stocked with smokes of a popular brand, and in another pocket I found another cigarette case—this one small and gold. It had three thin reefers in it. The reefers were hand-made, of white high-grade paper, and looked like the kind sold under the counter by a guy named Ameno the Greek who ran a ratty saloon in San Pedro.

I WAS just tucking this case back into the dead man's breast pocket when a chill draft touched icy fingers to the back of my neck and the front door slammed. I glanced over my shoulder and saw the blonde.

She held one of those tiny Colt twenty-fives in a gloved hand, and the hand trembled. The color had gone from her cheeks again, just leaving twin unnatural rouge spots, and her eyes were wide and blue and almost as glassy as Patrick's.

"You shouldn't… have done this…." Her voice was so low I could hardly hear it. "What made you find him?"

I didn't try to answer that.

The blonde took a halting step closer to me. The little pistol in her right hand pointed directly at my face. It was like looking at the fangs of a rattler—small but not harmless.

"Put him back in the closet," she said.

"Now wait a minute…."

"Did you hear what I said?"

The tiny gun trembled, and she was close enough that I could see she had the safety off. It's no fun to be that close to a nervous gun.

I stooped, as though to heft Patrick's body, but instead I grabbed the edge of the throw rug on which she was standing and yanked. Her legs tipped over a table, spilled a floor lamp, and as she finally fell, her full sleeve caught in a metal smoking standard and the cloth ripped open to the elbow.

I got to her in two long strides and snatched the tiny Colt from her. She tried to bite my hand. I slipped the gun into my pocket and slumped into a chair by the telephone. I picked up the handset and dialed for the cops.

The blonde remained on the floor where she'd fallen and stared at me with wide horrified eyes. "Don't call the police! I didn't kill him! I swear to you that I didn't…."

"Give me Homicide," I said into the phone. "I want to speak to Captain Hollister…."

CHAPTER TWO
FIVE GRAND FOR THE DUKE

IN THE morning I walked around to the corner drug store near my apartment and bought the papers and sat down at the counter to have my breakfast and read them. All the morning editions carried approximately the same story.

Kim Patrick, the band leader, had been found murdered in his beach cottage some miles north of Santa Monica. An unidentified woman was being held incommunicado. My name didn't appear anywhere in any of the papers. They just said that a local taxi driver had found the body and had caused the arrest of the woman.

After breakfast, about ten, I walked down to police headquarters.

I went in and found Captain Hollister. He had been up all night on the case.

I closed the door and slouched into a chair near the desk. "Well, Captain, is the blonde guilty?"

He drummed a handful of fingers on the desk-top. "I wish it was that easy, Steve. But I'm pretty sure she didn't do it."

"Reasons?"

"A couple of them. We've just had the medical report. The guy was shot with six slugs from a Colt thirty-two. The gun in the blonde's bag—the one she pulled on you— was a twenty-five. And there's an alibi too."

"One you believe?"

"Sure," Hollister nodded. "The medical examiner says Patrick was killed between six and nine—P.M.—yesterday. The blonde was at the Sunset Club all afternoon and until after ten last night."

"She told you that?"

Hollister shook his head wearily. "No, we established it. She didn't give us the information. She even tried to hide it. And it's the first time in my life I ever found a murder suspect trying to hide her own alibi. That's why I believe she didn't kill the guy."

I said: "The papers claim you haven't identified her yet."

"Just the morning editions," he corrected. "The afternoon papers will carry the story. We identified her several hours ago—fingerprints."

"Who is she?"

"Gal named Donna Wyant. She used to pal around with Duke Rentano, back in Chicago, before the feds nabbed him on an income tax rap."

I KNEW about Duke Rentano, of course. He was just about as well known as Capone. He'd been a big-shot gangster during the spiked beer days and, like Capone, had moved into sidelines—liquor and women and gambling.

Rentano had been locked up on Alcatraz Island for the past six years. But less than a week ago he'd pulled one of the smoothest escapes ever known in the history of "The Rock." He'd gone over the wall one night, and had disappeared into the foggy waters of San Francisco Bay. He was still "at large."

I said to Captain Hollister: "There's your answer. Rentano crushes out of stir and comes to Southern California and finds his blonde playing sweetheart to a trombone tooter.

THE MAN FROM ALCATRAZ 63

So the Duke goes up to the love nest and fires half a dozen slugs into the guy. Have you thought of that angle?"

"Sure, I've thought of it. But Duke Rentano'd never use a light gun like that. He'd use a forty-five Colt, or a Tommy, or maybe a sawed-off shotgun. I don't think he'd kill Patrick with a thirty-two."

"Maybe you've overlooked an angle," I suggested. "Rentano just escaped from Alcatraz a week ago. He's on the dodge, and guns are hard for fugitives to buy. Maybe a thirty-two was all he could get."

Ashes dribbled in gray flakes from the end of Hollister's cigarette. He squinted at me narrowly over the desk. "You might be right. But I don't think so. I don't think Rentano killed the guy. And I don't think the blonde did either."

"Then who did?"

"I don't know yet, Steve. About all I know is that this won't be any cinch case. This Patrick was never a tin angel. He's been in a lot of jams in his time, and he smoked reefers. We found three of them in a gold case in his vest pocket. Anything can happen to a man with the marihuana habit.

"Here's something else we found on him—a ticket to Chicago. A lower berth, for one, on last night's Santa Fe Super-Chief. He bought it yesterday afternoon."

"Why was he going to Chicago?"

Hollister said: "I don't know. And nobody else seems to know either. I talked to the boys in his band, and they don't know anything about it. I talked to Rosalie Martin, the band's torch singer, and to Mike Magruder at the Sunset Club. None of them heard Patrick say anything about a trip to Chicago. None of them even knew he had a ticket for last night's train. It's all a nightmare."

I glanced at some of the papers on Hollister's desk.

There were half a dozen police photographs of Duke Rentano, taken at the time of early Chicago arrests, and pictures taken later at the time of his incarceration at Alcatraz Island. He was a heavy-set dark-haired man with a fighter's jaw, and deep belligerent eyes. He looked just as tough as he was—the kind of gangster that even the feds couldn't hold.

I said to Hollister: "Maybe I'm just superstitious, but I have a hunch that if you find Rentano you'll find out who killed the trombone player."

Hollister smiled wearily. "You think I wouldn't like to find Rentano? There's a five-grand federal reward on him right now. Every cop in the country is looking for him."

I RIFFLED through other pictures on his desk. There was a police photo of Donna Wyant, the tall blonde who had tried to get away in my cab last night. Notations on the photo said she had been arrested for questioning, six years ago, at about the same time the feds picked up her boy-friend—Duke Rentano.

I leafed through other papers—autopsy reports on the body of Kim Patrick, a ballistics report on the .32 caliber bullets, a sergeant's report on the examination of Donna Wyant's luggage which had been taken into custody at the time of her arrest last night. Also, there was a complete set of police pictures of all the gangsters, grafters, ward-heelers, bums, and shyster lawyers, who had ever had any connection with Duke Rentano during his lawless reign in Chicago. In that collection I found another blonde.

She was smaller than Donna Wyant, plump, with an oval childish face, and wide eyes that looked startled in the harsh police photos.

"That's Rentano's kid sister," the captain told me. "Her name's Rose. The feds picked her up at the same time they nabbed her brother. They released her, of course, but they kept a shadow on her until she managed to drop out of sight."

"Why the shadow?"

"Don't you remember about that? Rentano had the biggest criminal lawyers in the country battling for him on the income rap. The feds discovered his sister was paying off the lawyers in hundred-dollar bills, so they knew the rumors were true about Rentano having a bunch of money ditched somewhere. They figured only his sister knew the hiding place, and that the cache might run as high as half a million dollars. So they kept a watch on her in an attempt to recover the money for the government."

"But they lost her?"

"Well," the captain said, "there's never been a warrant out for her arrest. And if the kid really knew where the Duke's money was, she played too smart to lead the feds to it."

I thought of the Duke's very recent escape and said: "They'd probably like to find her now, though."

"You're damn right," Hollister agreed.

I kept fingering the police photos of this plump blonde, Rose Rentano, and wondering if I hadn't seen her somewhere before. But I couldn't think where, and dismissed it as an illusion. I glanced again at the photo of Donna Wyant, ex-mistress of Duke Rentano.

"How about this one?" I asked. "You holding her on the Patrick kill?"

Hollister wagged his head. "We released Miss Donna Wyant about an hour ago."

"You what?"

"Released her. I can't pin the kill on her, so why hold her? Besides, she might do me more good on the outside. I turned her loose, but I've got detectives shadowing every move she makes."

"She make any?"

"Not yet. Took her luggage over to the Southland Hotel. Went to bed to catch up on her sleeping. She needs plenty of it after the grilling we gave her last night."

"And you still don't think she shot Patrick?"

"I wish she had," Hollister sighed. "It would be so much simpler that way. But I know damn well she didn't. What I want to find out now is why she tried to conceal her own alibi."

I got up from the chair and clapped on my hat. "If I hear anything," I said, "I'll let you know."

He grinned lazily. "Thanks, Steve. And don't forget about that five-grand reward."

CHAPTER THREE
AMENO THE GREEK

THE GREEK'S name was Amenopopolas, or Amenopapadakis, or something equally difficult. Nobody knew how to pronounce it—let alone spell it—so everybody just called him Ameno the Greek. He stood about five-foot-two, a moonfaced little man with a leathery complexion and a mouthful of cheap gold dental work. He owned a crummy tavern in the harbor district.

I drifted in there sometime early in the afternoon.

I selected the deserted end of the bar and whistled for Ameno. He broke himself loose from the cash register, where he'd been busy counting the take, and came briskly along the bar to me.

"By golly! Is Steve Midnight! I don't see you lots of times, eh, Steve? Where you been all these times?"

"Let's have a drink," I said.

He grinned deeply, the gold teeth sparkling. "By golly, Steve, we both have couple of drinks! Is on the house!"

He poured rye whiskey from a special bottle kept hidden, and I leaned toward him over the bar.

"What do you think of this fellow Patrick getting shot last night?"

"Is terrible thing, eh?" His dark eyes attempted to be innocent but nevertheless they had a crafty glint in them. "By golly, I wonder who shoot that fella? Is funny thing, eh?"

"What do *you* know about it, Ameno?"

"Who, me?" He turned the whiskey glass slowly in thick brown fingers. "I just know what I see in the papers. Somebody shoot that fella. Is too bad. He always play nice music."

"Did you know him, Ameno?"

"Who, me? No, I just hear his music on the radio and on the phonographs. I never know him myself personal."

"You lie like hell, Ameno," I said.

"Who, me?" A little whiskey slopped over the rim of the glass onto his fingers.

His eyes squinted up at me from under shaggy dark brows. "By golly, you got no right to call me the liar!"

"Keep your temper cool, Ameno," I said, and leaned closer to him over the bar and spoke to him in a whisper. "A cab driver panders to a lot of lugs, Ameno—even reefer addicts. I've brought a lot of bums here to buy reefers from you, and I know what your weeds look like. I can tell your brand just as easy as I can tell Luckies from Camels. And

Kim Patrick had three of your reefers in a gold case in his vest pocket when he died. The cops haven't traced the reefers yet. If I tipped them off, they'd come right down here and put the pinch on you."

The Greek's eyes glinted like black steel. His thick lips worked nervously over gold teeth. He tossed down his drink of rye in one long swallow.

"We better go in back room, Steve. We gotta talk about this private-like, by golly!"

THE BACK room of Ameno's was a place where men played poker and shot craps on Saturday nights. Now it was empty and dark. There weren't any windows in it, and the floor was cluttered with cigarette stubs and stogie butts, and you could smell last night's misses on the cuspidor mats.

Ameno closed the door on us and locked it. He lit a single grimy bulb in the ceiling, and crossed to a battered buffet. "I get you another drink, Steve," he said.

But he didn't get me a drink from the buffet. He took a long-barreled Luger pistol from the top drawer and whirled suddenly and pointed it at me. I tried to be unperturbed.

"What's the idea, Ameno?"

The muzzle of the gun hadn't the slightest waver as he pointed it at me.

"You make too much damn trouble for me, Steve. You think I want to go to jail? By golly, you don't tell the cops yet about how I sell reefers, so I shoot your big damn face off! How you like that, huh?"

I said: "Keep cool. I haven't called copper. I'm not here to make trouble."

He studied me suspiciously without lowering the gun. "Then what the big hell you come here for?"

"I want to find out some stuff about Patrick."

The Greek thought that over for some time, scratching the back of his scalp with stubby fingers of his left hand. "Is none of your damn business, Steve," he said finally. "You work for the taxi company. You don't work for the cops."

"I have a reason to make this case my business," I told him. "And I don't see why you won't play ball with me. I've steered a lot of reefer bums your way, Ameno. I've never liked it, but a cab driver has to satisfy his customers or he can't stay in business. I've pulled a lot of shady stuff in order to stay in business with the rest of them, but I try to keep clear of real trouble."

The Greek got crafty again. "Did you have something to do with bumping off this music man, Steve?"

"Don't be a stupe," I said.

He did some more thinking and then asked reluctantly: "What you want to know about this fella?"

"Who killed him," I said.

"I don't know this stuff, Steve. How do I know about who killed this fella?"

"You might help me with some tips, Ameno."

"Tips? By golly, I don't have no tips."

"You might. Put that gun down, Ameno. It makes me nervous."

HE GRINNED with gold teeth at the Luger in his right hand and lowered it to his side but still held it ready. "I keep it just like this, Steve. What you want to know about this music fella?"

"How well did you know him, Ameno?"

"Well, I been selling him reefers."

"When Patrick used to come down here to buy reefers did any of his band come with him?"

"No, Steve. He always come alone."

"Ever a woman with him?"

"No, Steve."

"Did you ever hear him mention a blonde named Donna Wyant?"

"No, Steve." His eyes came up to me with a deep, reminiscent look in them. "But that name, she's familiar. I heard her somewhere before."

I said: "Donna Wyant used to be the gal friend of a big-shot Chicago gangster named Duke Rentano."

"By golly!" he nodded vigorously. "Sure, Steve. I read about that dame in the papers. Six years ago in Chicago." The Greek cocked an eye. "You hear about this fella Rentano? He bust loose from Alcatraz about a week ago. He's damn tough fella."

"I heard about it," I said. "And Donna Wyant was the blonde in Slim Patrick's beach house last night when I found Patrick's body in a closet. This blonde had called our cab company. She was packing up to take a train from Union Depot. So it boils down to this, Ameno. The Patrick murder is somehow tied up to Rentano. I want to find him."

"Sure!" Ameno exclaimed impersonally. "All the cops in whole damn country, they want to find Rentano. What you want to find him for, Steve?"

"On account of a possible connection with the Patrick kill," I said, "but mainly because there's five thousand dollars reward on his head. Five grand is a lot of money,

Ameno. It's a hell of a lot of money for a guy like me—just a cab driver."

"Is hell of a lot of money for anybody, Steve."

"I'm willing to split the reward with you, Ameno."

"Who, me?" His dark eyes narrowed craftily. "Where the big hell you get the idea I know where Rentano is? And anyhow I don't monkey with guys like that. You think I want my face shot off? No, sir!"

I sat one-hipped on a crap table and studied him fraternally through the dim light of the back room. "Rentano has the reefer habit," I said. "I read about it in the papers. He kept the habit at Alcatraz, and there was quite a stink up there about cons smuggling reefers into a federal pen." I paused and lit a cigarette and blew smoke in a gray cloud toward the Greek. "If Rentano's hiding out anywhere in L.A., he's getting reefers. Maybe you're not selling to him yourself, Ameno, but you ought to be able to find out who is."

Ameno caressed the Luger pistol and stuck it into his pants pocket. Most of it still protruded. He said: "Why should I find out for, Steve?"

"Five grand," I reminded him. "Or anyway a split of it."

The Greek made a snorting sound through his nose. "You think I want to squeal on a guy like that? You think I want my damn throat cut?"

"That's where I come in handy," I told him. "You can stay out of this and save your neck. All you have to do is slip me the tip. I'll stick my own neck out. I'll front for the reward money. Nobody has to know how I got next to the tip. And you can stay in the clear, Ameno."

HE TURNED his back to me suddenly and went to the buffet. He poured himself a drink and tossed it down,

then poured himself another. All that time he was thinking… and he was no doubt deeply tempted by a proposition that would net him a piece of change without risk.
He faced me abruptly.

"By golly, Steve, maybe I play ball with you. Only if you
double-cross me, by golly, I have your damn face shot off!"

"That's understood," I said, and added in a whisper:
"Where's Rentano?"

"I don't know, Steve. Not myself. But I know a couple
of fellas. They been buying reefers off me the last couple
of days. I think maybe they been buying the smokes for
Rentano. They don't use the stuff themselves."

"Who are these guys?"

"Is couple of fellas on the lam, Steve. You ever hear of
Al Seeley and Frankie Norell?"

I shook my head.

"Is couple guys used to work with Rentano in Chicago.
They been five years in Leavenworth, and they just got
parole. But they jump the parole, and they come out here
to the Coast. They are damn good friends with Rentano."

I said: "If they're good friends, they won't turn him in,
you dope."

The Greek's eyes gleamed. "Sure! But these here guys
are only friends with Rentano because they are damn
scared of Rentano. They would turn in that guy in a
minute—as long as he does not know who it is that turns
him in. So that's why they gotta have a front to collect the
reward on the Duke. They gotta have a front on account
of they jump parole from Leavenworth, and account of
they are damn scared of the Duke."

"It sounds screwy to me. How do they know where the
Duke is?"

His eyes narrowed craftily. "Didn't you never hear about the prison grapevine? These here two guys been sending messages in to Rentano even when he was on the Rock and they was at Leavenworth. Since they got out of Leavenworth they send reefers in to Rentano. They even send him news about how to get out—when he told them he has to get out."

I said: "Alcatraz is the tightest clink in the world. Nothing gets smuggled on—or off—the Rock. You don't know Alcatraz."

The Greek closed one eye in a surreptitious wink. "You don't know Rentano, Steve. That guy, he's plenty rich and plenty damn tough. If he die, he smuggle reefers into Heaven. Or maybe he smuggle messages out of Hell. He's damn tough."

"But you still think Seeley and Norell will double-cross him on the reward money?"

"Sure, Steve—as long as somebody fronts. So we will cut both these guys in on the reward. And cut me in too. You gotta front for all three of us, Steve."

"What's it gonna cost me?"

The Greek poured another drink and brought it over to me. "Is cost you three grand. That's damn cheap, Steve. You collect five grand on Rentano. You keep two. You pay three. I split my end with Frankie and Al. Then everything is jake, by golly."

He left the room and was gone about ten minutes. In that time I sat on the edge of the crap table and kept my eyes on both doors. I still didn't trust this Greek very much. He played with the rattiest of criminals, and it wouldn't be beyond him to turn around right now and double-cross me.

I had a chair in my hand, ready to throw it, when the door opened. But I didn't have to throw the chair. The Greek came back alone, his eyes blandly innocent, the Luger bulging from his pants pocket.

He shut the door carefully behind him and closed one eye in a broad crafty wink. "Is all jake, Steve. I just phone them fellas. They like to collect some money on the reward for turning Rentano in to the cops. You collect these money from the cops, and we split 'em up. Then everything is all jake."

"O.K.," I said. "Where's Rentano's hideout?"

He shrugged. "I don't know, Steve. You gotta go see these here two fellas. They give you the tip."

"Where do I meet them?"

"They want you should go downtown to L.A., Steve. They gotta be careful on account of being on the lam. They want you should go to Seventh and Main at seven o'clock tonight. Then you start walking north on the side of the street with the Burbank Follies and all them flop houses. You gotta wear your taxi cap and a white flower in the lapel. You just walk slow. Just keep walking. These guys, they pick you up after a while."

"O.K.," I said.

CHAPTER FOUR
SLEEPING BEAUTY

I GOT downtown early that evening, and there was plenty of time for dinner in a steakhouse and the late papers. Most of the front-page news concerned the war in Europe, but there was a prominent column about the murder of Kim Patrick, the Prince of Swing. Each of the afternoon editions announced that the blonde woman arrested by police, after a taxi driver had found the swing-ster's body, was now identified as Donna Wyant, former mistress of the Chicago gangster, Duke Rentano. Each of the papers hinted of a love nest on the beach shared by Donna Wyant and the Prince of Swing, and each alleged that Donna had thrown over her gangster boy-friend for a tragic romance with a trombone player. Miss Wyant, the papers said, had been held overnight by police, then released.

The second pages of the papers carried a story on Duke Rentano, the Alcatraz fugitive, but each paper's article differed widely from the others.

One headline read:

RENTANO BELIEVED DEAD
Thought Drowned in Wild Swim from Alcatraz

Another:

MASKED MAN ROBS GAS STATION
AT MEXICAN BORDER
Believed to be Duke Rentano

Still another read:

LOS ANGELES POLICE SEEK
RENTANO IN LOCAL DIVES

And the fourth paper, the *Coast Daily News,* carried still a different item through *Associated Press.* The News claimed to have information from "reliable sources" that Rentano was now making his way to Chicago. The paper claimed State Police were watching all highways into the Windy City, and reminded its readers that Rentano, before being sent to Alcatraz six years ago, had boasted of hiding half a million dollars in some secret place. The *News* stated

further that Chicago police were on the lookout for Rose
Rentano, the gangster's blonde sister. Rentano might try
to join her, they said. She might be waiting for him—to
tell him where the half million-dollar stake was hidden.

THE RAIN had started again when I got over to Seventh
and Main. I wore my Red Owl Taxi cap, a rubberoid
raincoat, and I had gone to a florist for a white gardenia.
The flower made me damned conspicuous on Main Street.

At exactly seven o'clock I started strolling north. I took
it slowly, glancing in the windows of pawnshops, second-
hand clothing stores, and pausing to look at the gaudy
lobby displays in front of nickel movie theaters that ran
all night.

I crossed Sixth Street in the rain, then Fifth, strolling
into a neighborhood that became crummier with each
step.

I kept glancing into the wet windows of stores, and
finally a man in a leather jacket came up beside me, and
we were both looking through the same plate glass.

He said from the side of his mouth: "Did you want to
meet somebody, pal?"

"It all depends," I said.

"Is that a taxi cap you're wearing?"

"It's *your* guess," I said.

"I like the flower, too." He grinned lazily. "Do you know
a guy in San Pedro that runs a bar?"

"You mean a Greek called Ameno?"

His grin broadened, but he kept looking at the pawnshop
display. He said: "We got a mutual friend, I guess. Let's
take a walk, pal."

He was a tall thin man with a haggard ageless face. The
collar of his jacket was pulled up about his throat and he

looked cold and damp from the rain. Brown corduroy trousers clung close and wet to bony legs, and his shoes were the cheap kind you could buy for a dollar in any store on this street. I could tell by the bulge under the leather jacket, under his left armpit, that he carried a gun.

"The name's Al," he said. "What's yours?"

"Steve," I said.

We walked straight ahead at a fast stride. He spoke without even glancing toward me. "Pleased to meetcha, Steve. I got a pal named Frank I want you should meet. We been watching you stroll up the street. We both hadda be sure you didn't carry no cops around in your pockets."

"My pockets are empty," I assured him.

We walked up to Main and Fourth, and then Frankie Norell joined us. He was a smaller man than Al Seeley, but he had a heavy healthy build and wore flashy clothes. He wore a Homburg hat with a tiny red feather in the band, a wide-shouldered Chesterfield overcoat, and his shoes cost money and had a shine on them. He strolled out of a corner drug store, smoking a cigar, and eyed me over, nodded to Seeley.

"Is this the guy, Al?"

"This is the guy. The one the Greek sent."

Frankie Norell studied me again, from head to foot, and lipped his cigar. "Let's all three of us take a little walk."

WE STOPPED at an alley far up Main, and there was no more traffic passing. Frankie Norell said: "Let's get down to business, pal. You're a hacker, and you want to earn a piece of change. The cops'll pay five grand for Rentano."

"Sure," I said agreeably, "let's get together."

Norell pulled down the brim of his hat to an aggressive angle. "This ain't so damned easy as you think. Duke Rentano ain't nobody's sissy. Guys that double-cross him don't live to regret it."

"I understand that," I said. "But Ameno the Greek tells me you two guys know where he is, and that we can split up the reward. I'll be front-man."

"That's the idea," Norell said, nodding. "You front for the money. We'll split it four ways—Al, and me, and the Greek, and you yourself. You think that's a deal?"

"It's fair enough," I agreed. "Is Rentano in California?"

"Yeah."

"In L.A.?"

"Yeah."

"All right," I said, "where?"

Norell removed the cigar from his mouth and studied it thoughtfully. "Don't get any fast ideas, pal. We know where Rentano is, but we want four grand for the tip. It's a big chance we take. Rentano is tough. So me and Al will split four grand, and you and the Greek will split the other. And naturally you gotta front for us on the reward. Al and me's got personal reasons why we both gotta stay in the dark on this deal."

"Naturally." I nodded.

Norell eyed me with sudden suspicion. "Naturally *what?*"

And then I made my mistake. I said: "Both you guys have jumped parole, so you can't front for the money."

Norell's suspicion deepened. "Who told you that? Do you know our names, pal?"

"Why not?" I shrugged. "You're Al Seeley and Frankie Norell. Used to work for Rentano in Chi. That doesn't make any difference, does it?"

Norell yanked his hat lower over his eyes. He glanced shrewdly at Seeley, then back at me. "It makes a big difference, pal. That Greek talks too much. He had no right to shoot his mouth off. We didn't know he told you our names. So the deal is off, pal. Me an' Al can't take no chances with cops, or with Rentano. So just forget about it, pal."

He snaked a flat Colt automatic from under his Chesterfield coat. He shoved the muzzle of it against my ribs and forced me abruptly into the alley.

Al Seeley also produced a flat Colt and shoved it at me. Both guns pressed into my ribs like a chiropractor's thumbs, and both men staggered me far back into the darkness of the alley.

"Now, wait—" I said.

"Don't get scared," Norell told me. "We won't sting you, pal. It's just that the Greek shot off his mouth too much, and the deal's off. I'm sorry, pal." He turned his head, saying briefly: "Kiss the guy, Al."

Al Seeley snatched a blackjack from a pocket of his leather jacket, got it out with his left hand. I saw it swinging, and I ducked a little, but not very much.

After all, it was better to be put to sleep with a leather-covered billy than with slugs from a pair of Colts.

WHEN I woke up I was lying in that same alley, and my head felt as if someone had dropped a ten-ton tractor on it.

I managed to get to my feet and every step I took sent a stab of pain into my brain. I staggered into a bar near Seventh Street and had a couple of quick ones and three aspirin tablets.

Then I phoned for a Red Owl cab and rode on employee rates to Pacific Park.

I got off at the Southland Hotel.

Light rain misted fog-like about the street lamps, and a man in a dark shaggy overcoat stood across the street and pretended to be waiting for a trolley. I recognized his coat and his bulk. It was Sergeant O'Keefe of the Homicide Squad. Further along the block, standing at the mouth of an alley which commanded a view of the hotel's side entrance and the fire escapes, was another man in a shaggy overcoat. I didn't recognize him, but I could safely bet my last dollar that it was another of Captain Hollister's men— assigned to shadow Donna Wyant.

I pushed through the revolving door into the warm lobby of the Southland and crossed to the marble desk. A clerk was sorting mail in the pigeon holes. He glanced at me through thick-lensed spectacles and gave a mechanical smile of greeting.

"Good evening, sir." His hand spun the register around, dipped a pen in the inkwell, offered the pen. His pale eyes behind the spectacles dreamed in some other world. "We have a fine sunny single on the second floor front...." Then he noticed my taxi cap. The smile faded. "Did you wish a room, or are you just calling for someone?"

I said: "I'd like to see Miss Wyant."

"Yes, of course. Certainly." He picked up a phone, said smoothly into it: "Room four-three-seven." And to me: "Whom shall I say is calling?"

"Mr. Midnight," I said. "I think she'll remember."

The phone in his lean white hand gave off a steady muffled ringing while he beamed at me over the marble desk. The ringing continued unanswered for nearly a minute, then he put the phone back in its cradle. "Sorry. Miss Wyant is not in. May I take the message?"

I knew she must be in, despite the unanswered ring to her room. There were two reasons for that. No key in the pigeon hole numbered 437, and the fact that those two detectives were on duty outside the hotel. If she'd gone out, Hollister's sleuths would have followed her.

I said to the clerk: "I'll wait."

I strolled across the lobby to its darkest corner near the plush-treaded stairway and sat in a fat chair behind a potted palm. I had no intention of waiting. I just remained there until the clerk turned back to his job of sorting mail, and then I slipped up the stairs.

I climbed three flights that twisted around the elevator shaft, and on the fourth floor I drifted along the narrow corridor looking at numbers on doors. The one I wanted, 437, was back by the service elevator. I'd lived in the Southland at one time, and now I remembered that the service elevator went to the hotel's basement, and that the basement had a small door, usually not locked, into the kitchen of a restaurant next door. I wondered if those two heavily coated city sleuths, watching the hotel from outside, had thought of it.

THE DOOR to 437 was closed, of course, and I didn't knock. It stood to reason that if she wouldn't answer a ring, she wouldn't respond to a knock. I tried an eye at the keyhole and didn't see anything. The key might be on the inside.

I tried the knob, and the door opened, and when I stepped in I found the paddle of the key hanging on the inside of the lock. All the lights were burning in the room, and a small radio on a table was distorting dance music.

I closed the door carefully behind me and stood looking at Donna Wyant.

She seemed to be sleeping, but it didn't take two glances to tell that she wasn't. The silk lavender spread hadn't been removed from the bed, nor had Donna Wyant undressed.

She wore the same black tailored suit I'd first seen her in last night—the suit she went to jail in—and she wore the same black sport shoes. Her Robin Hood hat had been carefully placed on the radio, her suede bag on the nightstand.

I went closer to the bed, and I found it hard to believe she was dead, because there was beautiful life to her—even in death. Her blond hair hung about her face in loose waves, her lips a little parted, as if smiling, and her eyes almost closed, as if sleeping. There was just a slight stain of blood on her blouse.

I loosened the blouse and found powder marks from a gun fired at close range, and a trickle of blood that had started to congeal.

Only one shot had been fired, but it had been close enough, and expert enough, that only one was needed.

I stood back from the bed and noticed again that she was wearing the same black tailored suit she had worn last night. I remembered the rip in the sleeve. She'd torn it against a smoking stand when I'd shoved her across the room at Patrick's beach cottage.

An idea began to dawn, and I glanced around the room and saw the same steamer trunk, the same suitcases, the same grip—all the stuff I had helped her pack last night when she'd called my cab. None of the luggage had been opened in this hotel room. My idea got stronger.

A woman—a fastidious blonde like Donna Wyant—doesn't go through an arrest, and go through the following day, without changing her clothes. She doesn't continue to wear a black tailored suit, with a torn sleeve, when she has a trunkful of changes. Not unless....

I broke open one of the grips and got out a fistful of feminine shoes. They were all too tiny to fit the feet of a tall girl like Donna Wyant.

I opened the steamer trunk, and the first gown I got my hands on was that fancy white one with the puffy shoulders like an angel's wings and the narrow delicate belt of entwined gold leaves. You didn't have to be a dress designer to see that this gown couldn't possible fit Donna Wyant, and that none of the other clothes could fit her, either.

I put everything back where I'd found it, and used my handkerchief to wipe away any fingerprints I might have left. I looked cautiously into the room's one closet and found nobody hiding, and there was nobody in the adjoining bath, either.

I returned to the bed and bent over her and looked again at the wound in her breast. A sharp, hard-hitting bullet had done it—the kind of high-velocity bullet that goes through you so fast you're dead before you can fall. Possibly the kind of special cartridge made for a Smith & Wesson .38/44.

I backed from the room into the corridor, leaving Donna Wyant forever in sleep, and shut the door on her and left the key hanging as before on the inside of the lock. I used my handkerchief on the outside knob, and then used it to mop nervous sweat off my face and forehead.

There was nobody in the hall.

I punched the button on the wall by the service elevator, and the car came up automatically, without anybody in it.

I rode the elevator to the basement, and used the side door into the restaurant, and said hello to a cook and a dishwasher.

When I came out on the street, through the restaurant, it was still raining, and Captain Hollister's pair of sleuths were still lurking around the hotel in their shaggy overcoats and waiting for Donna Wyant to make the next move.

CHAPTER FIVE
THE ANGEL DRANK ABSINTHE

I **HIKED** four blocks over to the Sunset Club and pushed through frosted glass doors into the foyer. Soft Hawaiian music drifted from the dining-room, polite murmur of conversation from the bar. The hat-check girl gave me a freezing glance as if I'd insulted her by my presence.

"The cab stand is outside," she said coldly. "I'll have the head waiter inform your party."

"Don't work yourself into a lather, honey," I said. "This is a social call. Go tell Mike Magruder that Steve Midnight wants to see him."

She tilted her chin haughtily, and stomped on high-heeled shoes through a door marked *Private*. She came out again, smiling, as if she now loved me dearly, and Mike Magruder, sole owner of the Sunset Club, followed her into the foyer with a jovial grin and an extended hand.

"Hi, Steve! Long-time-no-see. They tell me you're driving a cab for a living instead of spending your dad's money in clubs. It's a change for the better, eh?"

We had a laugh over that and concluded that the Red Owl Cab Company might someday turn a mouse into a man.

"Did you want to see me about something, Steve?"

"Yeah, about your orchestra leader." I cocked an ear toward the sound of strings coming plaintively from the club's dining room. "It sounds like you've replaced him already."

"Patrick? It's not that easy, Steve. He had quite a following at the club. He played sweet music, and you can't replace a guy like that with a bunch of beach boys from Honolulu. Have the cops got any lead yet? I mean about Patrick?"

"Not yet," I told him evasively. "But Captain Hollister is a friend of mine, and I'd like to steer him a tip—if I have any."

"You think I might know something, Steve?"

"You might."

"Such as what, Steve?"

"Well, about the woman Patrick used to go around with."

"I don't know anything about his woman, Steve."

"How about this little love nest north of Santa Monica? Didn't you read about it in the papers?"

"Yeah, but it's all news to me. When I hire a guy to provide dance music, I'm just interested in his music and the way he draws customers to the club. I don't care a damn about his love life."

"Did the boys in his orchestra know about his women?"

Magruder shrugged. "Probably not. The Prince had a habit of keeping to himself when he wasn't working. I didn't even know where he lived till the papers came out.

And while I've seen this tall blonde—this one the papers call Donna Wyant—hanging around with him, I never suspected there was any romance."

"There wasn't any," I said.

His gray brows lifted a trifle. "No? But the papers said—"

"They said wrong," I cut in. "Donna Wyant may've known him, but she wasn't sharing his roof and board."

He studied the long ash at the end of his cigar. "You mean some other woman? Who, Steve?"

"That's what I'm asking," I said. "How about this singer—this Rosalie Martin?"

He glanced up at me sharply. "Her?" He jerked a thumb toward a full-length colored portrait hanging on the wall in the foyer. "Rosalie was just the band's canary. I don't think Patrick had anything to do with her outside of work. Of course, it's just a guess on my part. It's possible.... Hey, what's the matter with you, Steve?"

I was staring at the portrait and my heart had skipped several beats. I was looking at a small brunette wearing a long, full-skirted organdie gown, with puffy fragile shoulders like wings, and a belt of entwined gold leaves.

It wasn't just recognition of the gown that caused my heart to stop. It was a haunting recognition of the girl's face. I felt like a man who doesn't believe in ghosts but can't deny one when he sees it.

There she was, in the portrait on the wall, in the club's foyer. Underneath the picture was a small neat card reading:

ROSALIE MARTIN
Now appearing here in person with
KIM PATRICK
And his Seven Swingsters

I tried to make my face look normal again when I turned to Magruder. "She's a nifty one, Mike. I don't suppose you'd crack out the phone number?"

Magruder grinned. "For an old friend, I might." He fished a small black book from the side pocket of his dinner jacket, thumbed a card which had been thrust loose into the pages. "She gave me this address just this morning, in case I wanted to reach her about continuing to work at the club without Patrick. Here it is. No phone—just the address. Las Flores Court, Bungalow Six, Las Flores Avenue. I'm not supposed to give out the addresses of employees, Steve."

"You've done it for me before."

He gave a jovial laugh. "Still the same old rake, eh, Steve?"

I WENT home and got my Colt out of the top dresser drawer. Too many people had been shoving guns at me in the last twenty-four hours, and I knew I'd feel a lot safer if I carried one of my own.

It was going on eleven when I got over to Las Flores Avenue and hunted out the numbers of the small Spanish-type bungalows in the court. I found the number I wanted at the back of the garden, hidden in wet shrubbery.

No porch light was burning, but I could see yellow light sifting under the drapes at the front studio window. I groped for the bell-button, gave it two confident rings, and the door jerked open so suddenly that you'd think it operated by some electric device connected with the bell. A woman's voice from behind the door said in a tense whisper: "Come in, Duke! Quick!"

I stepped through the door with the Colt in my hand, and shut the door swiftly behind me. I was looking at the small brunette who had her portrait hanging on the foyer-wall at the Sunset Club. She wasn't wearing the angel's gown of white organdie, of course. She wasn't wearing much of anything—just a flimsy silk negligée over her bare body, and the negligée was too large for her. It had been made for a taller girl. The sleeves had been rolled back, and the skirt was so long it trailed on the floor.

Her eyes flashed at me angrily. "Who the hell are you?" She noticed the gun in my right hand, at my side. Her eyes widened. "What do you want? You've got the wrong apartment—get out!"

I groped behind me with my left hand and turned the lock on the front door. "This is the right apartment, *Rose*. It's probably Donna Wyant's. That's obviously Miss Wyant's negligee you're wearing."

She glanced with frightened eyes at my cap. "I didn't call any cab...."

She backed away with halting nervous steps, and tripped on the negligée, and sat suddenly on the green mohair sofa. Her eyes didn't seem quite sane.

"You've got the wrong place," she said. "My name's Martin—Rosalie Martin."

"Rosalie Martin," I repeated slowly. "Didn't they ever call you Rose—for short? Or maybe it was Rose in the first place, and you changed it to Rosalie—for long? And the last name's not Martin—it's Rentano."

The way she looked at me then, you'd think somebody had knifed her in the back. Her voice got down to a throaty whisper. "Rentano?"

"That's it, and we don't have to kid each other. You're the Duke's sister. I saw your picture, this morning on Captain Hollister's desk. Only at the time of the picture you were a blonde. Now you're a brunette. Six years, and beauty parlors, and reducing, and new styles, can make a big difference. But you're still Rose Rentano."

SHE SLUMPED back on the sofa and giggled. The giggle was inane. She reached for a frosted glass at her elbow, took a sip of it. She giggled again.

"You're cute!" she exclaimed coyly, and it sounded like a kid talking baby-talk to a doll. "I think you're real cute! But you shouldn't come here like this. My brother would get mad." Her eyes became cautious for a moment. "Besides, my name isn't Rose Rentano... and besides, I don't have any brother." Tears began to trickle from long lashes and streak mascara down her cheeks. "You think I'm a liar? I am not! You have no right to say it... to say any such a thing... and besides, my name is Rosalie Martin—everybody knows that... and besides...."

I snatched the frosted glass from her hand and sampled it gingerly. Absinthe. Enough absinthe to make any girl turn into a giggling incoherent maniac.

I put the glass down on a table by the sofa and said: "How much of this stuff have you been drinking?"

She eyed me coyly from under smeared lashes, then frowned and abruptly became angry. "Who the hell you think you are, coming busting in here like this? You get out of here! Besides, I want my drink back!"

She reached for the drink and upset it. Liquor made a sudden wet stain on the negligée that didn't fit her. She began to weep hysterically, with her face in her hands.

I backed away from her toward an inside door, tried the knob. The door opened, and I found a closet full of feminine clothes. Clothes that might fit Donna Wyant—not Rosalie Martin.

I tried another door into a bathroom, another door into a kitchenette, another to a wall bed.

All this time Rose Rentano, alias Rosalie Martin, was crying hysterically.

I said: "When do you expect him, Rose?"

"Who?"

"Your brother."

She glanced at me sobbingly. "I haven't any brother!"

I said: "How long have you been living on this absinthe?"

She peeked up at me coyly, through spread fingers, and giggled inanely. "You sound just like Donna… always trying to make a lady out of me." She reached for the bottle of absinthe on the table, but I managed to ease it away from her hands. Again that senseless giggle. "You're just like Donna…."

I said: "You didn't kill Kim Patrick, did you?" And I answered my own question. "No, you're too dumb, and too full of absinthe. Do you know that the cops, and even the feds, are looking for you? They're hunting you under the name of Rose Rentano."

Again the giggle. "I'm Rosalie Martin. I'm a torch-singer…." She had a hard time tonguing the last word.

I said: "Where's your brother's stake? Let's play a game. Let's find it."

"Where's what?"

"The half-million."

SHE STUDIED me thoughtfully for a full minute, red lips showing signs of another giggle that never fully got under way. "You sound just like Kim… want to know where it is. The joke's on Kim… He's dead. The joke's on him because I know the Greek too, and I've been down there a few times, to San Pedro. That Greek likes to talk. He'd tell dirt about his own grandmother—that Greek."

I tried to seem confidential, and I knew she'd had enough absinthe to do a lot of talking herself. She didn't need prompting, either—just rambled along in a semi-coherent way, mostly talking to herself. At times she was hardly aware of me.

The gist of what she told me went like this: Al Seeley and Frankie Norell wanted to hijack Duke Rentano's half-million-dollar stake, but they were too afraid of the Duke to make a bold stab at it. A few remaining wings of the Duke's gang machine—those not yet broken by the feds—were still in operation, and anybody that double-crossed the Duke might find himself dead in an alley.

So Norell and Seeley avoided any plot which might lead them to trouble with their ex-boss. They carefully pretended to remain his friends. They had smuggled him reefers into Alcatraz. They had kept him in touch with his sister via the prison grapevine, and they had even assisted in his escape.

"But those tramps don't fool me," Rose Rentano said slyly. "They talked to the Greek. They fixed it with the Greek for them to meet Kim Patrick, and they made a deal. That trombone hooter didn't know who I was when I started with his band. They told him. And after I moved to his dump he tried to pump me about Duke's money…."

Her eyes narrowed into crafty slits. "Kim was supposed to make love to me and pump me, the big cupid! The hell with Kim Patrick. The hell with all these damn hijackers. If I told my brother about those guys, he'd knock them off."

"Didn't you tell him?" I asked.

She made a vague gesture of disgust. "Why bother? And Kim got knocked off anyhow. I'm loyal to my brother. I got wise to that guy Patrick the first time he tried to pump me. So I played the corn-fed country girl and I told him where the Duke hid his kitty. I told him the Duke hid it in Chicago—that was yesterday. You know what address I gave the guy?"

I said I couldn't guess, and she laughed drunkenly, as if we had a great joke in common. "I gave him the address of the Michigan Avenue Police Station! Can you imagine that poor sap going back there and trying to find the kitty in a precinct-house? It's too bad he couldn't go back and look up the address and find out what a sucker he was...."

She eyed me as steadily as she could, and a new thought entered her absinthe-fogged brain.

"Say! Who're *you?*" She got angry, and reached for the bottle of absinthe which I'd taken away from her. "You get the hell out of here! I never even saw you before! I don't even know your name! Who let you in here, anyhow?"

There was no necessity for me to answer. Somebody had rapped knuckles in a swift signal on the panels of the front door.

CHAPTER SIX

THE MAN FROM ALCATRAZ

BEFORE THE absinthe angel could utter any cry of warning I quickly unlocked the door and flung it wide. "Come in, Duke," I invited.

The man on the stoop was taken by surprise. He saw the Colt in my right hand. His own hands, long and boney, hung at his sides.

He said, in a cold bitter voice: "Eight hard days off the Rock, dodging tough cops and feds, and I get caught by a punk that hides behind doors...."

Rose Rentano rushed me suddenly, rushed at my back, but she was awkward from the effects of the absinthe. Out of the corner of my eye I saw her coming, and I reached out with the flat of my left hand and shoved her away. She tripped on the negligée. It ripped apart and she sat abruptly in a corner, on the floor, her body half-naked. That made her silly again. She giggled in that foolish way, and a bit of saliva formed at the edges of her lips.

Duke Rentano said to me coldly: "You try that again—pushing my sis—and I'll kick your goddam teeth out—gun, or no gun!"

He stepped on into the room, and I slammed the door behind him. I frisked him carefully and found just one gun, a heavy-duty Smith and Wesson .38/44. I ejected the shells with my left hand and tossed the unloaded gun clear across the room.

"All right, Duke," I said, "have a chair."

He walked away from me to the table and picked up the bottle of absinthe which his sister had been drinking. He looked at it disgustedly. He dropped it on the floor, as if the sight of it made him sick. He picked up a bottle of Scotch and studied the label. That seemed to please him, in his solemn way, and he uncorked it and took a long drink from the neck of the bottle.

"Don't try to throw the bottle," I cautioned.

He gave a wry smile and sat on the edge of the sofa. "You punks—you all scare easy." He wearily placed the Scotch bottle on the floor at his feet. "What shall we do now?"

I said: "I intend to call copper on you, Duke."

He stared solemnly at his own hands, shrugged. "Yeah. The hell with it. I don't care. Call it."

"You made one terrible mistake in your life, Duke."

He glanced up with a haggard sneer. "Leave off the sermon, punk. You got me. Pick up the marbles. The cops'll give you five grand on me. Go ahead and collect it. What the hell are you waiting for?"

"To tell you about that mistake you made. I'm not talking about your past life, or about what sent you to the Rock. I'm talking about the mistake you made just a couple of hours ago."

He studied me sharply.

"I mean about Donna Wyant," I told him. "You made a mistake when you killed her."

His jaws set grimly. "Who says I killed her?"

"I do, Duke. You read in the papers about your sweetheart getting arrested in a love nest. The cops didn't prove that Donna Wyant had shot Kim Patrick, but that didn't matter—not to you. All that mattered was that you thought Donna two-timed you for a trombone player. So you went to the Southland Hotel a couple of hours ago, sneaked up through the service elevator, and you shot her with one straight slug from that Smith & Wesson .38/44. And that's where you made the biggest mistake of your life, because Donna Wyant hadn't been sharing Patrick's roof and board. She wasn't untrue to you—the slightest. You murdered her for nothing, Duke."

HE STARED at me blankly, while his sister sat in the corner and giggled and drew her negligée about her and smiled at us coyly.

"Rose is the real trouble," I continued. "She drinks too much absinthe. She's practically ga-ga from it."

"Get to the point," he demanded.

"The point," I said, "is that after you went to Alcatraz six years ago, your sister dropped out of sight. The feds wanted to keep track of her, but they didn't have any warrant for arrest. They just wanted to shadow her because they thought she knew where you had hidden about half a million dollars."

Rentano cocked an eyebrow. "Yeah?"

"But Rose dropped out of sight. She dyed her hair, changed her name, took off thirty pounds of plumpness, and let time and beauty parlors and styles take care of the rest. She wasn't so much hiding from the feds. She was really hiding from any hijackers that might want to make a half-million, while the great Duke Rentano was on the Rock. And just a few months ago a couple of hijackers got warm."

"Yeah? Who?"

"A couple of pals of yours," I said. "Al Seeley and Frankie Norell."

Rentano's narrow face got both cynical and bored. "You slice the baloney too thin, guy. Al and Frankie are a couple of buddies of mine."

It was my turn to say, "Oh, yeah?" and to add: "Well, listen to this, with both ears open. Al and Frankie have been playing you on the sucker side. They've played ball with you, but that's only because they're scared of you and what's left of your machine. They've been a regular team of Boy Scouts keeping in touch with you in stir through the grapevine, and working the grapevine to keep you in contact with your sister. They even helped you off the Rock.

"Those two guys," I continued, "have been double-crossing you all along the line. They've been in Leavenworth five years, and the reason they jumped parole was to work on your sister while you were still on the Rock. They had to help you get off the Rock because you'd grapevine them a death warrant if they didn't. At the same time they were after your stake, and they were after it by working on your sister."

"Yeah?" he asked cynically, but his dark eyes were beginning to believe me.

"So get this," I said. "Al Seeley and Frankie Norell know a Greek in San Pedro that sells reefers. That's where they've been buying yours. And in that same place they meet a trombone player named Kim Patrick for whom your sister was singing. So they arrange with Patrick, who was just a heel anyhow, for him to work with them, and act the cupid with your sister, and pump her about where your stake was hidden. They played the romantic angle on your sister.

"Patrick would like to make a cut of half a million, so he plays ball with the two guys he met at the Greek's. He gets your sister to move in with him and he pumps her about the stake. But your sister gets smart. She gives him an address in Chicago where the money is supposed to be hidden, but the address is a phony… the Michigan Avenue Police Station."

"Patrick doesn't know your sister gave him a phony steer. He thinks he has the answer to half a million dollars, and he thinks he'll double-cross Al Seeley and Frankie Norell. So he sneaks downtown and buys a ticket on the Santa Fe Super Chief to Chicago. He figures he'll collect the money for himself, and then turn Seeley and Norell in to the cops. To a marihuana addict, it no doubt seemed like a fine idea.

"But the trouble was that both Seeley and Norell didn't trust the guy from the start. They kept watching him, and when they found he'd bought a ticket for Chicago, they went out to his beach cottage and put the blast on him."

Duke Rentano studied me with hard black eyes. "You sure of that? Why?"

"Everything checks," I said. "Captain Hollister, of Homicide, tells me Patrick was killed by bullets from a Colt thirty-two automatic. I met both those guys tonight, on Main Street, and both of them carried Colt thirty-two automatics."

DUKE RENTANO put his thin face in his hands, elbows on knees, and became deeply thoughtful.

I said: "When your sister came home to the beach cottage and found Patrick dead, she was plenty scared. So she phoned Donna Wyant."

Rentano took his face from his hands and looked up sharply.

"It's a miracle how some women can love some men," I said. "Donna Wyant loved you so much she went right out to the cottage and chased your sister out. And Donna stayed behind—to handle things."

Rentano's bony face was now a pitiful thing to see. He was outguessing me as I talked.

I said: "Donna wanted to save your sister from being apprehended on a murder rap, or even for questioning. Donna wanted your giggling sister to make good as a torch singer, and Donna went the limit for her."

As Rentano looked at me now, he seemed to ignore the gun in my hand. "Keep telling it, punk."

"So Donna took charge. She knew she had to get your sister's clothes out of there. She called a cab and said she wanted to get to Union Depot to catch a train. The cab—that was me. And Donna packed all your sister's clothes, and cleaned out the cottage—but I happened to find the body of Patrick in the closet. I called the cops.

"The cops arrested Donna and questioned her, but she nobly kept her mouth shut—and even hid her own alibi—to protect your sister."

"Then what?"

"So the cops released the luggage when they released Donna. They thought the clothes belonged to Donna. Why not? Captain Hollister only saw a sergeant's report on the contents of the luggage, and the cops had no reason to suspect the clothes wouldn't fit Donna. It was only a routine check, and I wouldn't have suspected the difference in sizes either—if I hadn't had a hunch on a certain white gown with wings like an angel's, and a belt of gold-entwined leaves.

"I had the bulge on the cops," I continued, "because I used to be a playboy, a matinee dancer, a tea-cup-balancer. So I know more about women's clothes than the average cop. To the average cop, a woman's dress is only a bill which his wife submits to him on the first of the month. If it hadn't been for that bulge I wouldn't have identified your sister as Rosalie Martin, the torch singer at the Sunset Club. I spotted her picture, wearing that white gown, in the lobby of Mike Magruder's Sunset Club. And that's why I'm here."

DUKE RENTANO was looking at his hands, and his face was a thin mask of new enlightenment.

"So now you know the answer," I said. "You killed Donna Wyant for nothing. You killed her without knowing what she'd done for you… without waiting to find out that she'd just been trying to save your own sister from a police tie-up to murder. You…."

"Shut up!" he said, and got up off the sofa. His dark narrowed eyes made him the killer you read about in newspaper accounts. He said: "You can lay off the rest of it, buddy. I know where I'm at, and I know what I done. I killed an angel." He glanced disgustedly at his sister.

"Listen," he said to me quietly, "a couple of guys double-crossed me, and they made me shoot my own woman for something she never done. I'm all washed up, but I got one more thing to do before I cash in my chips. And I need my gun back. Will you sell me my gun?"

I shook my head.

He said: "Did you ever hear of a guy paying half a million bucks for a gun? That's my offer, and if you pull down that wall-bed and cut open the mattress, you'll find the dough. Century notes and small bills, all on the up-and-up—all from the U.S. Treasury." The sinews of his thin hands twitched a little. "You hear me, guy? I'm offering a half a million bucks for one minute with my gun!"

I didn't have to pull down the bed and cut open the mattress. I knew he was telling the truth. I knew the half-million would be there.

He said: "Maybe you're too honest to take it. Maybe you'll just turn it in to the cops when you get me pinched. Maybe you're—like Donna." His eyes narrowed into crafty slits. "I got another idea. If you won't take a half-million bucks for my gun, maybe you'll bargain for my neck. The feds'll pay five grand for me. And you can have the five grand, punk, as soon as I even up the score. I got a personal matter to settle with Al Seeley and Frankie Norell. You don't want a couple of rats like that to get away, do you?"

"No," I said.

His eyes brightened. "Then play ball with me, huh? Let's go down to the Greek's. When we get there, you give me my gun—loaded. I'll do my job, and I'll give my gun back to you. I been a rat all my life, but this time I'm on the up-and-up. Will you play ball with me, fella?"

"I'll play," I said.

CHAPTER SEVEN
A HUNDRED GRAND
A SLUG

IT WAS between midnight and two A.M. when Duke Rentano and I got over to San Pedro. We pushed through the glass doors and walked along the bar in the Greek's.

The place was crowded, with all the booths filled, every bar stool occupied, and the whole joint was thick with cigarette smoke and the music from the electric phonograph.

We walked along the bar, Duke Rentano and I, and found the Greek at the cash register.

He looked up at me and grinned. "Is Steve Midnight, by golly! I'm damn sorry you have trouble with them fellas I send you to. Is too bad. But this fella Duke Rentano, he's bad tough fella...." The Greek recognized Rentano, and his grin faded. "Hello, Mr. Rentano...."

"Let's go talk in the back room," the Duke said.

"Sure!" The Greek got paler. His eyes glinted with fear. "I'm certainly glad to see you, Mr. Rentano...."

"The hell you are," the Duke said.

The three of us walked into the back room and closed the door. Rentano cuffed the Greek roughly, the way you might cuff a dog. He said "Phone Al Seeley and Frankie Norell. Tell 'em to get over here in a hurry. You want to see 'em about something important. Make it sound honest."

"Sure, Mr. Rentano!"

Rentano said further: "If you try to double-cross me, greaseball, I'll grind a heel into your puss, and they'll have to wipe you off the floor with a mop."

The Greek tried to grin. "Is big joke, huh?"

And Rentano said: "There's a phone right in here—ditched in that buffet. Use it, and don't make any mistakes."

"Sure," Ameno nodded, trying to be friendly. Then he got serious. "I got the wife and kids, Mr. Rentano!"

Rentano just smiled wearily. "I'm not gonna hurt you, Archipopulous. Not if you behave on the phone."

Ameno didn't look much relieved as he got a desk phone out of a drawer in the buffet and dialed a number. His hands were shaking, but he managed to make his voice sound unafraid when he spoke to Al Seeley and Frankie Norell. He told them he wanted to see them right away—about rubbing somebody out. He made the speech sound convincing.

His round face dripped with sweat when he'd finished phoning, and his brown eyes got big as the Duke said to him: "Chase all the drunks out of your saloon, or they might get hurt."

AT SIXTEEN minutes to two, I handed a loaded gun to Duke Rentano. He said: "Thanks, pal. I won't double-cross you."

"Didn't think you would," I said, "or I wouldn't give you the chance."

He grinned wearily. "Thanks a lot, pal. You're too honest to mooch that half-million I told you about. But you know where it is. Give it to Uncle Sam for income tax. And thanks for putting me straight about Donna...."

At fourteen minutes to two the place was empty of customers....

At thirteen minutes to two the front glass doors swung open and Al Seeley and Frankie Norell walked in.

They both stopped suddenly when they realized the place was empty.

Ameno the Greek was behind the bar, his hands shaking over the cash register. "Hello, Frankie," he said. "Hello, Al."

Both men exchanged short nervous glances and reached into their pockets.

Duke Rentano came around the end of the bar with a gun in his hand. "You dirty sneaking rats," he said. "You monkey with my sister, and you make me kill Donna Wyant. I just paid half a million bucks for a gun, and I only need five shots, so each slug costs me a hundred thousand dollars. You can have the first one, Frankie...."

The crash of the gun sounded like dynamite exploding in a cigar case.

Frankie Norell bent over, as if somebody had slugged him in the belly with a baseball bat. His Homburg hat bounced off his head.

"Here's another one," Rentano said. "It cost me another hundred grand....."

The heavy pistol wanged again, and cut Frankie Norell in the middle, and spilled him to the floor, to his hands and knees.

All this time I stood in the phone booth, calling the cops. I got Captain Hollister and said to him: "The Patrick murder is cleared. And you owe me five grand for the capture of Duke Rentano. The Duke is just putting the finishing touches on a couple of ex-comrades—Al Seeley and Frankie Norell.... Can you hear it, Captain? I'm at Six-fifteen Wilmington Boulevard, San Pedro, at Ameno the Greek's...."

I glanced out through the window of the phone booth, and saw Frankie Norell try to kill Rentano with another shot. But Frankie's gun slipped from his fingers... he was crawling on hands and knees over the sawdust floor, as if looking for a place to vomit. Then he collapsed.

Al Seeley had a gun out, a flat Colt automatic, and he fired seven times—blast after blast—and the slugs caught Duke Rentano where it hurt. But the Duke didn't fall.

"Here's a couple of hundred grand," the Duke said, and he fired twice. The bullets hit Al Seeley in the neck and threw him across the room, as if you'd hit him with an axe.

Then the bar was silent, the Greek hidden under the counter, and I could hear the wail of a police siren as a prowl car came across town.

Duke Rentano walked unsteadily to the phone booth, leaving two men dead. The Duke looked almost dead himself. Blood leaked from his shirt, blood leaked through his coat and down his shoes. His face was drawn and pale as he handed me the heavy revolver which had killed Donna Wyant as well as these men.

He said, "Thanks a lot pal... and slumped to the floor.

He was dead a full minute before Captain Hollister arrived.

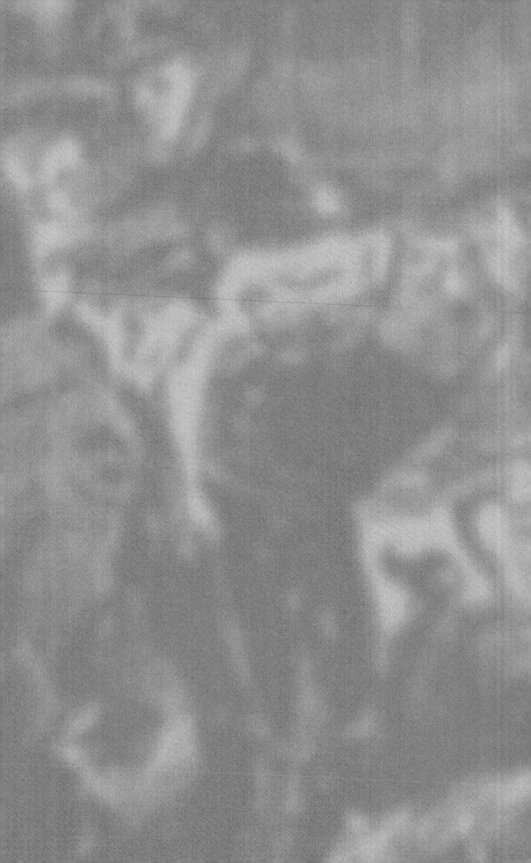

HACKER'S HOLIDAY

IT BEGAN JUST LIKE ANY OTHER DULL MONDAY NIGHT WITH FARES FEW AND FAR BETWEEN, BUT COME 12:00 A.M.—AS THOUGH TO PROVE HIS NICKNAME REALLY MEANT SOMETHING—THE RED OWL CAB COMPANY'S HARD-LUCK HACKER STARTS IN TO DEMONSTRATE JUST WHAT IT MEANS TO BE BACK OF THE 8-BALL. BEFORE 1:00 HE ACQUIRES A BLACK EYE, LOSES HIS JOB AND GETS THE COPS ON HIS NECK FOR MURDER—ALL IN ONE FELL SWOOP.

CHAPTER ONE
THE CANARY
AND THE PUG

IT BEGAN just like any other dull Monday night, with no activity along the Drag and nobody in need of a cab. There was a cold wind blowing in from the ocean, swirling clouds of fog before it in sullen eddies, and snapping the shabby awning in front of the Corinthian Club. Even the weather was dull. I hadn't had a single fare all evening.

Along about midnight I was considering a cup of coffee at the corner drug store when Lola Loomis came briskly through the steamy glass doors of the Corinthian and headed straight for my cab.

She said gayly: "Hello, Ben Hur. Gas up the chariot for a two-bit ride."

She was a small, sad-eyed blonde with a veneer of glamor. She always dressed to the hilt and wore the latest screwy hats and affected the glib sophistication of a telephone operator out on Saturday's date. The veneer was an attempt to cover the disappointment in the tough life she had to lead—singing in cheap clubs like the Corinthian, mailing money to her folks in Kansas, and at the same time supporting a stumble-bum prize fighter named Poke Haley who divided his time between being counted out on the ring canvas and taking alcoholic cures in all the local sanitariums.

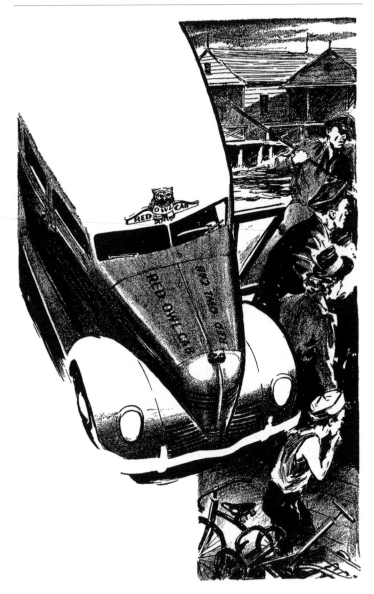

I swung open the door, dropped the *For Hire* sign, switched the meter. "You're through early tonight," I said.

"I wasn't working tonight, Steve. Just barged around to see a couple of guys that claimed they could put me in

She had been bound with lengths
of clothesline to an old-fashioned
iron stove and there wasn't any
need for the pulmotor squad.

radio. Played my records for them." She had half a dozen
recordings of her voice in a flat leather case which she now
placed on the seat beside her.

"Get a job out of it, Lola?"

She sighed and shook her head wearily. "The radio guys wanted me to come up to their apartment—for a personal audition. I've heard that one before. It's a great life, Steve."

I tramped on the starter, rolled the cab away from the curb. "Where do you want to go, Lola?"

"Home," she said. "You can escort me inside, and then wait while I lock the doors and bolt the windows."

I grinned back at her. "The radio guys?"

"No, it's Poke. He's on another binge. You'll probably get a sock in the eye when you take me home, Steve. I hope you won't mind."

"I'll try to be pleasant about it," I said.

LOLA LIVED in a Los Angeles suburb known as Venice, and her cottage was on one of the canals. The shortest way to get there from Pacific Park was over a street called the Speedway. It was really, an alley rather than a street—no sidewalks, dark as the inside of a derby, and you passed the back doors of restaurants, with their platoons of battered garbage pails.

We hadn't gone more than a mile when I became sure we were being tailed. A small closed car, which had been parked across from the Corinthian Club, had pulled away at the same time we did, had made a U-turn, and was now cruising along behind us. I slowed to ten an hour, and the headlights in my rear-vision mirror got no closer. I throttled up to thirty-five, and those headlights didn't get left behind.

I said over my shoulder: "Poke Haley's got us tagged already."

"Poke?"

"Yeah, there's a car tailing us."

"Oh," she said. "But that's not Poke."

"The radio guys?"

She giggled. "Uh-uh. It's somebody else."

"You don't sound worried, Lola."

"Of course not. This goes on and on. Six months now. I have to pull my shades at night. You probably haven't noticed it before, but this same car has followed us every time I've been in your hack. Or anybody else's."

I said: "If it's a masher I can nab him for the cops, Lola, if you say the word."

"It's not a masher, Steve."

"You mean you know who it is?"

"Well, I know his name. One time I sneaked out the side door of the Corinthian and he wasn't in the car. It's a Ford '36 coupé. I looked at the registration. Belongs to a man named Charles West."

I said: "All you have to do is give that information to the cops and they'll find out about West."

Her voice was tired. "I already know about him."

"And you don't want the guy taken out of your hair?"

"No, Steve."

"But if you're in some kind of a jam, Lola...."

"Forget it, Steve. I know why West tags me around, and if anything ever happens, I've got a little friend." In my mirror I saw her open her handbag. She took something out and reached it over to show me—a Colt .32 automatic. "I can use it too," she said. "Don't think I can't."

"You want to be careful with a gun like that, Lola."

"Sure. But it's a handy little friend, and it saves me a lot of worry. In fact, the only worry I've got right now is that Poke Haley might bounce knuckles off your eye when you take me home." She leaned toward me, sitting on the edge of the rear seat. "Steve?"

"Yes."

"Forget what I said about West. Keep it under your pink bonnet."

"Sure," I agreed. "We hackers are like the Chinese—see all, hear all, say nothing."

WE TURNED up the main street of Venice, where garish lights flamed from garish buildings, and I swung the cab over the trolley tracks and into the district of the canals. It was quite a district—not beautiful, but at least unusual. All the streets running east and west were salt-water canals filled by seepage from the ocean. The canals were about forty feet wide, ten deep, and the shacks and cottages faced them in rows. When you saw it at night, it wasn't so bad—you couldn't see the empty beer bottles and refuse floating in the sluggish water.

Our road bisected the district and we crossed the canals on narrow concrete bridges which rose steeply and dropped steeply, like the arched bridges of Japanese gardens.

I flipped on my spotlight after we crossed the fourth bridge and hunted for the street sign. It read: Napoli Canal. I put the cab in low gear and bumped over an empty lot, grown thick with weeds, driving behind the cottages that fronted on the canal.

Lola said: "You'd better stop here, Steve. It gets muddy further on. You might get stuck."

The meter read forty-five cents when I parked. I gave Lola a nickel change from a fifty-cent piece, and she didn't tip me, of course—since cab drivers don't take tips from their friends.

I got my flash and guided her along the muddy trail, through thick weeds, to a dark cottage. Glancing back, I could see the headlights of a car bumping across the lots near my cab. Then the headlights went out. That would be Mr. Charles West in a '36 Ford coupé.

Fog rolled thick and damp over the marshes, with the chill of the sea in it. We groped our way to Lola's cottage and I helped her with the key in the lock. We lit lights in a small living-room with bare rustic furnishings and an old-fashioned pot-bellied iron stove in one corner. We lit lights in the kitchenette, and in the bath and the bedroom. We even looked in the closet.

"I'm safe," Lola said at last. "I guess Poke hasn't found me yet."

I said: "You told me Poke was taking the cure again."

"He was, but he got away this afternoon. Thinks he's fighting Joe Louis tomorrow night, and he beat up a fellow downtown, and beat up a cop. The police want him for resisting an officer. He phoned me an hour ago at the Corinthian—stinko drunk—and he thinks I've got secret boy-friends. That's why I said you might get a sock in the eye for bringing me home."

"Well," I suggested kiddingly, "maybe I better shove along now—while I can still see out of both eyes."

Lola laughed and put the phonograph records down and took my hand in a brief friendly clasp. "Thanks a lot, Steve."

"Got the windows all locked?"

"Sure. Everything's fine now, Steve. Guess Poke is blotto in some bar. See you tomorrow night. I'll be wanting a ride home from the Corinthian at two A.M."

"I'll be there," I promised, and as I stepped out the front door Poke Haley bumped me back against the jamb, clipped an awkward blow to my jaw, jolted a fast left into my belt-line.

"You'll be where?" His speech was thick with liquor. "So *you're* the guy, huh?"

"Listen...." I said.

He slapped my face with a meaty palm. He was a big hulking guy who looked like Frankenstein's monster when he loomed out of the fog. "Listen to *what?* You listen to me, louse! You monkey around Lola, huh?" His bleary eyes took in the whipcord uniform which I wore for the Red Owl Cab Company. He glared blearily at my cap. "Who the hell you think you are? A Nazi soldier? You think I'm scared of the Germans? Nuts to *you*, pal!"

He started to swing at me, and then Lola had him by the arm. She shook him like a mother reprimanding a child.

"Poke Haley, you're drunk! This is just a taxi driver that brought me home...."

Haley shoved her away as easily as he'd brush a bug off his sleeve. He brought up his fists, in fighting position and danced toward me on the balls of his feet.

"Lousy Nazi soldier—that's what he is—monkey around my woman—damn louse-"

Haley led with a left. I slipped it easily over my shoulder but his right snapped up like a whip and smashed me in the eye. I fell backwards into the weeds, and while I scrambled to my feet Lola had both arms about Haley.

She cried to me: "Beat it, Steve! Let's not have any trouble! I'm sorry if he gave you a black eye He doesn't know what he's doing...."

I picked up my cap and dusted it against my pants. "I'm staying right here, Lola. Just as long as this lug gives you trouble—"

Poke Haley wrestled drunkenly in Lola's grip. " So I'm a lug, huh? Well, no lousy Nazi can call me a lug—"

"Please go away, Steve," Lola insisted.

My left eye felt as if somebody had swung at it with a twenty-pound sledge. The swelling got bigger and sore as a boil. Poke Haley kept trying to get at me again, swinging his arms, crouching.

Lola said firmly: "Please *go*, Steve!"

So I told her good-night, while she hung onto Haley, and walked back to my cab and drove away from the district, passing again over the arched bridges of the canals.

And that's the last I ever saw Lola Loomis—alive, I mean.

CHAPTER TWO

THE FIRE AND HIRE SYSTEM

I GOT back to my cab stand before one, and sat there for the rest of the night without another fare. The fog settled thicker and colder, like chill smoke in the street, and it was nearly five A.M. when my phone rang. The call-box at my stand hangs on the wall outside the Corinthian Club, and when the bell rang I climbed out of the cab, crossed the sidewalk and unlocked the phone from the box.

The voice of Pat Regan, the chief dispatcher, barked belligerently into my ear. "What the hell you been doing? You drunk again, Steve?"

"Drunk? I haven't been drunk in a year."

"The hell you haven't! How did you get the black eye?"

I stared at the phone in amazement, wondering vaguely if it had some television attachment on it. I couldn't think of any other method by which Pat Regan would know I had a shiner.

"Well?" he snarled.

"Well, what?"

"Have you got a black eye, Steve?"

I was still in a kind of daze. "Yeah, Pat—just a little mix-up when I was taking a lady home. It's nothing serious...."

"The hell it ain't! When one of our drivers gets a black eye, it's a black eye to the whole Red Owl Cab Company! You think nice people want to ride our cabs when our drivers got shiners? It makes us look like a bunch of gangsters. How'd you like to ride a cab when the driver has his face in a sling? By golly, you bring that hack back to the garage, Steve! You're fired!"

"Now wait a minute...." I protested.

"Wait for what? I'm damn tired of you getting in these jams!"

"I'm not in any jam, Pat."

"No? The hell you ain't! Two different guys been phoning this office and asking which of our drivers has a shiner. The last one even got your license number."

"Who are they?" I asked.

He snorted in disgust. "You think I'd ask 'em questions? Hell, man, the Red Owl Cab Company don't mess in these jams. As far as Red Owl is concerned, we just want that hack! And don't forget the meter receipts!"

He banged up the phone, hard, and I stood there for nearly a minute, staring blankly at the call-box. It's not pleasant to lose your job, particularly at the dreary hour of five A.M.

Finally I locked the box and turned back to the cab, and a man was standing there at the curb, smiling at me.

"Hello," he said.

He was tall and lean, in a military raincoat and crusher hat. He wore a white ascot scarf in a loose knot about his neck, under the raincoat, and his face was thin and hard and boney. His lipless mouth held an unlit cigarette that moved sideways with the smile. I didn't know him from Adam.

"You have some hard luck?" he asked.

"What do you mean?"

Both his hands were sunk deep in the side pockets of the raincoat and he didn't remove them to point. He just shrugged one shoulder expressively. It pointed toward my eye. "That shiner," he said. And again he shrugged, this time toward the call-box. "You didn't sound so happy on the phone. Lose your job?"

"What if I did?"

"Nothing. Except I might be able to give you another. Want it?"

"That depends," I said.

"It's honest. How about coming downtown to L.A. and talking it over with me?"

"What's the risk?"

"No risk. Just a simple way of making some money. I've got a car here, and I can trail you into the Red Owl Garage while you turn in the hack. Then I can ride you downtown. You're safe all the way—like in church. Want to take the gamble?"

"O.K.," I said, and returned my cab to Red Owl and paid in my meter receipts.

HE FOLLOWED me in a green Chrysler sedan with muddy wheels, and picked me up at the garage. Then we rode downtown in the dreary morning. On the way he was silent, smiling liplessly, always intent on his driving. I couldn't get a word out of him all the way. Finally we swung down a concrete ramp into the basement parking of the Wheelan Building.

That was a new building, and not for pikers. An attendant in white overalls took the sedan, and a blonde elevator operator dressed like a drum majorette rode us to the eleventh floor in a cage that was deeply carpeted, paneled in walnut, with indirect lighting glowing from frosted glass.

We walked along a marble corridor past the swank offices of important law firms, large-scale business enterprises, the offices of well-known physicians and surgeons, and came at last to a door marked simply—*SANDERS & WALLACE, Investigations.*

I knew what that name meant, and was impressed. I was more than impressed when we entered the reception-room. It was about twenty feet square, as comfortable as a living-room in a Beverly Hills mansion, with thick rugs, dark oak walls, deep chairs and divans. There were new magazines to read, and cigarettes available on the end-tables, and a tall brunette receptionist behind a desk in the corner. A discreet brass plate on the desk read: *Miss Barker.* She wore a gray tailored suit over a figure good enough for the Follies, and her hair was cut short and mannish, combed back over her ears. Her fingernails were long on slim hands, the nails tinted the same crimson as her lips.

She smiled at us aloofly and said: "Good morning, Mr. Millan."

Her eyes had a tired look, as if she'd been working all night, and Millan patted her shoulder affectionately as he passed the desk. "We don't want to be disturbed, Flo." He gave me a nod. "This way."

We entered a small private office decorated as extravagantly as the reception-room, and he closed the sound-proof door and motioned me to a chair. He sat behind a broad shiny desk, not bothering to remove the raincoat or the crusher hat. He pulled out a drawer and put his muddy feet up on it, rocking back in the chair, and leisurely lit the cigarette which had been a dry smoke since I'd met him.

"Want a drink?"

"It's too early."

"Smoke?"

"O.K.," I said, and took one of the foil-wrapped cigars he shoved across the desk.

"Well, I guess you wonder why I brought you here." He stared sleepily at the cigarette in his lean fingers. "Just for a talk. And the job. I know cab drivers are a pretty square bunch, and I thought you'd trust me better if you saw the company that's back of me." He waved a hand around the office. "You ever hear of Sanders and Wallace?"

I'd heard of them, of course. Sanders used to be an ace G-man working under Hoover in Washington. Wallace used to be district attorney in Chicago and was an equally famous crime buster. The two of them had formed a part-nership in California now, with a reputation as sound as a federal bank. Private detectives, you could call them, but private detectives of a very high standard. They rejected such drab work as divorce cases, domestic probes, blackmail, and things of that class. They worked with corporation lawyers on big-time investigations, collected evidence on insurance swindles, and even worked for the State Senate in probing isolated cases of public graft. Their reputation was unimpeachable.

"I've heard of them," I told Millan.

He nodded solemnly and squinted at the burning end of his cigarette. "I'm Rush Millan, one of the investigators for this firm."

HE REACHED across the desk to tap his cigarette against a bronze ashtray, but I noticed that his little finger flipped the switch on the interoffice dictograph.

"Let's talk about you," he said. "Your full name is Steven Middleton Knight. They call you Steve Midnight as a sort of pun, and because you used to be a midnight playboy on a nation-wide scale. Right?

"Your father was a financier who shot himself after Wall Street losses. You have a mother and a sister, and you've sent them to a ranch in Arizona, because your sister has lung trouble. The Knight money is gone. You now work as a cab driver to support your family. That's very commendable, Steve. You've made a man out of a playboy." He sighed sleepily. "It's unfortunate that you just lost your job with Red Owl, but it's no reflection on your character. Cab drivers have a way of seeing life in the raw, and you happen to be a man who always manages to land in some sort of jam."

I said: "Wow! Where'd you promote all that?"

"Sanders and Wallace never sleep," he said. "I can tell you more. You know a girl named Lola Loomis, a torch singer at the Corinthian Club. You took her home to

Venice at about midnight, and a drunken friend of hers called Poke Haley socked you in the eye."

I said: "So you're one of the men who tried to trace me through Red Owl's chief dispatcher."

His eyes lost some of their sleepy look. "One of them? Were there two of us?"

"That's what the dispatcher told me." "He put out his cigarette thoughtfully. "I don't know about any other one. I checked your license number, and I figured there was a good chance you'd have a stand somewhere near the Corinthian Club, since you took Lola Loomis home from there." He dug into his pants pocket and found a roll of currency big enough to plug a leaking dike in Holland. From this roll he peeled off two crisp fifty-dollar bills and dropped them carelessly on the desk.

"That's yours," he said. "And maybe there's more."

I said: "We hackers don't go in much for murder."

Again the sleepy smile twitched at his lips. "You don't have to kill anybody, Steve. Sanders and Wallace merely want some information, and we want it kept confidential. You might work yourself into a nice job with us here."

"I'm not much of a detective," I said.

"I question your modesty, Steve. So let's begin with the information. How well do you know Lola Loomis?"

"Only casually. A regular fare of mine. Nice square girl who wants to get in radio, and who supports a stumble-bum named Poke Haley." I touched my black eye. "That's about all I know."

"Is Lola Loomis her real name?"

I hadn't thought of that till now. "It does sound a little phoney," I admitted. "Probably a professional name."

"Ever hear her mention her real name?

"No. Why?"

"Because we've had her under surveillance for a couple of months and we have confidential reasons for wanting to check on her. I hope you won't ask the reasons."

"I won't," I said. "The reputation of Sanders and Wallace is good enough for me."

"Thanks. What other friends does Lola have?"

"I don't know."

"Where've you been taking her in your cab?"

"Just home nights from the Corinthian. She used to live in a Santa Monica hotel. Lately in a shack at Venice. Guess she's hiding from Haley."

"Did she ever mention any names to you—friends, enemies, ex-employers? Anything like that?"

I THOUGHT about Charles West tagging Lola in a dark '36 Ford coupé, but ethics prevented me from telling him that. Lola had been a fare, and a driver keeps confidences when requested to do so. "No," I said.

He removed his feet from the desk and produced a bottle of brandy from a cabinet behind him. He poured himself a small drink.

"Ever hear of the Rightman Plan, Steve?"

I'd heard of it, of course. Another Utopian pension scheme aimed at the old people of California. A man named Silas Rightman developed the scheme about a year ago, and it was supposed to be better than the Townsend Plan, or the "Thirty Dollars Every Thursday Plan," or half a dozen other plans aimed at protecting Old Age. Rightman was now trying to lobby the plan through the State Legislature backed by the support of thousands of oldsters who sent their nickels and dimes to campaign headquarters.

I nodded to Rush Millan. "It's in all the papers," I said. "It's on the radio."

"You ever hear Lola Loomis mention anything about the Plan?"

"No," I said.

He studied me shrewdly for a moment. "One other question, Steve. Suppose Lola Loomis gave up her job at the Corinthian and suddenly went away. Would you have any idea where she'd go? Or why?"

"She might be dodging that drunken pest—Poke Haley. But I don't know where she'd go. New York, maybe, to get into radio. Or maybe back to her folks. She said something about her family in Kansas. She might go there. It's just a guess, of course. Why? Did she go away?"

Millan smiled blandly, like a good poker player who might be sitting pat on anything from a pair of deuces to a royal flush. "This is all under your hat, Steve, and I can't tell you any more—not now. But if you want the job, you're working for Sanders and Wallace beginning this minute. You report directly to me, and I'll try to line you up driving for another, cab company. You work entirely under cover, and we find out all we can about Lola Loomis. As a cab driver, you can get a line on her friends without arousing suspicion. This is a big case, Steve. It's so big, we're on a secret investigation for the government of California. That's all I can tell you right now. But I know you're reliable, and if you want the job, you can take it. What say, Steve?"

I'd lost my hack job less than two hours ago, and wondered how I could support my mother and sister down in Arizona, and now I had another job already. It was a grand feeling.

"Sold," I said to Millan. "What's the salary?"

"Fifty a week, Steve. Two weeks in advance." He flipped the twin fifties further along the desk. "And when I line you up with another cab company, you keep the driver's salary. We're glad to have you in the firm, Steve."

We shook hands, and I said: "When do I start?"

"Right now. Go home and get some sleep. Call me back tonight. You can reach me at this office, or at Barney's Bar in Pacific Park."

I left his office walking on air—even that early in the morning. I flashed a smile at Miss Florence Barker, the receptionist, and I felt so fine about life in general that I almost invited her out to breakfast.

CHAPTER THREE

ONE WEST—ONE EAST

ON MY way home from L.A. on the suburban trolley I stopped in at the Elite Cafe for coffee and sinkers. Alex McDougal, the counterman, when he passed me the steaming cup of coffee, said: "You hear the news, Steve?"

"What?"

"Guy knocked off last night. Right here in Pacific Park. Joe Gault, the milkman for Green Valley Dairy—he found the guy. Joe was just in here a few minutes ago. He told me about it.... Try one of these chocolate-coated dough-nuts, Steve."

A platter was shoved across the counter to me, and McDougal sampled one of the doughnuts himself. He went on: "Anyway, Joe is driving his milk route like usual and he sees a car jammed against a fence down on Ocean Avenue. Just about an hour ago. Joe gets out to look at the car, and there's a guy sitting in it. The guy's dead as a post, covered with blood. Maybe the guy's been sitting there all night—dead like that. Joe calls the cops, and they can see the guy stopped some slugs, but they don't know how, or why. According to the registration on the car, the guy's name is West.... What's-a matter, Steve? That coffee too hot?"

I put the cup down. "It's fine, Alex. What did you say the guy's name was?"

"Charles West, I think."

"What kind of car was it?"

"Ford coupé. With red wire wheels. And it was jammed against this fence. The cops let Joe Gault finish his milk route, but Joe's gotta go to headquarters this noon."

"Where'd you say he found the guy?"

"Ocean Avenue. Just down off the street in that gulley that used to be the city dump. You want some more coffee, Steve?"

I got away from the Elite Cafe as soon as possible. The fog had turned to a thin misty drizzle, and I had to hike six blocks through it to the place where the milkman had discovered the body.

There were a couple of dozen cars parked along the avenue, including three official police vehicles. A small knot of excitement-seekers stood in the morning rain and peered over the embankment. Down the weedy slope, below street level, there was a gully, and beyond the gully a white rail fence which blocked off the former city dumping ground. A black Ford coupé, with red wire wheels, was jammed against this fence, and several cops and detectives had gathered around it, smoking cigarettes in the rain. Among them I spotted Hollister, of Homicide, so I heel-skidded down the weedy embankment.

A uniformed cop blew his whistle at me and waved a hand. "All right, buddy! Get back up on the road!"

"I want to see the captain," I said. "Friend of his."

HOLLISTER TURNED. He was a big man in a shaggy tweed overcoat which he'd owned for the past twenty years. His battered porkpie hat was on the way to becoming almost as historic. His face was full and broad-jawed, and his steely eyes had a reputation for being better than 200-watt incandescents when it came to grilling a suspect. The stubby cigar in his teeth shifted from one side of his mouth to the other, with a vigorous jaw movement, and he waved one hand in friendly greeting.

"Hi, Steve. You implicated in this?"

"Any grounds for suspicion, Captain?"

"Nothing concrete, Stevie. But whenever anything happens in this town, you're usually implicated in some way or other. You don't happen to remember shooting a fellow last night, do you?"

"Not particularly."

I went over to the car and peered in. The dead man was slumped across the seat, as if he'd fallen asleep while driving. There was dried blood on his raincoat, more of it on his clenched thin hands, and a lot of it matted in his hair. His cap had fallen off and was lying upside down on the floor boards, with caked blood on it. His mouth was partly open, with rusty stains on his chin and lips. I noticed that his coat was covered with mud, as if he'd fallen out of the car and been put back again.

Hollister said: "About the mud on him, I don't know. Funny, isn't it? There wasn't any marks around the car, except those made by the milkman who found him. The city doc just had a look, and he found five holes that might be from an Army Colt. The first slug hit him in the side, but there's a handkerchief wadded against it. That means the guy was shot somewhere else and tried to get away in his car. But somebody tailed him along Ocean Avenue in another car and threw four more slugs at him. The last four hit him while he was driving. We can see where they went through the car door. Those last four knocked him off the Avenue and down here against the fence. But that first slug had to be fired somewhere else—before he got in the car."

"You know who he is?"

Hollister nodded. "The car's registered to a Charles West. Stuff in the guy's wallet makes him the owner of the car. I don't know what his business was, but we found bundles of pamphlets in the rumble. It's the kind of literature they circulate to the old people about this Rightman Plan. Sixty Dollars Every Tuesday, or Seventy Dollars Every Wednesday—something like that. If the guy's been working for this old-age-pension outfit his murder is gonna be a helluva sock in the puss to the Rightman Plan. They've got a Holier-Than-Thou reputation to hold up, and it'll shoot their lobby all to hell if it turns out their workers are getting knocked off."

"Or maybe it's good advertising," I suggested. "You sure this fellow was working on the Rightman Plan?"

"I don't know. All I've got to go by is the bundles of pamphlets. But I phoned Rightman. He's got campaign headquarters in L.A., and he's been in town for the last week. He ought to be able to explain about the pamphlets." The captain glanced up the embankment at the parked cars. "He ought to be along any time...."

SILAS H. RIGHTMAN arrived in a stately black limousine with a uniformed chauffeur. Mr. Rightman himself had long gray hair, a benevolent face, and wore the dark clothes and high reversed collar of a preacher.

Rightman's chauffeur didn't appear so benevolent. He was a burly red-headed man, with fists like a ring-fighter, and he looked tough enough to rob a metropolitan bank single-handed.

The chauffeur assisted Rightman down the muddy embankment and led him by the arm over to the circle of police officers. Rightman, with a sad expression on his lean, wrinkled face, inquired: "Did a Captain Hollister wish to interview me?"

"Yes," Hollister said. "I'm sorry to get you over here this early in the morning, Mr. Rightman, but the fact is, we've had some trouble. Fellow was shot last night. And the reason I called you is, this fellow had a batch of propaganda stuff in the car. Pamphlets on the Rightman Plan."

The lean face of Mr. Rightman took on a somber flush. "Over half a million Californians support my pension plan, Mr. Hollister. Half a million elderly citizens demand the care of the government in their declining years. I can vouch for the fine character of my flock, Mr. Hollister, and if there is a black sheep in our midst, I'm unable to understand how he was led astray."

The red-headed chauffeur added smugly: "What Mr. Rightman means is he don't know who knocked this bum off, and he don't even know who this bum is, and furthermore, if you want any more dope, you gotta see our lawyer."

Silas H. Rightman shot a shocked glance at his chauffeur. "Please, Brick! Your language!"

"Ever hear of a Charles West?" Captain Hollister asked.

Rightman's benevolent eyes looked gravely into the eyes of the police captain. "Yes, that name is quite familiar. Is that the man who met his death here?"

"Yeah, that's him."

Rightman stared sadly at the ground. "About all I can say to you, Captain, is that a Charles West has been my chauffeur—in the past. Until I got Brick."

"What the boss means," Brick added, "is that this bum Charley West used to work for him, but the guy turned out a load of mashed potatoes, so we give him the air. We ain't responsible if the guy got chilled, and furthermore you got no right to chin us like this. If you want any more dope, then you gotta see our lawyer, or else you gotta soup-eenie us into court. A fine man like Mr. Rightman ain't got no time to mess in these here knock-offs."

"Your language, Brick!" said Silas Rightman again, indignantly.

"The hell with the language, boss. We're talking to cops now, and when you talk to these babies you gotta speak their language."

Captain Hollister said quietly: "You'd better put a halter on some of that language, tough guy. Somebody might kick it down your throat, and you might choke to death on it. What's your name?"

The chauffeur's grin, was smug. "Ben Shultz is the name, Cap. My friends call me Brick."

"What *I* call you," Hollister said, "is a mouthy punk."

"Brick," Silas Rightman intervened apologetically, "is a product of an unfortunate early environment. I hope, Captain, you won't take offense at his language. I hope someday to elevate him to the level of his soul."

"That'll take a tractor," Hollister grumbled. "And get this, Mr. Rightman. I'm conducting a murder investigation here, and I demand some respect along with cooperation."

"Certainly, Captain, certainly. I quite understand your position, but I can't tell you more than that Mr. Charles West formerly worked for me as a chauffeur. I dismissed him several months ago, and if he had pamphlets in the car pertaining to my Plan for old age pensions, then I can only say that he was a true follower of my ideals. I can't give you any information on Mr. West's personal life. I can only say that this whole affair is—er—unfortunate."

By this time, of course, I was fed up with the pious Mr. Silas H. Rightman, and fed up with his new chauffeur. I didn't think either of them would contribute any further information on the death of Charles West—except through their lawyer, or in court—and I turned away and started climbing the muddy bank to Ocean Avenue.

Captain Hollister waded through the wet weeds after me. "You leaving, Steve?"

"Why not?"

He took the cigar stub out of his mouth and studied it. "Ever hear of this Charles West?"

I shook my head.

"Your black eye doesn't look so bad," he told me. "Did you see the drunk yet?"

"What drunk?"

"The guy that gave it to you."

"He probably doesn't remember me," I said.

"You mean you didn't see the morning papers?"

"Sure, I saw 'em."

"Then maybe you don't bother to look at the classified ads. Cops do. It's part of our business."

He produced a rolled newspaper from his pocket and folded it back to the ad section. His finger ran down the personal column and pointed out a single item.

SORRY about the shiner. Will the cab driver in Pacific Park who got a black eye last night please get in touch with the intoxicated fellow who gave it to him? You can see me at the Surf Hotel. I would like to make amends.

Signed: SORRY.

Captain Hollister smiled knowingly at my shiner while I read the item. He said: "As soon as I saw this I told Lieutenant Ross, it'll be Steve Midnight, that driver for Red Owl. Because if ever any black eyes run loose around town, Steve'll get 'em." He reached out a forefinger and stabbed at the swelling. "It's a beaut, too! A work of art, Steve!"

He was calling suggestions for cures—applying raw steak, frog spit, or a gold wedding ring—when I climbed up through the wet weeds to the avenue.

THE CLERK at the Surf Hotel watched me cross the shabby, sunless lobby. He took in the whipcord uniform, the Red Owl cap, the black eye, and before I reached the desk he knew what I wanted.

"Oh, yes," he said. "I guess you're the gentleman to see Mr. Hailford. Room 318. He's expecting you."

There was no elevator at the Surf so I climbed two flights of musty stairs to the third floor and rapped.

Poke Haley opened the door immediately. He must've had a hell of a hangover, because a stubble of black whiskers stood out aggressively on his jaw, and his eyes were bloodshot, with deep fleshy bags under them. He glanced at my shiner, said: "Yay, man, I really slipped you one, huh?

Come in, guy, and meet my friend Kathy Walsh. I don't know your name. They wouldn't give it to me when I phoned the cab company."

"The name's Steve Midnight," I said.

"Come right in, Steve."

I stepped past him and he closed the door.

An attractive dark-haired girl sat in the room's one comfortable chair. She wore a camel's hair swagger coat over a plaid dress, galoshes over high-heeled shoes, and a small smart hat that was speckled from the rain. She didn't look at all like the type of girl who would be a friend of Poke Haley.

She nodded politely toward me, after Haley's casual introduction, and then her face got a frightened look, and she cried: "Don't, Poke! Don't hit him!"

Haley's swing hit me just over the ear with a hard-knuckled contact that made flashes in my brain and knocked me to the floor. He jumped down on top of me and got my throat in his big meaty hands.

"All right," he demanded, "where's Lola? I didn't bring you around here to say no apologies for that shiner. You thought maybe I'd slip you a few bucks, huh? Well, that's all baloney. I just got you here so I could find out about Lola."

The funny part of it was that I'd come to see Haley for the same reason. I wanted to find out about Lola too. But I didn't tell him I was working for Sanders and Wallace.

I said: "Take your hands off me, monkey. I happen to know you socked a cop in L.A. last night, and there's a wanted tag out on you. All I have to do is create a little noise, and there'll be so many cops around here, it'll look like the Germans in Holland."

"I'm not scared a bit," he said. "Where's Lola?"

He had me flat on my back, his knees on my biceps, pressing down his full weight. He felt like a ten ton truck. Now he took his hands from my throat and boxed me briskly, like a cat playing with a mouse.

"Where's Lola?"

Kathy Walsh had come from the chair and was standing over us. "Leave him alone!" she snapped. "Don't be such a drunken fool!"

"This lug is gonna talk," Poke said. And to me, "Listen, lug. Lola went away last night. Maybe she went in your cab. Where'd you take her?"

"I didn't take her anywhere."

"Don't try to kid me. She had to take a cab, or something. She always went around in your cab, I guess. So I guess you're the man that knows." His fist smacked me painfully on the swollen eye, but his swing was so hard it threw him off balance, and I rolled out from under him, spilling him sideways.

I got to my feet quickly, and his next movements were all too slow. He had too much of a hangover.

I slugged him three times in the face while he was still getting up, kicked him on the knee-cap, and he sat down stupidly and began to weep. He was a wreck of a man, an alcoholic, nerves and emotions shattered to hell, and he began to sob, sitting there on the floor, while big tears trickled down his whiskered cheeks. He sobbed so much he couldn't talk, and then he crawled along the floor to a table and took from it a pint bottle of rye, still half full.

"Don't be a fool!" Kathy Walsh snapped at him. "You want to get sent back to the sanitarium?"

She tried to snatch the bottle, but he nudged her away and drank greedily. "Where's Lola?" he barked. He threw the empty bottle at me. Then he put his head in his big meaty hands and cried like an hysterical woman.

I picked up my cap, saying to the Walsh girl: "If this is an example of what the hooch habit can do to a man, then I'm even swearing off coffee and tea. How long's he been like this?"

"Four years," she told me. "Lola's had him take all the best cures. He just can't help it. He drinks till he goes crazy."

I'd started to go out the door when she touched my arm. "I'd like to talk to you," she said. "Not here. We'll leave Poke here. He'll be all right."

THE RAIN fell in a hard spring downpour as Kathy Walsh and I left the musty lobby of the Surf Hotel.

She owned a small DeSoto roadster which was parked against the curb, and we sat in it, Kathy under the driver's wheel, while the rain pattered on the top and trickled down the windshield. She held out an imitation silver case, but I shook my head. She selected a cigarette herself, tapped it against the wheel, lit it from a dashboard lighter.

She said: "You don't really know what happened to Lola, do you?"

"No. Why should I?"

"Well, I thought you might. Poke says you took her home last evening."

"Around midnight," I said.

"Didn't you see her after that?"

I shook my head.

"You didn't go back to the cottage and drive her to a train or anything?"

"Nope."

"And she didn't say anything to you about leaving town, or anything?" When I shook my head to that too, she flipped the cigarette out into the rain and turned her face toward me, worried. "You'd tell me the truth, wouldn't you?"

"I have no reason for lying."

"I'll tell you," she said, "how important it is for you to help me. Something terrible might've happened to Lola."

"Such as what?"

She hesitated only a moment. "Well, I guess there's no reason not to tell you all of it. I'll probably be going to the police—or maybe I won't. I don't know. Lola's been mixed up with something for a long time. I've known her for the last two years—met her when we were both working in a burlesque show in Dallas. We've been pretty good friends ever since. She never told me exactly what it was all about, but one night in San Francisco, less than a year ago, she said a funny thing."

"What?"

"Well, we were sitting in the apartment we shared, and she was reading the newspaper while I did some sewing on a dress. She put down the paper and said to me, 'You know, Kathy, if I wanted to do some talking, I could make it awful hot for a certain man that once did me dirt.' So I asked her what she meant, and she said her name was really Loretta Burdick, and that Lola Loomis was just a stage name. She once married a man in Denver, but he turned out to be a confidence man. When Loretta, or Lola, found that out, she left him."

"Was it Poke Haley?"

"I don't know. But Lola said this man had changed his name now and was in another business. She said she might even make some blackmail money if she wanted to stoop to that sort of thing. That's all Lola said about it—until about a month ago."

"Then what?"

"Well, we were both working here in Pacific Park, singing in the clubs, and Lola told me one night that I shouldn't ever repeat what she'd mentioned in San Francisco that time. Not unless something happened to her. She said she had to keep her mouth shut, and she showed me a pistol she'd bought to protect herself. She said she wasn't interfering with this man who used to be her husband, but she didn't entirely trust him, and he didn't trust her, either. So Lola gave me a letter that night, and told me to keep it hidden, and if anything ever happened to her, I was to take it to the police."

"What was in the letter?"

THE WALSH girl flushed, and then looked annoyed. "I didn't read it, of course. And anyway it was sealed."

"You've got the letter now?"

She shook her head worriedly. "That's the terrible thing. It was stolen from me."

"When?"

"Just this morning—early. Lola called me on the phone, at my apartment in Santa Monica, about three o'clock. She sounded nervous and said she was leaving the city suddenly and made me promise never to tell anybody she was in any kind of trouble. She told me to put the sealed letter in another envelope, and not to read it, and to mail it right away to her folks in Kansas. She insisted I put it in the mailbox right then. I asked her to come see me, but she said she was boarding the train right away."

"Then what?"

"So I did as she asked, and went out to put the letter in the corner mailbox, and a man stepped out of an alley and knocked me down and took the letter."

"You tell the police about that?"

She shook her head nervously. "No. On the phone, Lola made me promise not to say anything to the police—no matter *what* happened." The Walsh girl rested gloved hands on the steering wheel. They were trembling a little. "So I don't know what to do. I don't know whether to go to the police—or what."

I said: "Did you tell Poke Haley?"

"Yes, but his brain is just about pickled in alcohol. You can't talk sense to him. He thinks Lola ran away with some man. She called him on the phone this morning, at three, about the same time she called me. She told him she was going East and never wanted to see him again. So he tried to get in touch with you, calling the cab company, putting that ad in the paper. He thinks you must've driven her to the station with some man."

I began to get an idea. I said: "Are you sure it was Lola herself that you spoke to on the phone? After all, Poke Haley wouldn't be able to tell one voice from another, but *you* would."

"Yes, I think it was Lola. She has a funny kind of accent, part Kansas, part Brooklyn. It's that accent and voice that makes her go over so well when she sings in the clubs. So I'd know it. Or I think I would. And naturally, she sounded nervous. And she wouldn't give me any reason why she was leaving town, bag and baggage. I just talked to Pete Sondergaard—he's the manager of the Corinthian where she's been working—and Pete said Lola got him out of bed by ringing his home phone at about five this morning and saying she was taking a train."

I said suddenly: "Oh-oh. Are you sure she called Sondergaard at five?"

"That's what he told me."

"And she called you and Poke Haley, respectively, about three?"

"Yes Why?"

"There's a discrepancy in the time," I said. "At three A.M. Lola was just boarding a train. But two hours later, at five, she still had time to call Sondergaard. Are you sure she really left town?"

"I hadn't thought of that. But Lola's gone all right. Poke Haley came to my apartment early this morning to see if I knew where she'd gone. We drove down to Venice. The cottage is practically empty. Even the furniture gone."

"Furniture?"

"Yes, some chairs and the sofa, and a few other things."

I said: "She wouldn't take furniture on a train. Maybe we can trace it through the local moving companies. Did she own the furniture in that cottage?"

Kathy Walsh gave me a startled glance. "Why, no! I just remembered—that place was rented furnished!"

"We'd better take a drive down there," I said.

CHAPTER FOUR

SHE VANISHED IN VENICE

THE RAIN that morning had been just another California shower and it let up as suddenly as it had started. By the time we reached Venice there were people headed for the beach in swimsuits, and in one of the canals some kids were playing deep-sea diver with a home-made diving apparatus constructed cleverly of an old wash-boiler, a length of garden hose and a bicycle pump.

Kathy Walsh drove the roadster smoothly over the arched bridges and turned into the marshy lots along Napoli Canal. It was muddier than ever after the rain, and we left the roadster and walked the rest of the way to the cottage.

The door had been smashed open and was leaning crazily on a broken hinge.

Kathy said: "Poke Haley did that when we came down here this morning. He thought Lola might be inside with some man. He's as screwy as a mouse in a cage, you know."

"I know," I said.

We stepped into the cottage, and it was vacant, all right. Rugs gone, pictures removed from the walls, the furniture itself gone. But the thing that struck me immediately was that even the old pot-belly stove was missing. I couldn't think of any reason why Lola Loomis, a nightclub canary, would want to steal a wood stove.

Kathy said: "Strange, isn't it?"

I'd found something else that was strange. The floor had been swept, a thoughtful gesture on the part of a tenant who's stealing the landlord's furniture, and a spot in the center of the room had been scrubbed clean. A rug had once been in this spot. You could tell by the darker, unfaded tone of the pine planks.

I thought about that, and then began looking around the place. In the bedroom part of the furnishings had been left—the heavier pieces. In the kitchen, the tiny gas range was still there, and most of the dishes. In the bathroom there was a musical powder box on a shelf, and a couple of costly little bottles of French perfume.

I didn't think Lola Loomis was the kind of girl who would steal an old stove and leave behind that imported perfume, so I returned to the living-room again and gave it a more thorough check.

In the ceiling, the last place you'd think to look, a sheet of tin had been tacked to the plaster, as if to cover a leak. The tin was rusty, but the heads of the tacks looked as if they'd been hammered recently. And the most interesting feature of all was that this ceiling leak was directly over the spot where the floor had been scrubbed.

I got a straight chair from the kitchen and stood on it to pry the tin loose with my pocket-knife. There was a sharp round puncture in the plaster.

Kathy said: "Good Lord! You don't think a bullet did that?"

"I certainly do," I said, and stepping down from the chair, examined the room once again. This time I found a sprinkle of soot near the glass doors to the porch.

The porch was on the canal side, its planks joining the planks of a small boat wharf that extended over the water.

I walked out on the wharf and the planks were still wet from the rain. I stooped down and ran my finger between loose boards and when I looked at the finger it had wet soot on it.

Kathy Walsh was beside me now, watching me curiously, her eyes round and frightened.

I stood up suddenly, and by accident—or not quite accident—I bumped against her and knocked the leather handbag from under her arm. It fell into the water with a splash, sank.

"I'm clumsy," I apologized.

She accepted the accident with a good-natured smile, bending over the edge of the wharf, peering down. "Gosh," she said, "the water's so dirty you can't even see where it went."

"We'll get it," I promised, "even if we have to hire a deep-sea diver." Then I snapped my fingers as if I'd just thought of something. "Those kids… I'll get them. Wait right here, Kathy."

I HIKED up the edge of Napoli Canal and crossed the bridge and went over to the next canal.

The kids were still there, with their homemade diving apparatus. They took me for a truant officer and started to run. I lured them back by jingling a pocketful of change.

"Listen," I explained, "a lady just dropped her purse off a wharf on Napoli Canal. I'll pay a reward of a dollar to anybody that can get it for me. How about it, fellas? Is Napoli too deep for your diving equipment?"

A tow-headed kid glowered at me scornfully. He looked like a ten-year-old edition of James Cagney. "Listen, mister," he said, "for a buck I'd dive off the Santa Monica breakwater." Then he got shrewd and winked at his partners surreptitiously. "But it's muddy down there. How about a buck and a quarter to cover the whole five of us?"

"It's a deal," I agreed, and when I returned along Napoli Canal I had the five-man diving crew with me. They ranged in ages from the Cagney urchin, ten, to a kid about six who peddled a tricycle. The tricycle towed along a toy wagon for a trailer, and on the trailer was the diving equipment.

Kathy Walsh was waiting for us on the wharf, and the miniature Cagney instantly took charge of operations. "All right, you guys," he barked, "get that stuff ready. Don't worry, lady, we can get your purse."

The wash-boiler, inverted, was a diving helmet. This settled down over young Cagney's head, and stretched rubber drawn tight about his scrawny neck. He wore nothing but swim-trunks, otherwise he was naked. You could see his glowering face behind the glass window which had been fixed into the front of the helmet.

His crew worked efficiently. They thrust the bicycle pump up and down, hissing air into the helmet, and air escaped through a makeshift valve in the top. They tied a rope around the diver's waist, and attached a belt which carried cumbersome pieces of scrap iron.

"We're ready," they said.

The youthful diver waded into the water at the side of the wharf, his bare feet oozing mud. He waded deeper and deeper, until the water closed over his head, and bubbles rose rapidly to the surface from the valve. Then he was down out of sight, while we followed his progress only by the movement of the rope attached to his middle, the path of the bubbles.

None of us spoke. The crew took turns on the bicycle pump, and suddenly there came a yank on the rope.

"He's got it!" one of the kids said.

But I knew the diver didn't have it—not the purse, because I'd started him in the water on the other side of the wharf from where the purse had fallen in.

We dragged him back up the bank by the rope, and the crew removed the helmet. He was shivering—not just from the cold water. His skin had goose-prickles. His thin freckled face was scared.

"Gee!" he cried. "There's a lady down there!"

I pretended I hadn't sent him down there to hunt for anything like that. "A what?"

"A lady! She's drowned! Honest, mister! I ain't fooling—
it's a real lady!"

Kathy Walsh said: "Good God, maybe it's Lola!"

"Honest," the boy diver went on excitedly, "she's down
there, and she's tied to something that looks like an iron
stove—like you heat a room with!"

I wiped the fingers of my right hand against my pants,
removing the stove soot I'd found in the planks of the
wharf. "It couldn't be a stove," I said. "How could it be?
You boys go call the cops."

A POLICE radio car arrived fast. Following that, by a
few seconds, came the pulmotor squad from the fire department. Then more sirens announcing the life-guard
crew from the beach, a traffic cop on a motorcycle, and
Captain Hollister, of Homicide, in a small white official
sedan that bogged down in the mud outside the Loomis
cottage.

The life guards had worked speedily, bringing up the
body from the bottom of the canal. It was Lola Loomis,
blonde hair plastered like wet straw to the shape of her
head, her dress hugging her wetly, her chin battered with
an ugly wound. She'd been bound with lengths of clothesline to the old-fashioned iron stove, and there wasn't any
need for the pulmotor squad.

Captain Hollister came striding out on the little wharf,
the tails of his tweed overcoat stained with mud and the
antiquated porkpie hat jammed down over his ears. When
he saw me he said glumly. "You sure get around places
where things happen. Huh, Stevie?"

I said: "This one happened before I got here, Captain."

"You always arrive a little late. What's her name?"

"Lola Loomis. Torch singer at Pete Sondergaard's Co-rinthian Club—until now. I brought her home last night in my cab. A boy-friend of hers gave me a shiner. He was drunk. That's the last I saw of her, until now."

"How'd you happen to find her in the canal, Steve? Diving for pearls?"

I introduced Kathy Walsh. "Kathy," I said, "was a friend of Lola's. She was worried about Lola leaving town all of a sudden. Lola called her early this morning and said she was going away. I met Kathy through Lola's boy-friend. Just met her a little while ago."

"The guy that socked you?"

"Yes," I said. "Ex-fighter named Poke Haley."

Captain Hollister had a marvelous memory. That's part of what made him a good cop. He remembered the ad in the personal column of the morning papers, and remembered the name of Poke Haley. He turned to one of the radio cops and said: "Go around to the Surf Hotel and pick up Haley. He might be there under a phoney name, on account of he socked a cop in L.A. yesterday, and there's a wanted tag on him. Pick him up, Dave." Hollister's eyes came back to me. "How'd you happen to find the body in the canal?"

"We were looking for Lola, that's all. Happened to walk out here on the wharf, and Kathy's purse fell in the water. I got these kids to dive for it. They found the body."

"You wouldn't hold out on me, Steve?"

"Why should I?"

He shrugged. "I don't know, Steve. I think you're a straight guy, but it's damned funny how you get mixed up in these jams. Who do you think killed this Lola Loomis?"

"I don't know," I said.

"You think it has any connection with that Charley West case?"

"I don't suppose so."

"Awful funny that two of them happen on the same night. This Lola looks like she's been shot."

HE SENT for the medical examiner, and a hasty investigation there on the wharf was enough to indicate death by shooting.

"A single bullet," the M.E. told us, "fired upward under her chin, pierced the brain, lanced out the top of the skull. Contact wound. Might be a .38."

"Or a Colt .32," one of the life-guards offered. "An automatic. Here it is."

He had found it inside the stove which had been brought up from the bottom of the canal with Lola's body. He passed the gun to Hollister. It was Lola's own gun, the one she'd showed me in the cab last night. But I didn't mention that.

"I'll be damned!" Hollister said. "Take that rod, doc, and send it to ballistics. I'll try to locate the slug. Also we want to give her hands the paraffin test—see if she shot herself." Hollister's eyes came back to me. "As for you Steve—you seem awful hot stuff around here. Got any ideas?"

"Two," I said.

"Give, fella."

"First—about the furniture in the cottage. It was moved away. I don't think a moving company is responsible, since the furnishings belonged to the landlord, and Lola Loomis was too dead to steal it. Whoever took that stuff away had to bring a car in here to get it. I suggest you take plaster casts of the tire tracks around the front of the cottage. The rain makes it a cinch for you to get good ones, and I only saw one set of tire tracks when I came up here this morning. Of course with all these sirens blowing, and the police cars—"

"Nuts to that," Hollister said. "None of our cars came within twenty yards of the shack. What's the other idea?"

"The other's about Lola Loomis. Some years ago she married under the name of Loretta Burdick. That was in Denver, Colorado. So I suggest you contact Denver and find out the name of the man she married."

Hollister said: "You seem to know a hell of a lot about this killing, Steve."

"I only know what I pick up driving a cab, Captain."

He turned on Kathy Walsh. "Do you have any information, Miss Walsh?"

"Well—just what you heard. Lola was worried about something, and she told me once about her real name being Loretta Burdick, and about a man who used to be her husband."

"You'd better come up to headquarters with us, Miss Walsh."

"How about me?" I asked.

"I'll want to talk to you, Stevie, after I question Miss Walsh. Don't be hard to find."

CHAPTER FIVE

RIDE WITHOUT METER

AS SOON as I got away from the canal district I strolled into a drug store on the main street of Venice, and used the pay-phone to call the office of Sanders and Wallace.

"I want to speak to Rush Millan," I said, trying to sound casual.

"Who's calling, please?" It was the sultry voice of Flo Barker, the sophisticated receptionist.

"Steve Midnight," I said.

"Oh, yes. You're the taxi driver. He's not in the office right now. You might reach him at Barney's Bar, in Pacific Park."

So I called Barney's, but Millan wasn't there. I was pretty anxious to get in touch with him about what had happened to Lola Loomis, so I called back to the office and asked to speak to either Mr. Sanders or Mr. Wallace.

The receptionist put the veto on that. "They're not here at the moment," she said, "and anyway you're supposed to work with Mr. Millan personally on this case. You'd better wait for him at Barney's."

I strolled out of the drug store and there was a Red Owl cab parked at the curb. Olie Greenberg, one of our drivers, grinned up at me from his newspaper. "Hi-yuh, Steve. I heard about Pat Regan yanking your hack from under you. How's the eye?"

I was getting damn tired of people's concern over my eye. "It's fine," I said.

"Did that guy get in touch with you?"

"What guy?"

"The fella that was going around asking all us drivers which one of us had a shiner and where was he?"

"Yeah, I saw him several hours ago."

"Several hours? He must be looking for you again. He only asked me ten minutes ago."

"A big guy with a black beard and a hangover?"

"No, a red-headed guy dressed like a chauffeur."

So it wasn't Poke Haley—not this time. It was Ben Schultz, whose friends all called him Brick.

Toward noon, big dark clouds rolled in again from the ocean and fought a thunderous battle in the skies. I rode a suburban trolley from Venice to Pacific Park, and got off at my station and wondered which way to go. I could stroll up the drag to my hotel and maybe find Brick Schultz, or I could stroll up Fourth Street to Barney's Bar and wait for Rush Millan. While I was debating that, somebody else made a decision for me.

I'd seen this dark sedan move up the street past the trolley station. I didn't pay any attention to it. Then the clouds clapped heavy thunder overhead, the rain came down in driving sheets, and the same dark sedan came back again and braked to a stop. A man stepped out of it briskly.

"Hell," he said, "I been looking all over town for you." It was Brick Schultz, and he held his right hand tight inside his pocket. "This is a rod," he said. "If you think I'm scared to blast you in broad daylight, then you can stay where you are. You want to get in the car, pussface?"

The cloth of his pocket bulged ominously with the shape of the gun inside it and the barrel seemed to be tilted at just the right angle to send bullets crashing upward between my good eye and my shiner.

So I climbed into the rear seat of the sedan, and he joined me there instantly. He slammed the door, took the gun from his pocket and held it across his lap.

"O.K., Harry," he said, "roll it."

There was another man in the front beside the driver. He was slumped down in the seat, his whiskered chin resting on his shoulder, his head tipped a little to one side. He hadn't moved since I got into the car, and his only movement now was the slight rock of his head as the car turned the corner.

I said: "What did you do with Haley? Kill him?"

Schultz gave a scoffing laugh. "Him? Say, if hooch don't kill that big bum, nothing will. I never seen such a souse in my life. Harry and me go up to his hotel, and the big gorilla is sitting on the floor and he's bawling like a baby. Somebody stole his woman, he says. So we get him out in the car and drive him around, but he won't talk. We even took his shoes off and gave him the old hot-foot, with matches. You know what he did? He fell asleep!" Schultz wagged his head in amazement. "Can you imagine a souse like that?"

The sedan had crossed the business district of Pacific Park and was now in a forlorn section of bare, rolling hills and abandoned oil derricks.

"Where'm I going?" I asked.

"Just a little ride, hacker. And don't let the meter worry you. We ain't got one."

AHEAD OF us there was only a dirt road now, muddy in the rain, and the sedan continued along this with no traffic in sight in any direction. We parked in a by way off the road, and Harry killed the motor and twisted around in the seat to look back at us.

"This all right, Brick?"

"This is swell," Schultz said. He swung up the heavy revolver and slapped me hard on the jaw with it. Instinctively I put my hands up to guard my face, and he slugged the top of my head with the gun, and then jabbed the muzzle into my ribs with the force of a railroad section-hand driving the last spike into the last tie at the close of a day's work.

He said: "Maybe you want to talk now, huh?"

"About what?"

Again the muzzle of the gun stabbed my ribs. "Don't try to kid me, hacker. I'm playin' cop now, and I'm ten times tougher than coppers. Charley West was my buddy, see? And furthermore I'm married to his sister, see?"

I said: "You didn't act like such a friend of West's when you talked to the cops up on Ocean Avenue this morning."

"Never mind how I acted in front of the cops. You're gonna tell me who bumped Charley, see?"

"What makes you think I know?"

"Listen, don't try to kid me. You took that Loomis dame home in your hack last night. So you was down there, and this bum Poke Haley was down there, so one of you has got to know what happened to Charley."

"Oh," I said, "I see what you mean. Charley West got knocked off while he was tailing Lola Loomis."

That stopped Shultz. He stared at me for a moment with profound amazement. "How the hell you know *that?*"

"I know lots of things. Maybe *I'm* the one that ought to ask the questions. West was working for Silas Rightman, wasn't he? All this about West being canned as Rightman's chauffeur is a lot of baloney West was doing the tail-job for Rightman."

Shultz made an effort to recover from his surprise. He said: "Mr. Rightman ain't got a thing to do with what happened to Charley. Charley was just tailing that dame around on account of he had a crush on her. And Charley's my brother-in-law. So I gotta find out who rubbed him. That's all it is, see?"

"Baloney," I said. "The way it stands now you might've bumped off Charley West yourself. Or this guy Harry did.

Or Rightman himself. You picked up Poke Haley because you knew he was down there at the Loomis cottage about the time Charley stopped the first bullet. You thought Haley might've seen something. You had to be sure he didn't. And now you've picked *me* up for the same reason. I was down there at about the same time, and you have to be sure my eyes didn't get too big."

SHULTZ EXCHANGED swift glances with Harry, the driver. Neither of them said a word to each other, and their quick exchange of glances carried a world of bewilderment.

"Listen," Shultz told me, "that's a lot of guessing and it's wrong. You're taking an awful chance saying I killed Charley, because if I had, I'd shut you up forever, right now, with a mouthful of slugs."

"But I'm not taking any chance," I said, "because I know my guessing was wrong. I can tell by the look on your pan, and the way Harry gapes like a fish, that neither of you killed West. And I know that if anybody connected with the Rightman racket did the job, you'd cover it up. You wouldn't spoil a million-dollar racket by letting West lie dead in a gulley with a bunch of Pension Plan pamplets in his car."

Shultz said: "Go on talking, guy."

"So when you picked up Haley and me you really did want to know who killed West. You're trying to cover the Rightman racket by keeping a murder from being tied up to it."

"What you mean by 'Rightman Racket?'"

"I mean," I told him, "that this pension plan is nothing but a high-caliber swindle that deludes half a million old folks into believing they can cease to be a burden on their children if they support this phoney pension scheme. You don't have any intention at all of ever putting the scheme into effect. All you do is collect campaign money."

Harry said: "He can't talk like that. Brick," and closed one eye in a crafty wink. "Mr. Rightman could sue him for libel—for talking like that."

I said: "I'll be glad to have Mr. Rightman sue me for libel. I might ask the court to learn his real name, and if he wasn't once a confidence man in Denver, and if he didn't once marry a girl there named Loretta Burdick. You want to hear some more?"

Brick Shultz nodded sullenly. "Tell us some more, bright guy."

"About the Rightman Pension Plan? There's a nice twist in that. Silas Rightman goes around the state addressing the old people and luring them to his miraculous plan that will pension all of them for a hundred dollars a month in their declining years. He paints a fine picture of happy old age, with nobody dependent on their children or the State. But to lobby this Plan he asks the old people to send him twenty-five cents a month. Nobody thinks he's a sucker when it only costs two bits a month. A mere two bits doesn't sound like a swindle. But there's over half a million followers of the Plan, and those quarters add up, pal. They add up! You don't have to be a cab driver to do arithmetic. Those half million old folks are sending a hundred and twenty-five thousand dollars a month to Rightman. They're sending over thirty thousand dollars a week—over four thousand dollars a day! And four grand a day is an awful big racket, my friend! No wonder the State is making an investigation."

Harry said: "What makes you think there's any investigation?"

Brick snapped at him: "Shut up, stupe. Let him talk."

"There's nothing more to talk about," I said, "except that if you two guys didn't knock off Charley West, and if you didn't kill Lola Loomis—"

"Geez," Harry said, "is Lola dead?"

And with the very name of Lola Loomis, Poke Haley came awake. He snorted and looked around. "Lola? For God's sake, she ain't dead?"

"In a canal in Venice," I told Shultz. "And if you and your boy-friend Harry didn't do either of those jobs you'd better leave Haley and me alone. The Rightman Plan is sunk. The cops will check with Denver and find out the name of the man Lola Loomis married there, when she used the name Loretta Burdick. You'll sink with Rightman on the pension swindle, but a rap in prison is better than a rap in the death-house. You can't cover the pension racket by killing either Poke Haley or myself. So you'd better take to the life-boats, boys. The ship is going down."

I'D MANEUVERED myself, temporarily at least, out of any danger from Brick Shultz and his stooge. They were glad enough to fall with a collapsing swindle rather than become involved in a couple of murders they hadn't committed.

The only trouble we had at the moment was from Poke Haley. He'd come out of liquor-sodden sleep with the knowledge of only one fact in his mind. Somebody had killed Lola Loomis. It might have been us. He wanted to fight.

Harry produced a leather-covered sap, flipped it expertly in the air, snapped it down and Haley's big body slumped down in the seat again, with his head canted as before, his bewhiskered chin resting peacefully against his shoulder.

Shultz said: "Thanks, Harry." And to me, "Say, you don't think this Haley is the one that bumped Charley? Or Lola?"

I laughed at that. "Poke Haley never killed anything in his life—except bottles of whiskey. I'm not so sure about your boss."

"Rightman? Say, that old wind might sell the Golden Gate bridge to tourists, or might mooch the gold fillings out of his grandpa's teeth, but I can't imagine him knocking anybody off. Besides, I know he didn't bump Charley, because I was with him last night."

"With Charley?"

"No, with Rightman. We was sitting in Rightman's hotel in L.A. last night and talking about old times—like when we used to sell gilt-edge bonds in Florida, and the time we had another old-age-pension plan that we worked in Kansas. Rightman was there all the time with me, in the hotel, so I know he didn't go out and kill anybody. Besides, Charley was working for him."

"Tailing Lola?"

"Yeah. Naturally, we had to keep an eye on her so she wouldn't squeal on Rightman's past. Charley phoned us about one o'clock in the morning and said there was a lot doing around the Loomis shack in Venice. He said a cab driver brought Lola home, and that her boyfriend, Poke Haley, socked him in the eye. Then he called again, about two. Somebody had caught him snooping, he said, and socked him over the head and tied him up and tossed him in the mud. But Charley got away, and went to a drug store to phone us. And the last we heard he was heading back to the shack to find out what was going on, and maybe nail the guy that socked him. That's the last we heard till the cops called us and made us come out to look at the body."

"And you don't know who killed Lola Loomis?"

Shultz wagged his head. "It couldn't be Rightman, because, anyway, he ain't the kind of guy to get his feet dirty.... What's a matter?"

I guess I must've had a funny expression on my face, but a whole line of reasoning had fallen into place with that one statement. I felt like a drowning man seeing his whole life pass before him.

"I know," I said at last, "exactly who killed Charley West and Lola Loomis. Let's call the cops."

Shultz glanced briefly at Harry and his mouth curled into a sneer before I saw his eyes again. "Listen, mister, do me and Harry look like a couple of suckers? When this Rightman bubble goes bust, me and Harry'll be a hell of a long ways from here."

"So you don't care who killed West, huh?"

"I care about Charley, all right. I'm really married to his sister. But I don't care enough about it to have a bunch of cops send me to stir on the Rightman racket. Harry and me want to travel places, brother, and we're starting right now." Then his homely freckled face got a shrewd look. "Say, if you really know who chilled Charley, you'd better spill it. Harry and me might have time to even up the score before we travel."

"I'm not positive enough to have you even a score," I said. "But if the guy I have in mind is really guilty, I know a way to trap him."

"You do? What?"

"Drive us back to Pacific Park. I'll show you."

Shultz said: "You wouldn't try to slip over a cross, would you, brother?"

I said: "You've got me in the car haven't you? How can I pull a cross?"

' "O.K., I guess you can't. But we don't want no cops in this—not till Harry and me shake off the dust of California."

"There won't be any cops," I promised. "Not directly. You'll be with me every minute of the time and you can stop me whenever you think I'm pulling something."

Harry and Shultz exchanged brief nods of agreement. Shultz said: "O.K., brother. Who's the guy?"

CHAPTER SIX

I PICK UP THE MARBLES

A T ABOUT four o'clock, with rain still falling from lowering skies, we parked on the deserted main drag. "What do we do now?" Shultz asked.

"We phone like I said."

So both of us got out of the car and entered a drug store and crowded into a phone booth at the back. Shultz still didn't trust me and kept his hand sunk deep in his pocket on the gun.

"Phone, brother," he said, "only when you talk to the cops, don't bring 'em here. You might get hurt if you try a cross."

I dropped a nickel into the slot and dialed police headquarters. I said to the desk sergeant: "There's a disturbance on the corner of Main Street and Ocean Avenue in Pacific Park. Please send a radio car."

I rang off immediately, dropped another nickel in the slot, and dialed the same number.

The same desk sergeant answered the phone.

I pitched my voice a little higher and said: "A man in blue overalls, who looks like a Mexican, just snatched a woman's purse in front of Barney's Bar in Pacific Park. He's about six foot tall, with work-shoes, and a straw hat. Better send a radio car."

I hung up instantly, dropped another nickel in the slot, and this time dialed the fire department. "There's a fire at the Surf Hotel!" I shouted excitedly.

Brick Shultz himself broke the phone connection by pressing his left hand on the receiver prongs.

"That ought to be enough," he said. "Now call your other number, like you told me. And no monkey-business."

I put another nickel in the slot and dialed the number of Barney's Bar. I told the man answering the phone that I wanted to speak to Rush Millan, and in a few seconds Rush himself was on the wire.

"Hello, Steve," he said cheerfully. "How's tricks?"

"It's a mess," I told him. "That girl Lola Loomis, the one you wanted me to find out about, she's dead. Somebody shot her and put her body in Napoli Canal. The police have a bunch of clues. I just found out from Captain Hollister they have plaster casts of tire tracks in the mud outside the Loomis cottage. All they have to do is find the tires that made the tracks. So Hollister is covering Pacific Park with a police drag-net. They're stopping all cars and checking the tires. They've got some more clues...."

Millan's voice became deeply calm, yet brisk. He said: "Listen, Steve, you're working swell. Go downtown to L.A. and wait for me in the bar at the Biltmore Hotel."

"Can't I see you now?"

Somewhere outside the drug store, sirens were scream-ing through the streets—probably the fire department heading for the Surf Hotel.

"Listen, Steve," Millan said, "I'm in a hurry. You're doing fine work, Steve. I'll meet you at the Biltmore as soon as I can."

The line went dead as Millan rang off, and I turned to Brick Shultz with a grin. "It's working, pal," I said.

We came out of the drug store, Shultz and I, and piled into the car and Harry cruised us past Barney's Bar. As we went past on the opposite side of the street, we saw Rush Millan stroll out of Barney's, trying hard not to hurry. We saw him try to light a cigarette in the rain, his hands fumbling with the match.

Across town the sirens were still screaming—the fire apparatus on the way to the Surf—and on the drag two radio police cars rolled slowly, one of them hunting for a six-foot Mexican purse-snatcher in overalls and a straw hat, the other investigating the report of a disturbance at the corner of Main and Ocean.

Rush Millan listened to all this hubbub and tried not to be worried. He watched the two police cars roll by, then he climbed under the driver's wheel of a green sedan and drove away fast.

"All right, Harry," I said, "let's tail him."

WE FOLLOWED the green sedan for three blocks up the drag, two blocks over a narrow side street, and then lost track of him when he swerved through the wide-arched doorway of a garage.

It wasn't the best garage in town—I knew that from my experience as a hacker. It was a cheap repair shop with grimy front windows and a mechanic named Joe Carlyle who specialized in secret repairs on hit-and-run cars, and who was once arrested for altering the motor number on a stolen roadster. The sign over the door read—JOE'S SUPER AUTOMOTIVE SERVICE—OPEN DAY AND NIGHT. I happened to know for a fact that he did most of the business at night.

Shultz and I got out at the next corner and walked back. That left Harry with the job of cruising the block while he waited for us, and it also left him with the job of keeping Poke Haley in line. That last would be quite a job, because Haley had gotten the idea we were about to locate somebody who had killed his sweetheart, and Haley was in a mood to break that somebody's neck.

I said to Shultz: "There's apt to be fireworks when we walk into that garage."

"I'm ready for it," Shultz said.

"But how about me? I haven't even got a gun."

"One of us has a rod," he said confidently, "and one's gonna be enough."

The interior of the garage was dark and cold, with bare concrete walls and a slab floor. Murky light filtered through the grimy front windows, revealing a dozen dilapidated vehicles nosed against the walls. The whole place was as silent as a long-abandoned tomb, but in the back, through another wide arch, we saw yellow electric bulbs burning over a workbench, and saw the front end of a green sedan hoisted a foot off the floor with a rolling-jack.

Carlyle, the mechanic, was removing the tire on the left front wheel, and Rush Millan, coat and vest removed, lent a nervous kind of assistance. Neither man saw us until we'd walked right into the shop. Then they both glanced up at the same time.

Millan's face paled. He said: "Hello, Steve. Thought I told you to meet me at the Biltmore.... How come?" He looked worriedly at Brick Shultz: "Who's your friend, Steve?"

I strolled over to the car and put a hand on the tire they were removing. "Still in good shape, Rush. Plenty of tread on it. Ought to be good for another ten thousand miles."

"I got a flat," Millan said.

"On all four?"

His eyes narrowed suspiciously. "Four?"

"Yeah, you wouldn't be changing all four tires, would you, Rush?"

"Now, listen here…" but he couldn't finish because Poke Haley had come into the garage and picked up a heavy steel monkey-wrench. I'd had an idea Harry couldn't hold Haley outside in the car, and Harry hadn't. I noticed that the knuckles of Haley's fist were bloody, and I could imagine what had happened to Harry's jaw.

Haley said: "Which one of these heels killed Lola?"

That seemed to be the match that set off the dynamite. Rush Millan yanked an Army Colt from his pants pocket. The blast of it was sharp and heavy, with three banging explosions, and Poke Haley's big rugged body slapped to the floor faster than it had ever slapped canvas in a fighting-ring.

In the same instant Joe Carlyle swung at me with an iron tire-tool. I ducked under it, with more instinct than plan, and kicked his knee-cap and slugged him. That staggered him backward. He slipped in some oil, and disappeared abruptly into a five-foot work-pit. He didn't come up again, and I found out afterward that he broke his collar-bone and left wrist in the fall.

While this was happening, Brick Shultz snaked his gun into action. He matched shot for shot with Rush Millan, as both men stood only spitting distance apart. The crash of gunfire filled the garage with blasting sound, brought drumming echoes from the concrete walls.

Shultz dropped the gun, pressed both hands to his body, and went down slowly, like an old man overcome with stomach-sickness. But Rush Millan, already shot twice, was still in action. He swung the gun on me.

But when Poke Haley dropped, I had snatched up the steel wrench, and now I slammed Millan's gun-hand. It shattered the bones in his hand, and I learned later he'd have been crippled for life—if he'd lived that long.

IT WAS ten minutes before any cops arrived because the neighbors, hearing shots in the garage, had chalked it off as back-firing. But Harry, our driver, called the cops. He called them anonymously from a Venice pay-station, told them to investigate trouble at Joe Carlyle's Super Automotive Service, and then abandoned his car and disappeared into thin air. No doubt he had a lot of traveling to do.

In the ten minutes before the cops came I had a long talk with Rush Millan. There was nobody else to talk to, because Shultz was dead, Poke Haley was dead, and Joe Carlyle was unconscious in the work-pit.

I rolled Millan over gently, placed a car-cushion under his head, propping him up so he could breathe easier. He'd stopped two slugs in the chest, and blood frothed at his lips. Shultz had done some nice shooting before he died.

Millan said: "Water, Steve."

I gave him a drink, holding the cup to his mouth.

"Thanks, Steve. You mind telling me something? How'd you get next to me?"

"Mud," I told him. "I remembered mud on your car and mud on your shoes. I remembered mud around the Loomis cottage. And you told me yourself you've had Lola under surveillance. So I figured you must've been down there at the time she got killed. And if you didn't kill her yourself, you ought to know who did. Or anyway you ought to know she didn't just move away last night."

"That's guessing," Millan said.

"Maybe, but there's a lot more guesses. You knew a cab driver took Lola home last night, and that he got a black eye from Poke Haley. So how did you know that—unless you were down there covering the place?"

A vague smile flickered over his bloody lips. "That all the guesses you had, Steve?"

"It's all I needed to start me. The rest of it fit in swell. I don't have to be a genius to smell the Rightman racket, and I don't have to be smart to realize a State Senate Investigating Committee hired Sanders and Wallace to check on Rightman and his Plan. You work for Sanders and Wallace, but you decided you could make more money blackmailing Rightman than you could make in honest salary. So you hid behind the Sanders and Wallace reputation, and you played both ends against the middle. This secretary down at the Sanders office—she's working for you."

"More guesses, Steve?"

"Lots more," I said. "The first time I saw Flo Barker she looked like she'd been up all night. Sure. Working for *you*—not in the office. And when I tried to get in touch with either Sanders or Wallace this afternoon she steered me off. That makes her your stooge."

"You sure of that?"

"I'm sure of everything. I know how you killed Charley West, and why, and I know how you covered the Lola Loomis killing. The only thing missing is exactly *why* you killed Lola. That has to be a guess."

"Try it," he said.

"All right, here's a try. You investigated Lola's past and found out she once married Silas Rightman in Denver. They married under assumed names. So learning that, you wondered why Lola didn't blackmail Rightman. You cornered her last night at the cottage and tried to proposition her to split blackmail with you. But Lola's a square girl, and told you to go to hell. She yanked a gun on you, and you slapped the gun, and a bullet enters her jaw and kills her. Is that a good guess?"

"It's good enough," Millan admitted, his lips dry and caked with crimson.

I SAID: "The rest of it is easy. You knew Charley West was tailing Lola around and keeping an eye on her for Rightman—so she wouldn't spill the truth on the pension plan. In order to see Lola alone you had to get rid of West. So you slugged him to sleep last night, tied him up, and left him. Then you waited till the cab driver went away—that's me. You waited till Lola's boy-friend went away—that's Poke Haley."

"Nice," Rush Millan said. "Go on."

"You had your talk with Lola, but she wouldn't play ball with you on blackmailing Rightman. She pulled a gun to chase you out, and maybe her getting killed was accidental, and maybe it wasn't. You'd land behind the eight-ball if Sanders and Wallace ever learned you were double-crossing their reputation. So Lola gets shot, and you have to get rid of the body."

Yes?"

"This part of it is nice," I continued. "Her blood is on the rug, so you have to take away the rug. And to cover the mysterious removal of the rug, you take a lot of the furniture out of the shack—all your car can carry. That makes it look like Lola just moved away. You scrub the floor where the stain was. You tack tin over a bullet hole in the ceiling. You sink Lola's body ten feet deep in Napoli Canal. You had to have something heavy to keep her sunk, so you tied her to the wood stove. That was a mistake, Rush, because I knew Lola wouldn't steal a stove, even if she stole the landlord's furniture, and also I found stove-soot out on the wharf."

"You're even smarter than I figured."

I said: "While you were covering the Lola Loomis kill, Charley West came back. He saw what you were doing, and you had to get rid of him before he could report it to Rightman, or anybody else. There was nothing you could do now but kill again. You hit him with one shot, but he escaped. You chased him in your car up Ocean Avenue and fired again and again, and finally he crashed down the gully into the city dump. That worked fine, but you were still in a tough spot on the Loomis kill."

"Tough spot?"

"Yeah, there were a lot of cards still out against you. You knew from your investigation that Lola had protected herself by giving a sealed letter to her friend Kathy Walsh. All Kathy had to do was turn that letter over to the police and the Rightman racket would go bust. You couldn't afford to have it bust, Millan, because you wouldn't be able to blackmail a racket that didn't exist. And that's where you played smart."

"Smart?"

"It was a good idea, though," I said. "You took the phonograph recordings of Lola's voice—took them to your friend Flo Barker and had her imitate the voice. Flo called Kathy on the phone and pretended to be Lola, and gave Kathy to understand that Lola was leaving town. You worked the trick neat enough to get that sealed letter from Kathy.

"Then Flo Barker called Poke Haley and told him she was Lola and that she was leaving him. And later you thought about the manager of the Corinthian Club, where Lola worked. You called him too, and let him think it was Lola calling. But you called a couple of hours too late for that angle—I figured Lola couldn't be just boarding a train at three A.M. and still boarding it at five."

"Is there more?" Millan asked.

"Just a little," I said. "Your next trick was trying to handle me. You knew I took Lola home last night. But you didn't know how well I knew Lola, or if I knew about her past, or her connection with Rightman. The only thing you could do was get in touch with me and pump me. And that's what you did. You figured the best way to pump me on my knowledge of Lola was to pretend you were giving me a job with Sanders and Wallace—offer me a nice job, bribe me with money. All you wanted to find out was how much I knew about Lola, and if I maybe had another sealed letter like the one Lola left with Kathy Walsh."

"You're right," he said.

"You weren't just covering a couple of murders. You wanted to blackmail the Rightman racket."

Millan shrugged, and winced at the pain in his lungs. "Pick up the marbles, Steve," he said.

I SPENT the next two days talking to Captain Hollister, and a bunch of cops, and the district attorney. The third day I was chief witness at the inquest.

On the fourth day I had a phone call at my hotel. It was Pat Regan, Chief Dispatcher for the Red Owl Cab Company. He said: "All this hero-stuff looks fine in the papers, Steve. But when do you return to work?"

"What work?"

"Driving a hack, Steve. Or maybe you're too snooty now to remember you're working for Red Owl. Get back on the job, Steve, and get back fast! Who the hell you think you are—Errol Flynn?"

"You fired me," I reminded him.

"Oh, so I'm a liar now, huh? Listen, you got a verbal contract with Red Owl."

"What verbal contract?"

"Listen," he shouted, "I ain't got time to bandy words. Either you're working for Red Owl, or else I'm a liar!"

And I'd learned from experience there was no percentage in calling an Irishman a liar.

"All right," I said. "Grease up the hack."

THE SAINT IN SILVER

IT TAKES ALL KINDS OF
WACKS TO MAKE UP THIS
SCREWY WORLD AND
MOST OF THEM WIND UP
RIDING THE CAB OF RED
OWL'S HARD-LUCK HACKER
THROUGH THE PURLIEUS
OF L.A. THE SILVER SAINT
WAS THE SCREWIEST OF
THE LOT AND, THOUGH HE
NEVER ACTUALLY GOT IN
STEVE'S TAXI, HE TRIED HIS
DAMNEDEST TO PAY THE
METER CHARGE—SEVERAL
THOUSAND TIMES OVER—
FOR THE MIDNIGHT RIDE
OF A TREASURE-HUNTING
BLONDE AND HER CORPSE
COMPANION.

CHAPTER ONE
A FARE FOR VALHALLA

IT WAS the drunk again. He had passed Siberia twenty minutes earlier in a low-swung cream-colored roadster doing at least fifty in the rain, on the wrong side of the street. Now he was coming back again, and still on the wrong side.

That night I'd done a pretty good business on account of the rain. About a dozen short local hauls and a couple of long ones. Altogether the meter had ticked off close to eighteen dollars. Tips had averaged well over a dime a ride. So I felt fine as I sat there in the hack counting over the night's winnings, and I continued to feel fine until this guy in the cream-colored roadster entered my otherwise happy existence.

I suppose it was just after two A.M., because the Corinthian Club had closed. The orchestra boys had come out into the rain carrying neat black instrument cases. The last car had coughed, with chill motor, out of the auto park and I had called good-night to Pete Sondergaard as he looked up. That left nothing on the main drag but the rain falling steadily and gurgling in the gutters, dim night lights burning behind the misty windows of the corner drugstore, an orange traffic globe blinking regularly at the intersection. No pedestrians, no passing cars, no patrolman— nothing. My cab stand after two A.M. might just as well

have been in Siberia. And Siberia is what I always called it, after two.

I was just slipping the count back into my pocket when the roadster came roaring up behind me, doing fifty. It

With the blade of the scalpel she
backed me into the hanging body.

passed like a breath of wind, plump tires hissing on wet
pavement. There was a guy at the wheel, laughing. There
was a girl beside him, trying to wrestle the wheel from

him. I just caught a glimpse as they went by. Then the car went out on the Amusement Pier.

I couldn't think of any good reason why they'd drive out there. In the first place it was against a traffic ordinance. In the second place the amusement concessions, from roller coasters to hot dog stands, had closed early. And in the third place there was nothing out there but darkness and rain and the Pacific Ocean.

I began to wonder if maybe they weren't a couple of lovers in a suicide pact. Drive the car right off the end of the pier. And while I was wondering that, not doing anything about it, the roadster came back again.

It was going slower now. It came down off the ramp at about twenty, couldn't decide which way to turn on Ocean Avenue, skidded a little, first right, then left, as if on casters instead of wheels. Then it came on across the intersection and straight toward me on the main drag, on the wrong side of the street.

I sat up in my hack and blasted the horn button. The sound of the horn was like a siren in the night. The drunk heard it, and saw my headlamps snap on, and decided not to have a head-on collision with a parked cab. He swerved the roadster to the other side of the street, his own side, and the girl grabbed the wheel and pulled the emergency brake. The roadster came to a jolting stop against the opposite curb, and the man's voice scolded drunkenly: "Hey! Wassa big idea?"

"Don't be such a fool," she said, and switched off the ignition and took the keys. There was a little struggle over that, but she pushed him, and his face came down limply against the wheel. He didn't struggle any more. He looked like he'd passed out.

SHE OPENED the door of the car and came across the street toward my cab, a small determined blonde in a yellow transparent rain coat with a yellow rubberoid hood drawn up over waved honey hair. She walked rapidly and aggressively on high spiked heels, the movement of her legs flapping the rubberoid skirt. She glanced once at the lettering on the side of the hack, the lettering which said: *Red Owl Cab Company*. Then she looked up into my face.

"You for hire?"

"Certainly."

"My boy-friend's too tight to drive," she said. "We need a cab. But you'll have to help me with him."

I got out of the cab. It occurred to me that maybe she was tight, too. Or anyway she had a peculiar combination of nervousness and rage.

"Come on," she said, leading the way back to the roadster. "I don't know how to drive, or I'd take the wheel from him. I hope he don't clip you."

But her boy-friend made no move to clip me. He was too drunk for that. With his head cradled in his arms, his arms folded on the steering wheel, he slept heavily.

I opened the door beside him and eased him out. He tried to get his feet on the ground, but his shoes skidded, and his body became dead weight in my arms.

"Wassa big idea?" he grumbled thickly.

I carried him over to the cab and propped him up in the back seat. He was nicely dressed in a tuxedo, trim-fitting, but now it was rumpled from his night's orgy. His black bow tie hung crooked on the white starched collar. He was a hefty man and hard to handle when his muscles turned to sand. His head rolled loosely and a lock of dark pomaded hair had come down over his eyes. He had lost his hat somewhere.

"Hey," he muttered. "Wassa...."

And then he was sound asleep again, in the corner of the cab.

The blonde got in with him and slammed the door.

"All right," she said. "Get rolling."

"You want to leave the car here?"

"The hell with his car," she said. "Anyway it's locked. I've got the keys. I guess it'll be all right here."

"There's a no-parking ordinance after twelve," I said.

"That's *his* worry," she said.

So I climbed into the front seat, switched on the meter and the headlamps, tramped a foot on the starter. The cab's motor growled and roared, and I called over a shoulder: "Where does he live?"

"It don't matter where he lives. We're not going there." She took a slip of paper from her purse and held it under the dome-light in the rear of the cab. "We want to go to Valhalla."

That was silly. I'd never heard of any apartment house, or hotel, or suburb, called Valhalla. The only Valhalla I knew was a cemetery on the other side of Los Angeles. And it wasn't an active cemetery. Nobody had been put to rest there in the last ten years. It was a neglected weed-grown burial park down near the Southern Pacific freight yards.

I said to the blonde: "What's the address of the Valhalla Apartments?"

"It's not an apartment," she said. "It's a cemetery."

"You want to go *there?* Tonight?"

"Yes," she said.

"The fare will run around nine dollars."

Her red lips sneered with impatience. "Did I say I was worried about the fare?"

So I got us rolling and didn't ask any questions. After all, you meet such screwy people when you drive a cab for a living.

IT TOOK us nearly an hour to get there, and Valhalla at three A.M., with dismal winter rain, was hardly what you'd label a romantic spot.

The front of it faced a macadam road, its surface battered and pitted by the passage of trucks during the day. There was a crumbling brick wall around it and behind the wall you could see the dark shapes of wind-lashed eucalyptus trees. There was a tall rusty gate, locked with chains, and back of that a small keeper's cottage that hadn't been occupied in ten years. I pulled up and came to a stop in front of the gate.

"Wait a minute," the blonde said, and passed a slip of paper forward to me. "See if you can make any sense out of this."

It was a note in a woman's handwriting, in green ink, and it read—

> The name is Valhalla. A place of the dead. Go around to the back. Dirt road above the railroad tracks. Find three trees by a break in the wall. Enter through the break, follow the trail to a marble crypt.
>
> Inside the crypt, where a forgotten body lies at rest, something awaits you.
>
> Have no fear.
>
> Seek and ye shall find.

There was no signature. That was all.

I returned the note. She took it in her left hand, her right being a support for the sleeping man. His shoulder leaned heavily against her. He looked like he might sleep that way forever.

"Well?" she asked. "Do you make any sense out of it?"

"A little," I said. "It tells you where to go."

"Let's go there," she said.

So I put the hack in gear and continued along the pitted macadam until there was a muddy road leading off to the side. I followed this in low gear. No cars had traveled on it in a long time. The wheels of the cab whirled and skidded in the mud, but I kept going and followed the road all the way around the cemetery wall to the rear of the park.

Below us now, down a long weedy slope, I could see the railroad tracks, half a dozen sets of them, gleaming like ribbons under the big headlamp of a switch engine as it puffed with a line of freight cars. All that was about half a mile down the slope.

To our right was the crumbling wall of the cemetery, and three tall dark eucalyptus trees beside a break in the wall.

"This is the place," I said.

"We've got to hurry," the blonde replied. "Hey, Lew! *Lew!*" She pushed him away from her into the corner of the cab. She smacked him open-handed. His head lolled with sleep. She took him by the shoulders and shook him. That didn't do any good either.

Then she turned angry eyes on me. "It's no use. He's out like a light. You'll have to go in with me. Do you mind?"

"Well—" I began.

Her red lips got that sneer again, and her eyes had a blue impatient sparkle in them under the interior dome-lamp. "What's the matter? Afraid of ghosts?"

"Do I look like a guy who might be afraid of ghosts?"

She studied my face appraisingly, studied my shoulders and hands. "No. You don't. Let's go."

I slipped out from under the wheel, killing the motor and the lights. I got a small pocket flash from under the seat and opened the rear door for the blonde and helped her step out into the mud.

"I'm not exactly superstitious," I told her. "Ordinarily, I'm not even curious. But this isn't any ordinary taxi trip. You can't blame me for wanting to know what that note means."

She laughed then, a sudden low-pitched throaty laugh. She reached out and patted my cheek with cool fingers, like a mother showing sympathy to a child. "Don't let it get you down, fella. This is only a treasure hunt. You know what a treasure hunt is?"

I thought I knew what it was. A party. People gather at somebody's house, and the host, or hostess, gives out notes to start them off. Then off they go, in couples, following the directions in the first note to find a second note. Then a third, a fourth—and so through the night, each couple trailing their own series of notes. The couple who returns first with the final note wins the hunt and the prizes.

"Is that what it is?" I asked.

"That's right. And I need a mink coat."

"You get a fur coat if you win?" Her hooded head nodded vigorously in the dark. "Not just fur—mink. And the man gets a gold watch. I don't care about Lew, of course. We'll just let him sleep it off in the cab. But a mink coat can come in awfully handy during the cold winter nights. Come on, cabby, let's take a look in the graveyard."

THE RAIN came down hard now, beating at us in the open places and dripping on us from the branches of trees. My flash cut a beam through the darkness, and we followed a narrow muddy foot-path from the break in the wall and back into the solemn silence of the cemetery. There were a few empty tin cans along the path, probably left there by railroad bums who hiked up from the freight yards to find temporary haven. The path itself, no doubt, had been worn by the weary feet of men who ride the rails and who have to hide from yard dicks whenever they reach a city.

On each side of the path orderly rows of granite stones marked forgotten graves. Some of the stones had settled in the mud, canted rakishly, most of them were almost hidden by the wild growth of weeds.

Through this neglected burial park we trod steadily, with no sound about us but our own shoes slopping in the mud, the hush of falling rain, the distant chug of the switch engine down in the yards.

"This must be it," the blonde said.

My flash had picked out the front of a tomb that looked like a tiny saddened cathedral. Part of it was below ground, with a narrow flight of stone steps leading downward to a heavy iron door. And part of it, the dome, protruded eerily into the night, covered with ancient vines.

I went down the broken steps and tried the door. It had no lock on it, but something prevented it from moving inward at my push. I pressed my whole weight against it. But I couldn't budge it.

The blonde said in a whisper: "There must be some way to open it. Or else how did they get the note inside?"

"Maybe they got in by some other way."

I came back up the steps and shot the beam of the flash over the dome-like roof. There was a glass skylight up there, most of it shattered by kids who played here during the day and practised their stone-throwing. It was probably a way to get in.

"I'll try it," I offered.

I grabbed a fistful of strong old vines and climbed up these to the skylight and lifted it on its rusty hinge. Broken panes of glass fell down inside the tomb and tinkled against stone. I pointed the flash downward.

"Can you get in?" the blonde called.

"It's a cinch," I told her. "But the fare is double. Ordinarily, the Red Owl Company doesn't figure on these extra services."

"I'll pay," she said. "What's ten or twenty dollars against a mink coat?"

By my flash, I saw I could climb through the skylight and step on an inside ledge, and then step to the top of an altar, and from there to the floor.

So I stowed the flash back into my hip pocket, and with both hands free, eased my body, feet first, through the opening. I groped downward until my shoes found the ledge. From there I slid my feet farther to the top of the altar, keeping hands gripped on a trail of vines that had grown inside through the broken skylight.

I was in absolute darkness now, hanging by my hands, groping with my feet. Rain lanced down from above and was cool against my face. That was good. I was sweating from the climb, and the interior of the crypt had a clammy warmness.

I got to my knees on top of the dark altar, then eased myself to the floor. I was just reaching for my flash again, when a pair of strong arms wrapped themselves about me and wrestled me back against the wall. My head struck stone with a blow that knocked my cap off.

It couldn't be a ghost, of course. This ghost was tough, and had a breath like garlic, and a fist that smashed me in the teeth like a straight left from Joe Louis.

I sat flat on the floor, with my back to the wall, and grabbed for something, anything, and got hold of an ankle. He jerked his leg away, kicked.

"You son-of-a———!" he said.

A ghost wouldn't say that.

We fought there in the dark of the tomb, and I kept trying to get up and fight him. Somehow I got the feeling he meant this fight to be my last one. He was in it for the finish, and his eyes had grown accustomed to the dark— mine hadn't. He kept slugging me time after time, slamming me hard, viciously. And then I knew it wasn't his fists he was using. He was slamming my body with something like a baseball bat or a pick handle. He got me twice on the shoulder and paralyzed my right arm. He swung against my kneecap, and I went down like a poled buffalo.

"You son-of-a———!" he said.

I could hear him grunt with each swing. He missed me a couple of times, and the heavy wooden weapon cracked against the stone wall, but I put my face into the next one. I got it right across the bridge of the nose.

Then the inside of the tomb became bright red, like water on fire, and I sank down through that fiery water, with a tremendous weight pressing against my nose and flashes blinding my eyes. I sank deeper and deeper through it, and nothing hurt me. It didn't matter when he kicked me in the ribs. It didn't matter when he snicked on a flashlight and put the beam into my face.

"What the hell?" he said.

Something smashed me on the side of the jaw, and brought new blinding flashes. It could have been a pick-handle, or a baseball bat, or a cane, or a stick, or even a toothpick. It just didn't matter.

CHAPTER TWO

THE MISSING MR. WALGREEN

WHEN I came around again, it was still night and I was still in the crypt. Something outside made a gentle scratching sound against stone. I fixed my eyes on the broken skylight and saw the branch of a tree moving sluggishly back and forth in the wind. The branch scratched and rustled.

I got to my feet with effort, and every part of my body had pain. I felt like a man hit by a truck and still lacking the knowledge of how seriously he's been hurt. A little rain pattered down through the skylight, touching my swollen face with cool drops. Nobody came out of the darkness to beat me down again.

In the upper pocket of my shirt, under my coat, I found the booklet of paper matches I always kept there. Striking a match, cupping its glow in my palms, I located my flash. I got it, snicked the catch, and it worked. It was good to have light again.

I groped for my watch to see what time it was; I didn't have any watch. I felt for my wallet and that was gone too. My pockets had been turned inside out. All I had left was a handkerchief, matches, cigarettes, and a handful of small change.

I shot the beam of the flash around the inside of the crypt and found the weapon that had slugged me but not the man who had wielded it. I was entirely alone in the tomb, with just my own laborious breathing for company.

The weapon was the handle of a pick. No wonder I still felt groggy.

I saw other things scattered about on the stone floor. An empty gin bottle. A tattered blanket which had once been somebody's bed. Empty tins with canned heat labels, a whole batch of empty bottles that had once contained rubbing-alcohol.

The beam of my flash moved upward on the far wall. Here was a marble slab with engraved words on it.

JONATHAN CARNES HOLBROOK

1862–1927

FLORENCE SHAW HOLBROOK

1864–1928

His Ever Loving Wife

Here They Shall Rest

I wondered how much resting they had done while railroad bums used their tomb for a camp, and for a place to get drunk on rubbing-alcohol and canned heat. I wondered if the Holbrooks, behind that marble slab, had enjoyed much rest while kids threw rocks at the skylight, and drunken adults used the place for treasure hunts, and while some guy tried to beat me to death with a pick handle.

While I was wondering that, my flash picked out a slip of folded white paper forced into a crack of the marble. I got the paper out and read, in a woman's handwriting in green ink—

> Find the small building at the end of the car tracks in Playa del Rey. Between a drugstore and a liquor store.
>
> The Doctor is out, or the Doctor is in.
>
> And behind a little cardboard sign are further instructions.
>
> Have no fear.

Seek and Ye shall find.

There was no signature; that was all. It was the next note of the treasure hunt—next in the series leading my blonde fare to the goal of a mink coat.

I put my turned-out pockets back in order again, stowed the note in one of the pockets, and further explored the crypt with the beam of the flash. There was only one more thing to see. The heavy iron door of the tomb now stood open a little. There was a marble statue broken on the floor beside it. The statue, even broken, was heavy to lift. It had made a good barrier to keep the door shut. But somebody had moved it aside to get out of here in a hurry. It would take strength to move it—the strength of a man who could wield a pick handle.

I got my cap, and followed the beam of the flash through the doorway and up the broken stone steps into the grave-yard again.

It was cold outside, with the rain coming down hard through the trees. I called: "Hello! Hello!"—meaning that for the blonde.

There was no answer. I followed the path down through the weeds and the orderly rows of forgotten tombstones, and climbed through the tumbled brick wall and stopped under the three eucalyptus trees.

My cab stood there as I had left it, dark and silent. I crossed over to it and shot the flash inside. The blonde wasn't there. Neither was her drunken boy-friend. My fares had skipped out on me. I glanced around the desolate, rainy landscape, and wondered where the hell they had skipped to. Their skipping would cost me their fares and tips. Furthermore, I had been robbed. And none of that was pleasant thinking.

I sat in the cab and tooted the horn. I kept that up for several minutes, hoping my fares would return to the cab. But nobody returned. There was just darkness and the silence of the graveyard and the lonely patter of rain. Far down on the railroad tracks a train came along with a fast flicker of lights. Then it passed on, leaving behind it only the memory of wheel-trucks hammering on rail-joints and the mournful toll of the big bell.

The hell with it, the hell with screwy people on treasure hunts, and husky thieves with pick handles who hide in forgotten tombs.

I started the motor of the cab.

Well, there was one satisfaction, anyhow. The blonde who ran out on me wouldn't win her mink coat.

IT WAS sometime after four A.M.—maybe going on five—when I got back to my stand in Pacific Park. Still rain, and more rain, and dark as coal. My call-box clings to the wall outside the Corinthian Club, and the phone in it was ringing harshly when I pulled up at the curb.

I got out and answered the phone and the voice of Pat Regan, Red Owl's Chief Dispatcher, didn't have the rasp of rage I expected. Instead it dripped with sugary sarcasm.

"Well, well, if it isn't Steven Middleton Knight! It's sweet of you to answer the phone, Steven. Just lovely of you to get out of your cab in all this wet—" Then came the expected rasp of rage. It came in one prolonged ear-splitting bellow. "Where the hell you been for the last couple of hours? Or is it tactless of me to inquire? Listen, you shiftless son-of-a-flat tire, I've had four calls in your district! Had to send Olie Greenberg over to cover 'em for you. Maybe I better have Olie cover your district *all* the time. Maybe—"

"Listen, Pat," I said, "I had a fare."

"Oh, yeah? Well, maybe you never heard it, but it's the custom of hackers to ring the office before they go out on pickup runs. Maybe you didn't know that. Or maybe you just wanted to be sweet and not disturb me!"

"The fare was in a hurry, Pat."

"Yeah? Probably some blonde. Well, get this, Steven: you can't play Romeo on the Red Owl's time! Now take the red rose out of your smiling teeth and get over to the Surf Hotel and pick up an old lady who wants to go to the bus depot! Will you do that for me, Stevie? Or is it too much to ask?"

"Well, as a matter of fact—"

I was stalling. How could I go pick up a fare when my uniform was a mess, my nose swollen and bloody, and there was a six-inch cut on my forehead?

Pat Regan liked his drivers to put up a smart appearance. He'd canned me once for the mere fact of a black eye. I was afraid he'd do a lot more if he got a complaint from the old lady that a Red Owl driver looked like he'd just come out of Dunkirk.

"You'd better send Olie," I suggested politely. "I've got another fare, Pat. In the cab right now."

"Yeah? Another cutie, huh? It's wonderful the business you do with the cuties!"

He rang off sharply and left me alone with the dead phone in my hand. And left me alone with a problem.

Pat went off duty at six A.M., didn't come on again till eight in the evening. That gave me exactly fourteen hours in which to patch up my face, clean up my uniform, and somehow find enough money to pay in the meter receipts I'd been robbed of.

There was no use trying to explain to him I'd been robbed—that's why I had no intention of notifying the police. Pat Regan wasn't the kind of man to believe robbery stories. He fully trusted me for a distance of about six inches. He was deeply fond of me—the way Hitler is fond of Winston Churchill.

So I climbed back into the cab, and listened to the rain patter, and brooded over the problem of raising about thirty dollars in fourteen hours. If I failed to raise it, I'd have to raise another job.

Well, there was still a chance. The long cream-colored roadster still stood across the street from me, one front tire jammed against the curb. Somebody would have to return for it. And whoever came would find a very aggressive taxi driver who wanted double payment on a nine dollar run to Valhalla Cemetery. That would give me eighteen bucks, anyhow. And left me still a few bobs to raise before Pat Regan came snorting around for my meter receipts.

I was just considering a hike across the street to read the roadster's registration when a police prowl-car cruised slowly up from the Ocean Avenue intersection. It was a small black sedan that glistened like gun-metal in the rain. In it were Officers Purcell and Lasker.

THEY STOPPED just opposite my cab, motor idling. A big spot-lamp cut a bright beam through the rain, examining the parked roadster. After the spot made a thorough examination, it snicked off. Lasker stuck his head out the window into the rain. His hands were resting on the driver's wheel. He wore white gloves.

He called: "That you, Steve Midnight?"

"In person," I called back.

"How long's this beautiful crate been parked here?"

"Since about two," I said.

"Then it gets a ticket."

"Swell," I said. "Give it a hundred tickets. The more the merrier. It's all okay with me."

Ed Purcell stepped out of the sedan and went over to the roadster. He got out a flashlight and a small book and a pencil. His big body leaned in over the door, his flat cap ducking under the rain-soaked fabric of the top. I saw the flash go on, as he examined the registration. Then the flash went out, and he didn't write a ticket.

"Walgreen," he said. "Lew Walgreen. You hear that, Jim?"

"I heard it," said Lasker, and got out of the police car and both of them crossed over to my cab. Rain-water dripped from the visors of their caps. They were suddenly stern, as if sore about something.

Purcell said: "Did you see the guy that left this crate here?"

"Sure. I took him for a ride. Stinko drunk. Had a blonde with him."

Purcell snicked on his flash and shot the beam at me—from close range. It made me blink.

"What's the matter with your face, Steve?"

"A little trouble," I said. "Beaten up. Robbed. Cab drivers get it all the time. Just part of the work."

"You report it?"

"No," I confessed.

"Why not?"

"Because the Red Owl Cab Company has a certain night dispatcher named Pat Regan. He doesn't believe his employees ever get robbed. Know what I mean?"

"I get it," said Lasker. "But there's a jam here, Steve. Where'd you take the drunk and the blonde?"

"Valhalla. The cemetery. It was a Treasure Hunt."

Lasker shot a solemn glance at Purcell, and Purcell returned it. Then both of them looked back at me, with the light still shining bright in my eyes.

Lasker said: "You'd better come over to headquarters with us, Steve."

"Headquarters? Why?"

"Because a fellow named Walgreen got knocked off tonight. Down in the Southern Pacific freight yards. Near Valhalla."

CHAPTER THREE

YOU CAN'T GET PRINTS OFF GRAVEL

THE ROOM was small and hot, and I sat alone in it for three long dreary hours. A steam radiator in the corner gave off hissing heat. I didn't know how to turn it off. I tried to lift a window, but it was stuck tighter than a window in an old-fashioned Pullman. I couldn't budge it.

I finally relaxed in a straight oak chair and smoked cigarettes until I ran out of them, and watched the rain patter against misty windows.

It was Captain Hollister's office, and nobody bothered me there until later in the morning when Hollister himself came in.

He was a tall, heavy-set man who smoked a ragged cigar and wore the same overcoat and battered hat which had done him service through many years. He had bushy gray brows, and eyes that could either smile on little children or make a condemned man squirm. The eyes were always changing—first pleasant, then shrewd.

He came briskly into the Homicide office and threw his hat at a brass hook on the wall. The hat missed, bounced off the wall and landed on the floor near a cuspidor. Captain Hollister ignored it. He went around the bare oak desk, plumped into a swivel chair, and put his feet on the desk. His shoes, his socks, the cuffs of his trousers, were coated with mud. He beamed on me pleasantly.

"Hello, Steve."

"Hello," I said.

"Poor old Steve Midnight. Whenever there's any trouble he lands right smack in the middle of it. Tough life, driving a cab—huh, Steve?" He laughed heartily, unlocked his desk and took out a box of cigars.

"Why am I under arrest?" I asked.

"Arrest?" His laugh boomed. "Nothing like that, Steve. Just a little talk. Seems you had a fare last night and the fare got knocked off."

"It's all news to me," I said. "The guy was drunk. Had a blonde with him. They were on a Treasure Hunt."

He waved a hand impatiently. "I heard all that from Purcell and Lasker. You got socked and robbed in a tomb down at Valhalla, Didn't report it." His eyes got shrewd. "Know who the blonde was, Steve?"

I shook my head.

"Neither do I," he said, "but I've got an idea. And the identity of your other fare is established. I traced him through some cards in his pocket, and some laundry-marks on his clothes. Lew Walgreen. Bugsy Walgreen. That mean anything to you, Steve?"

"Not a thing," I said.

"Bugsy used to peddle hooch back in Prohibition. After that, a little dope. The feds gave him seven years on a narcotic rap. They paroled him last spring. He seemed to be getting along all right. Nobody caught him at any crooked stuff. Had a night club up on Sunset Boulevard, in the Strip. Somebody financed him, we don't know who. I grilled all the boys up there, and they don't know either. Bugsy seemed to be living a clean life, driving a nice car, running a legitimate night club. No trouble till last night."

"You identified the blonde?"

He chewed the tattered stub of cigar. "Think so. Bugsy had a blonde singer working for him named Maybelle Knapp. Had a date with her last night. The boys at the club didn't know what kind of a date, but they knew where she lived. I went to her apartment. She'd moved out early this morning. No trace of her."

I said: "A small blonde with lots of red lips and hard blue eyes, and knows her way around?"

"That fits," he nodded. "Only we can't find her. I'd like to."

"So would I," I told him. "She owes me eighteen bucks and my job."

"We'll get her, Steve." He said: "Who started this treasure hunt?"

"I don't know," I said.

"She didn't mention anything about it?"

"Just a mink coat for a prize. That's all."

"Did Walgreen say anything?"

"He was too drunk. Just slept in the back of the cab. Both of them disappeared when I got robbed in the cemetery. I didn't know he got killed. I still don't know *how*."

"I can tell you about that," Hollister said.

IT SEEMED the police had had a call at four A.M. The call came from a track watchman in the S.P. Freight Yards. Walking up the tracks, just below Valhalla Cemetery, he had found a mangled body. It had been ground and pounded under the wheels of a fast freight.

"Suicide, robbery, or accident," Hollister said. "That's what it was supposed to look like. Too damned obvious. It missed by a mile."

I said: "Maybe some railroad bum robbed him and killed him. Maybe he wandered down there from my cab, and the bum got him. Maybe the same bum that slugged me and robbed me at the tomb."

"What makes you think a bum did it, Steve?"

"Well, bums use the cemetery for a hangout."

"Yeah," he nodded. "But most of the bums on the road don't fall into the killer class. Lazy, maybe. Drink a little rubbing-alcohol and canned heat, maybe. But not killers. No, Steve, there's something funny back of this."

"Was he robbed?"

"Sure. No money, or wallet in his pockets. But it doesn't have to make robbery the motive. It was just supposed to look like it."

"Couldn't be an accident or suicide?"

"Absolutely not," Hollister said firmly. I've got evidence on *that*. There's a water tower where Walgreen went under the wheels of the freight. Wooden tool-shed built under the tower. Somebody held Walgreen against the far wall of the tool-shed so the engine's big searchlight wouldn't pick them out. Then, after the engine passed, he shoved Walgreen under the wheels."

"Evidence of that?"

"Plenty. That's the crack freight from the Valley. Carries perishable fruit and travels like the very devil. A train passing that fast makes a big blast of wind—a fact this guy overlooked. He shoved Walgreen under the wheels all right, but the blast of wind knocked the killer back against the tool-shed. Walgreen's blood flew out from under those wheels like it had been thrown up from a bucket. The blood got on the killer, and some of it rubbed off his clothes when he fell against the tool-shed wall. There's a nice clear imprint of a bloody hand. It doesn't do us much good though. Not for fingerprints. The killer wore gloves. Cotton gloves. One of the gloves got torn on a nail. Doctor Dana, down in the Bureau of Criminology, tells me you can buy cotton gloves like that in any dime store in the country."

I thought that over as I lit one of Hollister's cigars. I said: "With all that rain, there was plenty of mud around. How about footprints?"

He wagged his head solemnly. "Too much rain. The water ran down that cemetery path like a spring creek. And the track-bed is all gravel. And gravel around the water tower. You can't get footprints off gravel."

"So that leaves you out on the limb, huh. Captain?"

"Way out," he said. "But I've climbed in off longer limbs than this. I'm gonna fingerprint everything in that tomb, Steve. I got a hunch the guy who slugged you in there was trying for Walgreen and didn't get him till later."

"Then you won't find prints," I offered. "He was probably wearing the same cotton gloves."

The Captain waved a hand impatiently. "Sure. Sure. But cops play all the angles. It doesn't pay to skip anything. I'll take your prints downstairs, Steve, just to clear them from any other prints we get at the crypt."

"Then can I leave?"

"Sure." His bushy brows drew together over a thin hawk-like nose, and his eyes gave me a stern third-degree. "You wouldn't hold out anything, would you, Steve?"

"Why would I?"

"Just asking, Steve. And you didn't get any identification on this guy that worked you over with the pick-handle?"

"He called me a son-of-a-bat. That's all."

"And you don't have any idea who started this Treasure Hunt party?"

I shook my head. "Can I go now, Captain?"

"Why the hurry, Steve?"

"Because," I said, "I've got less than twelve hours to scratch up thirty dollars for Pat Regan. Otherwise, I can scratch up a new job."

The captain chuckled. "This Regan sounds like a nice guy. If he heard about the robbery he'd think you faked it to chisel the cab company's meter receipts. That it?"

"Exactly."

"But you can't hide the robbery, Steve. It'll be in all the papers."

"That won't matter as long as I dig up thirty bucks."

The captain laughed. "This Regan is wonderful."

"He's a louse," I replied sullenly.

CHAPTER FOUR

SEEK AND YE SHALL FIND

IT WAS about ten in the morning when I got away from Headquarters. I went back to Siberia for my hack and drove it over to the Red Owl Garage. Pat Regan had been off duty for some hours, so he wouldn't be climbing into my hair over the meter receipts until eight o'clock in the evening. But eight o'clock didn't seem such a long way off.

I hiked back across town to my hotel, had to listen briefly to the clerk's wisecracks regarding my battered appearance, and then I went to my room to clean up.

That was quite a job. My nose didn't feel broken but it was swollen so much that fat blueish bags surrounded my eyes. The gash on my forehead was a superficial break of the skin, and under it was a swelling. There was a bloated bruise on the right side of my jaw, sore to touch, and my bruised knee gave me a limp.

I sat in a hot tub for a while, then showered off cold and drank a frosty highball. I began to feel hungry and like myself again. But in the mirror I didn't look like myself. Not at all. The swellings had gotten worse. I looked like a one-round stumble-bum who'd tried to take Joe Louis.

I dressed into clean clothes, from underwear to tan tweed suit, and then groped absent-mindedly through the pockets of my taxi uniform to find my wallet. That reminded me I'd been robbed. I didn't find the wallet, of course, but in one of the pockets I found a slip of paper, folded. On it was a woman's handwriting, in green ink.

I'd forgotten about that. It was the treasure hunt note I'd found in the crypt. The next note the blonde was after on the trail of a mink coat.

I reached for the telephone and called police headquarters. Captain Hollister wasn't there; probably out at the cemetery with the fingerprint men.

"No message," I told the desk sergeant.

I went downstairs to the hotel's coffee shop, swallowed a fast breakfast, then boarded a big red interurban trolley for Playa del Rey.

THE RAIN had stopped when I got to the end of the car line, but the sky hung low with dark angry clouds. The motorman climbed down from the trolley and strolled across the empty street to a little cafe. It was a deserted place—this end of the car line. Bare brown hills with scattered houses on them facing the sea; the Venice marshes, with tall skeletons of oil derricks. And right nearby, a grocery store, an abandoned real estate office, and a row of gloomy one-story stucco buildings near a gas station.

I limped over to these buildings, found a drugstore and a liquor store, and between them a narrow modernistic building with long glass windows and drawn Venetian blinds. The brass placard read simply—

Dr. Otto C. Jelks
Physician & Surgeon
Hours 9:00 to 5:00

There was a blue Chrysler coupé parked at the curb. Its glass had been cranked up and was misted from last night's rain. So it had been there a long time.

I entered a small foyer and rang the bell. I could hear it tinkle musically inside, but there was no response to it, even after repealed ringings. A cardboard sign hung on a hook above the bell. It said that the doctor was out and that he would return at nine A.M.

I lifted the sign a little, and a folded slip of paper fluttered to the damp brick stoop. I picked it up and read another note in a woman's handwriting in green ink.

You have found it! Return to the starting point! And if you are the first to return, then the reward is *yours!*

As usual no signature. And unfortunately, no information on the starting point of the Treasure Hunt.

I tucked the note into my breast pocket, rang the bell again, still got no answer, and tried turning the door-knob. It wouldn't turn. It was locked.

I limped across the sidewalk and went around the blue Chrysler coupé to the driver's side and unlatched the door. The interior of the coupé was cold from last night and had a musty smell. The State Registration on the steering post said the car belonged to Dr. Otto C. Jelks of 1444 Hobart Street, Los Angeles. A neat leather key-case hung from the ignition switch.

I removed the keys and went around the car again and up the brick steps into the foyer of the building. There were six keys in the leather case and the third one worked.

I stepped into a rectangular reception room, furnished with low modernistic chairs and chromium magazine racks.

"Hello?" I called. "Doctor?"

My own voice came back to me in muffled little echoes. I closed the door, locked it again, and used another key to enter the office.

This was sanitary and efficient, and full of gray daylight from frosted glass panels set slantwise up a slope of ceiling. Everything was white in the room except the floor—that was smooth green linoleum—white walls, a white roll-top desk, three white steel chairs, white filing cabinets, and a white enamel examination-table. Inside glass cases were rows of surgical instruments, laid out carefully on starched towels. The whole place was so sanitary and efficient, with a faint odor of disinfectant, that I felt glad the doctor was out and that I wasn't here to pay him a professional visit.

I found two other doors in the office. The first opened into a lavatory walled in white tile. The second opened into a dressing-closet—and that's where I found the doctor.

HE WAS hanging by his neck from an exposed water-pipe that crossed just under the ceiling. The noose was cinched with cutting tightness about his throat, forcing his tongue to stick out blue and bloated from between his teeth. The knot about the waterpipe had slipped a little, the rope had evidently stretched, and his feet, in black patent-leather shoes, dangled only a few inches from the floor.

I reached out and touched one of his hands. It was stiff and cold and lifeless, and just touching it caused his body to swing gently on the rope.

He wore a tailored Tuxedo, the trousers pressed into blade-like creases, and there was a wilting gardenia in the lapel of his coat. He was fastidiously dressed, except for the fact that his collar and tie were missing.

There was a small stepladder against the back wall, and it looked like he'd used this for his own gallows trap, standing on the top rung of it to fix the noose, to knot the other end of the rope at the waterpipe, before he jumped. And before he jumped, he had removed collar and tie and placed them side by side on the dressing-table. The tie had been folded. A very cool and calculated way to take your own life—if he had taken his own life.

I searched his pockets for a suicide note, didn't find any. Just a wallet with money and cards, a handkerchief, some loose change, and a small black case containing a hypodermic needle.

I looked up at his eyes. They were bugged from strangulation, but not the eyes of an habitual narcotic. So the hypodermic needle must've been intended for some patient.

I stepped out into the office and over to the desk. The top had been rolled up and there was a batch of papers but no suicide note. Most of the papers were bills he'd intended to mail, and ads from a physicians' supply house, and letters from patients explaining why they were unable to settle their accounts until next month.

But there was also a stack of dusty prescriptions—already filled—his personal copies. Those of them dated before July 1st of this year were on his own office pads, specially printed with his name and address. Those after July 1st didn't have his name printed, just serial numbers and his handwriting, and the paper was of fine quality—almost like the grade of paper the Government uses for currency.

I read his handwriting on all the prescriptions, and each was for Cocaine HCL, or Hyocine Hydro-Bromide, or for twenty-tablet bottles of morphine, one-half gram. The names of the patients were all different. The names of pharmacies where they'd been filled were all different too; some of the pharmacies were located outside the city of Los Angeles, and some even outside its suburbs.

I had just finished pawing the prescriptions when a bell tinkled musically behind me. I didn't quite jump out of my suit. It tinkled three times, the front doorbell, and I hoped it was some patient who would finally give up and go away.

I waited motionless for several minutes. The bell didn't ring again, and after a while I figured the patient had left. But he hadn't. A key clicked in the outside door and somebody entered the reception room.

I tip-toed into the lavatory and drew myself flat against the tiled wall.

Another key clicked in a lock and the door opened into the doctor's office and a young woman entered swiftly. She didn't even bother to close the door behind her. She went straight to the dressing-closet where the doctor hung by his neck, and a little choked sigh escaped her lips, but not a sigh of surprise.

She carried a black leather overnight case, and this she placed on the floor near his dangling feet. She yanked out drawers in a wooden chest and removed the contents and stuffed everything hastily into the case. It all took less than a minute, this packing. She then snicked the latch, shoved the drawers back, shuddered as she took one last frightened glimpse of the doctor, and came out into the room carrying the case.

"Hello," I called gently. "What's the hurry?"

Her eyes swiveled toward the doorway where I stood, but her eyes never quite reached me. Another shudder passed down her body from shoulders to ankles, and the start of a scream never materialized into sound. Her knees gave, and she crumpled to the floor in a dead faint.

CHAPTER FIVE
LADY WITH A KNIFE

I WENT over and picked her up and placed her on the white enamel table. That took effort; she was not small and light, and not the type for fainting. I must've given her quite a scare.

I loosened the ascot scarf from about her throat, found a bottle of ammonia in one of the cabinets. Uncorking that, I held it under her nose. It did the trick. It revived her.

The lashes of her eyes flicked. Then she stared at me, and stared at the room as if seeing it for the first time.

"Everything's all right," I assured her. "You're in Doctor Jelk's office."

That didn't remove any of the fright from her pale cheeks. She put firm hands on the table, lifting herself, swinging legs to the floor. They were strong legs, and muscular under tan silk stockings. With her feet on the floor, hips and hands on the table-edge, she regarded me thoughtfully and the fright began to dim.

"Who are you?"—that from a throaty competent voice.

"I was about to ask you the same question," I replied.

She shrugged a little. "I suppose you're one of the G-men."

"Suppose I am?"

"Nothing. You've found the doctor, of course. And you probably think I'm involved in it." That was a flat statement of fact and was followed with another shrug of her shoulders. "Well, so what."

"So you'll have to do some explaining," I suggested.

Dark eyes looked deep into mine, but no thoughts were given away by them. She was not pretty, but not unattractive either—if you like them strong and capable. She wore a plain gray suit, tailored like a man's, and her shoes were low-heeled, efficient. She reminded me of the girls' athletic coach in the local high school.

"All right," she said, "I'll explain. I'll have a drink first. Do you mind?"

I shook my head at that, and she stepped past me and opened a glass case. I didn't see anything to drink in it, just surgical instruments laid out on starched white towels. I saw her hand swoop down and I yelled at her and reached for her arm, but I was too late.

She avoided me as she turned, her back against the open door of the case. A gleaming knife was in her hand, a surgeon's scalpel, and she lashed it across my chest in one lightning movement.

"Don't be a fool!" she snapped. "Look at your coat."

My fingers went up instinctively and discovered a ten inch cut in the tweed material of my best suit.

"I can do the same thing to your face," she said. "But I hope I won't have to."

"Lady," I said, "so do *I*."

"I want to leave here. *Now*." The scalpel was steady in her strong hand and pointed at me like a gun. "I don't expect to be followed. You can remain with the doctor for a while."

The blade of the scalpel backed me away in slow steps, and advanced with me as I backed. My legs hit a chair and upset it. The blade still advanced, and behind it came this determined, grim-jawed woman who reminded me of an athletic coach. She backed me through the doorway into the dressing closet, and I reached behind me and gave a sly push to the doctor's hanging body.

"Good God!" I shouted. "He's still alive!"

Her nerves were so tense that another violent shudder shook her body. My sudden shout, and her brief glimpse of Dr. Jelks swiveling slowly by the neck, caused the scalpel to drop a little and her eyes to stare for an instant at the body behind me.

I took advantage of that instant. I knocked her arm aside and smacked her flush on the jaw. It was even harder than I intended, and I felt a little ashamed about it afterwards. Somehow you don't like to hit a woman that hard— even a husky capable woman with a surgeon's scalpel.

I picked her up and placed her on the table again. But I didn't get the ammonia bottle, not right away.

Her purse was a flat bag of gray cloth, matching her tailored suit, and it was well stocked with money. About four hundred dollars in currency, a fistful of silver. There

was a card in it that said she was Dorothy Tyler, a Registered Nurse. There was a personal check from Dr. Jelks
for twenty dollars—probably her last week's salary. There
was a railroad ticket for Omaha, Nebraska. Union Pacific,
Train No. 49, leaving L.A. Station at 3:45 P.M. The ticket
was dated today.

I put everything in the bag, closed it, put it where she'd
dropped it when she first fainted. I opened the black leather
overnight case and found it full of white starched dresses,
the kind nurses wear in a doctor's office. There were laundry
marks on them.

I closed that case too, and then got the ammonia and
brought her around again.

The lashes of her eyes flicked several times, and she
stared at me once more, and stared at the room.

"Hello," I said.

She lifted herself wearily and sat on the table and felt
the side of her jaw where I'd smacked her.

"Sorry," said. "It slipped."

"That's all right. I don't mind that. What gets me is your
gag about him still being alive. A gag like that stinks of
moth balls."

"It worked, didn't it?"

"Yes. And that's what gets me. It worked." She gave a
loose shrug. "Well, what do we do now?"

"That explanation," I said. "We're back where we started
from. Remember?"

"I remember."

"Will you talk?"

Her dark eyes had a shrewd look in them, like a Main
Street business man driving a hard bargain. "If I talk, does
it buy me out of here? A start?"

"It does," I agreed.

"A promise?"

"It's a deal."

"O.K.," she said, "what do you want to know—aside from the fact that I didn't hang Jelks?"

I WENT over to the roll-top desk and got the batch of dusty prescription blanks. I showed them to her. "He was peddling dope, wasn't he?"

She nodded, but her eyes remained on the papers. "Where'd you find those? He always kept them hidden."

"They were right out here on the desk. Maybe he got them out himself. Took one last look at them and hanged himself. The feds were after him. You mentioned something about G-men."

"Yes," she admitted. "They were after him. Before July first he could fill all the prescriptions he wanted, as long as he invented new names for the dope customers and sent them to different pharmacies. But since July first a new law makes doctors use blanks provided by the Division of Narcotics. He had to be careful then. But his dope customers kept bothering him. And I guess he made out too many prescriptions. A federal man was in to see him yesterday afternoon. I'm telling you the truth. I'm his nurse."

I said I believed her and I did. But there was a lot more I wanted to know. "For instance," I said, "when did you find the doctor?" I pointed with my chin toward the dressing-closet.

She lowered her eyes. "I found him at nine this morning when I came to work. As soon as I found him... hanging like that—I left."

"Didn't want to get caught by the feds. That it?"

"Yes."

"Then you went home and thought it over. The feds might be able to trace you through the laundry marks in your uniforms. You came to get them. You didn't want to be nabbed on a narcotic rap, along with the doctor. Right?"

"Yes."

"Did he give you any hint about killing himself?"

"None at all," she said. "In fact we had a date last night. A Treasure Hunt."

"A what?" I guess I barked it at her, because her eyes widened at my question.

"Treasure hunt. A kind of party where you—"

I waved a hand at her. "I know, I know. That's why the doctor is wearing a tuxedo. Did you go on the date?"

"No. He called it off. He phoned me early last evening and said he couldn't make it. So I didn't see him again until I came in here this morning and found him—like that."

"Who was giving the party?"

Her eyes got shrewd again. She said: "You ask too many questions. I don't think you'll stick to your bargain."

"I'll stick to it," I promised.

She glanced at a watch upon her wrist. "Can I leave in five minutes?"

"Yes," I said. "Who gave the party?"

"A Mrs. Rufus La Farge. The party was at her house. At 1924 Alpine Way, in Beverly Crest. She's been very friendly with the doctor for a long time. That's about all I know. I didn't go to the party when he called the date off."

"O.K.," I said, "one more thing. Did you ever hear of a man named Walgreen? Lew Walgreen? Or Bugsy Walgreen?"

The name brought a glimmer into her dark eyes. "I think the doctor knew him. He came into the office a few times. But he wasn't a patient. That's all I know. Can I leave now?"

"You can."

Hurriedly she snatched up the gray handbag, the leather traveling-case. She took one last worried look at me, at the doctor's body swaying gently, and then she fled, leaving only a slam of doors behind her.

I gave her just about enough time to reach the sidewalk. Then I picked up the telephone and double-crossed her.

CAPTAIN HOLLISTER was still out. A lieutenant of detectives answered the phone. He said: "The captain is in the morgue with the autopsy surgeon. He doesn't want to be disturbed."

"Well, here's something to disturb him anyhow," I said. "At the end of the trolley line in Playa del Rey there's a Doctor Otto C. Jelks. He's hanging by his neck in his office."

"You mean dead?" said the detective.

"That's what I mean. And he was supposed to go on a treasure hunt party last night. The one Lew Walgreen was on when he got killed near Valhalla."

"Say, wait a minute! Who's this talking?"

"Another thing," I said, ignoring his question. "Doctor Jelks has a nurse working for him. She was supposed to go on the party with Jelks last night. He called it off. The nurse knows he's dead and she's skipping town. She has a ticket for Train 49, Union Pacific, leaving L.A. Station at 3:45 this afternoon. You'd better cover the bus depots and the airports, too—in case she changes her mind about the train. Her name is Dorothy Tyler. Big husky gal in a gray suit tailored like a man's. The feds will want her for a witness against the doctor. He was peddling narcotics. You got all that?"

"Got it." And then the lieutenant gave a rasping cough to cover the sound of somebody at headquarters clicking into the line to trace my call. "Hold on a minute. Who shall I tell the captain is calling?"

"Steve Midnight," I said. "Tell him I'm still hot on the trail of my thirty bucks."

CHAPTER SIX
HEAVEN WITH A FENCE

IT WAS an hour's trip from Playa del Rey to Beverly. On Sunday afternoon the trolleys ran infrequently, and I had to change twice on buses in order to get there at all. I began to wish I'd called one of our Red Owl Cabs and bargained with the driver to ride me on company rates—I.O.U.

At about two P.M. I found Alpine Way, and hiked up the steep winding road into the swank district known as Beverly Crest.

There were mansions clinging precariously to the hillside, steep gardens behind vine-covered brick walls, and all the private garages had space for at least a half a dozen cars. In this retreat of luxury, lived movie people, oil tycoons, and retired industrialists who had accumulated wealth outside of California. It was a district where even the trees seemed to be shaped like dollar signs and the raindrops clinging to their branches were fourteen carat diamonds.

I followed the road to the very top of a mountain and there found a dream-palace of rambling roof and sweeping glass, the house itself set back in a garden of terraced lily-pools. A pair of downy swans paddled blissfully in one of the pools, and birds chirped and scolded through the trees, conversing about the recent rain. All the place lacked was sunshine, and the sudden appearance of a beautiful maiden riding a snow-crested steed. I felt like Ronald Colman discovering Shangri-La.

No wall surrounded this Heaven—just a steel fence which allowed you to enjoy the beauty inside but still guaranteed that you wouldn't try to touch it. I found a tall gate, locked, with the numbers 1924 made of bronze. I pushed the bell, and the birds stopped chirping and the swans craned their long graceful necks to give me the once-over through the fence.

There was a garage near the gate, built deeply into the side of the hill. Its roof was lawn and flowers. Only its gaping doorway opened out onto the road.

A man came out of this doorway and spoiled the serene picture by saying: "Hello. You want something?"

He wore a uniform of dark green whipcord, the flared trousers narrowing to a laced fit inside shiny black boots. His cap had a leather visor, was tall-fronted, like the cap of a German submarine commander. Under this, his face was square-jawed, freckled, and tough.

"I'd like to see Mrs. Rufus La Farge," I told him.

He looked me over carefully, from battered face to the slash across my coat, and I didn't let him think he worried me by the examination. I gave him the same thing, right back. I glanced down at his boots, then up at his cap. I studied the embroidered initials over the breast pocket of the uniform. The initials were *G.M.* Very fancy too. The *G.* interwoven with the *M.*

He said: "Mrs. La Farge ain't home. She's away at her Palm Springs estate. Did you have an appointment?"

"Not exactly an appointment. Since when did she leave for Palm Springs?"

"Day before yesterday," he said.

"Then she wasn't on hand for her own Treasure Hunt party last night?"

His eyes peered deep into mine and the set of his jaw didn't relax. He removed his cap and with the same hand scratched his head. He had red hair, thick, curling, and neatly combed.

"I don't know what you're talking about," he said. "She didn't have any party last night. The house is all closed up. Mr. La Farge is just back from Frisco and he's staying downtown at the church."

"Were you here last night?"

"No," he said. "Why?"

I began to wonder about Dorothy Tyler, the nurse. Maybe she'd tossed me a blind steer in the same neat way she'd slashed my coat with the scalpel.

I said to the chauffeur: "There was a treasure hunt party last night. A fellow named Lew Walgreen was on it and he got killed under a freight train down near Valhalla Cemetery. A Doctor Jelks was supposed to be on the party too. He didn't go. He's hanging by his neck down at his office in Playa del Rey."

The chauffeur put his cap back on, and his eyes never left me for a second. "You talk kind of funny. What's all this got to do with Mrs. La Farge?"

"It was Mrs. La Farge that held the party."

"Not here, she didn't."

MY EYES wandered away from him, and over his shoulder I saw the terraces of lily-pools and the swans now out of the water and moving across the lawn under the trees. In the house itself, way up beyond, a Venetian blind moved in one of the windows looking down at us. The slats of the blind tilted horizontal, then tilted to a steeper angle. My eyes came back to the chauffeur.

"And you say there's nobody home here at all?"

"Not a soul," he said. "They even sent the dogs to the boarding kennels. You must have the wrong house, mister. The wrong address. The wrong name."

"Maybe I have," I admitted. "Sorry to trouble you."

"That's all right. It's just some mistake. Mrs. La Farge wouldn't have any party where people got hurt."

"Not hurt," I corrected. "Dead." He nodded solemnly. "That's what makes me know it's some mistake. You know who Mrs. La Farge is? Her husband is Saint Rufus of the Thou Shalt Society. That's a church."

"I know," I said.

"So it's just some mistake. What did you say your name was?"

"I didn't say."

His eyes dropped to my shoes, then shifted to the paved road that led up to this hill-top from Beverly Hills. He got out a package of cigarettes and selected one and put it to his lips. "I don't see any car. You hike up?"

"No, I'm a parachutist. I came by air."

He flared a match on a thumbnail. "You don't have to get tough about it. I was only asking. If you want to clam up, then clam."

"You're pretty good on the clam-act yourself," I told him.

He dropped the match and his jaw tightened. "You think I'm a liar? Well, you listen to me, short pants. Personally, I don't think you're just a liar. I think you're a fugitive from a booby hatch. I don't know what you're beefing about, all this treasure stuff, and dead guys—and I don't like you hanging around here, so *scram*. I can call the cops to pick you up, or I can toss you down the hill."

"You'd better call the cops," I suggested. "If you try to toss me anywhere, you might get hurt."

"You think I can't?"

"You can try," I offered.

For a long moment he gave me a fighter's appraisal. Tiny muscles twitched along the line of his jaw. His hands worked and moved, started to become fists, then relaxed, and his facial expression changed from rage to disgust.

"Nuts," he said. "I can't be bothered."

He turned on his heel and strode back into the subterranean garage, a big handsome man whose uniform gave him swagger.

I started to hike on down the hill, but I only started. As I reached the far boundary of the estate, I took one last glimpse backward at the terraces, lily ponds and the swans. I saw the chauffeur emerge from a tunnel behind the garage and hurry through the garden. He was headed for the house itself, that palace of Shangri-La, and I saw him disappear through an arched doorway at the side.

I returned to the garage. It was a roomy place, with at least a five-car capacity, but now it had only two cars inside—one a long shiny limousine, a Rolls Royce, and the other an inexpensive little coupé. I looked at the registrations on both cars. The Rolls, of course, belonged to the La Farge family—Rufus La Farge. The coupé was registered to George Manning, of 37 Seaside Way, Manhattan Beach. The initials *G.M.* made a faded muddy monogram on the left-hand door, the same interwoven fancy initials he had embroidered on his chauffeur's uniform.

While I was examining the cars, I heard quick hard footsteps coming through a tunnel at the back, so I slipped out of the garage and ducked into thick shrubbery beside the doorway.

I was just in time. The chauffeur came out briskly and looked up and down the road. He went to the edge of it, where he got a good view of the lower turn. He waited there for several minutes. He was looking for *me*, of course.

After a little more sentinel duty, he strolled to the big steel gate and unlocked it. He returned to the garage, gunned up the motor of the long limousine and backed it out. Then he drove it through the gateway and up to the mansion.

I came out of my shrubbery and looked up the terraces of lily-pools. The Rolls stood outside the main entrance, like a battleship tied to a wharf, and the chauffeur was stowing luggage. Then a woman appeared, a large buxom woman who wore about a thousand dollars worth of fur coat. She was pulling on gloves, and I saw a flash of diamond rings. She stepped into the limousine, seating herself alone in the rear compartment.

George Manning slammed the door and got up front, and the big car rolled smoothly down the private drive and through the gate. By that time I was back in the shrubbery again.

Manning stopped the long Rolls and went back to lock the gate. He stepped over to the edge of the road and looked down it again. He still didn't see me down there. He returned to the car and said something to the woman. She nodded, and then the big limousine was rolling again.

It didn't go down the hill. It went up over the crest on another route, a back road which would finally reach Mullholland Drive. Evidently they weren't taking any chances on meeting me along Alpine Way.

I watched the car disappear over the crest, and wished I could follow it, of course. But after all I'm not a Spartan runner.

CHAPTER SEVEN
THE SAINT IN SILVER

A ROUND EVERY corner in Southern California you find mystics, fortunetellers, old-age pensions, shrewd real estate schemes, fake oil companies, phoney gold mines, quack dental offices, and Swedish massage parlors where the massage is not particularly Swedish. Grifters, hustlers, promoters, swindlers... all of them making an unending source of trouble for the law. And if it wasn't for the fine operation of that law-enforcement machine, both state and local, you wouldn't be able to cross a street without having some smooth-speaking promoter take your shirt and necktie as down payment on the L.A. City Hall.

The Thou Shalt Society was one of the newer innovations. Not entirely new, of course, since for hundreds of years shady swindlers have hidden behind a mask of religion in order to ply their graft. Hallelujah, praise the Lord! Put fifty cents in the collection basket and save thy immortal soul! Dig down, brethren!

The Thou Shalt Society was one of those. A racket plied against lonely people, against the sick, against the worried, against the aged. The lousiest racket in the world, hiding behind a cloak of spiritual religion and defying you to prove it's just a cloak. The Thou Shalt Society preached a doctrine that "thou shalt soon die. Therefore, thou hast no need for thy earthly wealth." Dig down, brethren.

So the congregation dug down, shelled out. And Mr. Rufus La Farge—Saint Rufus—lived in a fine mansion in Beverly Crest and last year paid the federal government over ten thousand dollars for income tax.

Saint Rufus, like the poor members of his congregation, might soon die. But his own pessimistic doctrine didn't prevent him from enjoying a hell of a good time while he was living.

I **TOOK** a bus down Sunset Boulevard to L.A. and reached the Temple of the Thou Shalt Society sometime late in the afternoon. It was a huge garish temple which might have been designed by a movie studio for use in a film depicting the future. Its walls were somber and gray with tall narrow windows of crimson glass. On the tremendous rounded dome was a colossal neon sign you could see across the roof-tops for miles—two words of brooding threat—

THOU SHALT!

There had been an afternoon service and people were just leaving. Most of them trudged along silently toward trolleys and busses. There were only a few automobiles—most of those battered and dilapidated, the cars of the poor. There were a few light delivery trucks loaded with families, and one ancient electric resembling a glass box set high on wheels. A pair of old ladies in lavender sat primly behind the glass.

I went up the broad steps to the doorway and spoke to a man who wore a cutaway frock coat and a full black tie.

His face held the feigned sadness of an undertaker as he said good-bye here and there to the departing members of the congregation. He was the head usher, and he frowned at me with annoyance when I spoke.

"I'd like to see Mr. La Farge," I told him.

He shook his head. "Saint Rufus is resting. He has just given a service. His health is not good, and he never sees anyone until after he rests."

"This is a personal matter. Important. It's something about his wife."

The usher glanced around us worriedly, as if fearing some member of the congregation had overheard me. But no one had. They'd all left, even the stragglers, and we were alone on the steps. The usher put a thin hand to his lips and coughed into it politely.

"Perhaps he might see you. What name shall I give?"

"No name."

"None?"

"None," I said.

The usher bowed and left me, but he wasn't gone even a full minute. He returned with a sad, loose-jointed walk, announcing wearily: "Step this way, please."

I followed him down a side aisle in the hall, past count-less rows of empty pews, and finally through a small door behind the pulpit from which Saint Rufus preached his doctrine of death and advised his brethren to shell out.

We went up a short flight of steps in a dark corridor, and the usher opened another door. "You may enter," he said, and promptly closed the door behind me, and de-parted with soft regular footsteps.

I was in the presence of Saint Rufus himself. He was alone in a somber consulting-room, but he was not resting. He sat behind a broad walnut table, smoking a cigar.

"You may be seated," he said, and I groped into a chair and looked at him across the table.

HE WAS something to look at, an amazing spectacle of a man. Not young, maybe over sixty, with a stern but healthy face, almost without lines. His hair was a silvery gray, brows bushy and silver, and under them a pair of deep-set, appealing eyes. He wore a fine flannel suit that was more silver than white. Under the table, his shoes were silver, even his socks silver. The only things not silver about him were the healthy glow of his cheeks, the tan of his hands and a full black ascot scarf about his throat. Even his voice had a silvery ring when he asked: "What was it about my wife?"

"It's about a party she had last night."

"Party?" His features sagged a little, showing lines of weariness and age in a face that hadn't had them when I first came in. "I wouldn't know anything about that," he went on. "I've been out of the city. I haven't been home at all. Too busy with duties of the faith. What kind of a party did you say?"

"A treasure hunt party. They met at the home in Beverly Crest. Sent out in couples following notes. The first couple back was supposed to win prizes. Fur coat for the lady, gold watch for the man. You didn't know about it?"

He shook his head. "I wish she wouldn't hold these parties. She's promised me she wouldn't do this sort of thing. I think you understand." He cleared his throat and made his voice silver again. His eyes held worry far back in their depths. "There was some... some sort of trouble last night?"

"Plenty. A man named Lew Walgreen was at the party. He was killed during the course of it. His partner disappeared. And a Doctor Jelks was supposed to attend the party with his nurse. Now Jelks is dead, and the nurse tried to vanish."

Saint Rufus paled. His face got almost as silvery white as his flannel suit. He fished out a handkerchief and dabbed nervously at his lips. They were moist. His eyes became deep green glass.

"You—you're from the police?"

"Not exactly."

He sat for a moment in silence. His body seemed to wilt. Then he straightened up, and got out of the chair, bracing hands on the table-edge. "Oh. I think I understand. Excuse me a moment."

He turned and opened a cabinet behind the table. Inside it, on a broad shelf, I saw money. Stacks of nickels, dimes, quarters, pennies—stacks and stacks of them. And on a lower shelf more money, this in currency, neatly assorted. Bunches and bunches of currency. And all this probably consisted of his collections over the week-end services.

He selected a fat wad of currency, counting it over. I only saw his back, the shrug of his shoulders. Then he slammed the cabinet door and returned to his chair at the table, with enough money to plug a dike in Holland.

"Let's get this conference over with as quickly as possible," he said, in a flat weary voice. "How much do you want?"

"Want?" I guess I gave him a puzzled stare. "What are you paying for?"

"Silence, of course. Isn't that why you came here?"

"Not at all. I came for information."

His moist lips twitched a little, and a deeper sadness crept into his eyes. "I think you have all the information you require. How much shall I pay?"

I didn't answer that. I said: "Then you know about your wife's party."

"No. Certainly not. And I don't care to hear the sordid details." He counted out several hundred-dollar bills. "How much, please?"

I waved a hand. "Wait a minute. Who's this Lew Walgreen?"

"A friend of my wife. A rather unpleasant friend. You must know that. Probably Mr. Walgreen sent you here."

"No," I corrected, "he didn't. And Doctor Jelks didn't send me either. Is the doctor another friend of your wife's?"

"Yes," he said.

"Your wife has nice friends."

HE FROWNED at that, became somehow pitiful in the way he rolled his eyes. "Please don't be sarcastic. I'm willing to pay your price, but I'd rather not listen to your comments." He shoved a cool thousand dollars across the table to me, and when I didn't touch it he peeled more off the roll and added another thousand dollars to the pile of money within reach of my hand.

I shook my head. "You don't seem to get the idea, Mr. La Farge. I'm not here to shake you down… though you're giving me a hell of a fight with temptation." I pushed the money back across the desk to him. "Information is still what I'm after. What kind of contact did your wife have with Walgreen and the doctor?"

"I don't know," he said. "And I don't care to learn. I'd rather not discuss it at all. My wife means a great deal to me, in spite of her unpleasant behavior. My temple, and the Thou Shalt Society, also mean a great deal to me. I'm willing to pay anything to preserve both. Will you take your money now and leave?"

He fingered the two grand, added more to it, built it into a pile that was like the jack-pot in a high-caliber. Wall Street poker game. He pushed all that money toward me, and resisting it brought sweat to my forehead. I'd gotten into this thing to collect only thirty dollars for Pat Regan and the Red Owl Cab Company. I'd been working like hell to collect only thirty bucks. And now I was having about five thousand dollars shoved at me, by a saint in silver, and I was trying to be noble.

The saint said: "I can't see what difference it makes, about information, and there's nothing you can say that will surprise me. I know my wife had some sort of an affair with this Doctor Jelks, know she then switched to some man named Walgreen, just in the last six months. And I know she's paid him a lot of money. I guess he made love to her. I don't care. When she gets over these… er, incidents… she always comes back to me. So you can't tell me anything that will surprise me. I even know she has a new man now. I don't know who he is, but my lawyers found out she goes to Manhattan Beach. It's undoubtedly some man. But she'll tire of him, like she's tired of the others. She'll come back to me."

"Did you say Manhattan Beach?"

"Yes. Some kind of a love nest down there. It doesn't matter. It doesn't surprise me. How much will you take for your silence? The Thou Shalt Society, as you must understand, can't afford scandals of this kind."

I stood up. I pushed the money back to him once more across the table. That amazed him.

"You won't take it?"

I shook my head, and a faint smile, bitter, flirted across his mouth. "You're a very unusual person," he said. "And if you're not a police officer, or a blackmailer, I can't understand you at all. It's something new. Will you have a cigar?"

It was a long thin smoke wrapped in silver foil, and the paper ring on it bore his name, Rufus La Farge, in crimson letters. The cigars were made especially for him, he said, by one of his flock in the tobacco business in Havana.

He got up and saw me to the door. "Are you going to wreck my temple and my reputation?"

"I'm not making a point of it," I said.

"And my wife," he went on, with almost a glimmer of tears in deep eyes.

"Sheila grew out of a sinful environment, but her eventual reformation is as certain as early death is certain to all of us. We all die, and most of us die sooner than we expect."

The way he said that gave me an odd feeling. I wasn't sure whether it was a statement of his doctrine, or a veiled threat. And I left him—not knowing.

CHAPTER EIGHT

LOVE NEST
FEATHERED WITH LEAD

I GOT out to Manhattan Beach, via trolley, as the light began to fade. Back of the prosperous little beach town were scattered cottages on the bare dunes.

A paved street groped its way through the dunes, past fewer and fewer houses, finally lost its sidewalks in drifts

222 THE COMPLETE CASES OF STEVE MIDNIGHT, VOLUME I

of sand. I turned off the pavement when I saw a lonely sign reading *Seaside Way*, and I followed a muddy dirt road for about half a mile and then found another small stucco cottage built in the dunes. There was no garden in front of it, just a broken garden gate in a leaning picket fence, and a tin mailbox on a rotting wooden post. The faded letters said: *37 Seaside Way.*

I opened the box and took out the letters. There were three of them, and they looked like bills. They were addressed to Mr. George Manning, which didn't surprise me, since I'd been guided there by the registration on his coupé—the one in the garage at Beverly Crest.

I looked up at the house. The shades were pulled at the windows, no light seeped out. The whole place looked like nobody had come near it in years. But, belying that idea, was the fact of mail in the box and the criss-cross of tire tracks in the muddy sand outside.

I bent down and examined the tracks in the fading light. The more recent tracks had been made by one car—since the last fall of rain this afternoon. Fat tires, with deep clear treads. You could see where the car parked, where it backed around to leave. And by the thickness of the tires, the long sweeping pattern they left as the car backed and turned, I had a picture of the great Rolls Royce battleship which I'd last seen leaving Beverly Crest.

I limped through the broken gate, went up to the front stoop of the house and tried the bell. It didn't ring. The button was rusted, the whole electrical system out of commission. I knocked on the panels of the door, but nobody responded. I tried turning the knob. It wouldn't turn.

Rain began to fall now, in far-spaced, pattering drops. Night was closing in fast.

I went around to the back door, tried the knob, and it turned readily.

I entered a rear service porch in which there was a washtub full of empty gin bottles, a rusty water heater, a clothesline with a pair of socks pinned to it. I opened another door into a kitchen, and found more gin bottles, and empty highball glasses which hadn't been washed. I went over to the drainboard and examined the glasses. Two of them had cubes of ice in them—not quite melted.

I pushed open a swing door into the combination living-room-dining-room, and the place wasn't empty. There was a woman in the house, and the first glimpse of her caused me to stop in the swing door. I thought she might sit up and scream, or reach for the phone to call the police.

But she did none of those things. She just lay flat on her back on the sofa, a fur coat thrown carelessly over her body, her face as pallid as death.

I said softly: "Hello. Pardon me...."

She didn't move.

I crossed the room and looked down at a smoothly beautiful face. It had no color at all, except rouge on cheekbones, and on her full lips. A wisp of dyed dark hair had come down over closed eyes, and she lay there on the sofa with no more motion than a hewn log.

I lifted the fur coat and placed the flat of my hand between her breasts. Holding it there, I could feel a little breathing, Soft, throbbing, not rhythmic.

I turned from her, and on a table found a pocket-size case containing a hypodermic needle, and a tiny vial with only a wad of cotton in it—no tablets. The glass cylinder of the needle was wet with moisture. There was a small enamel pan with warm water in it. The water had been boiling not so long ago. That's where the needle had been disinfected.

On the table also, I found a woman's suede handbag with a clasp of diamonds. I opened the bag, and it was full of money. There was also a check-book and club cards and a carbon copy of a voter's registration. But I really didn't have to use any of that stuff to identify her. I already knew who she was. The queen from Shangri-La. The big buxom woman who caused her husband so much trouble. The wife of Saint Rufus.

I EXPLORED, the rest of the bungalow. In the bathroom a tube of shaving soap and a razor in the basin, a man's suit of silk pajamas tossed into the tub. In the bedroom, socks and shirts crumpled on the floor, the bed unmade, a pair of pants hanging flat from the picture moulding—the kind of bedroom where a bachelor lived. A messy collection of clothes, but none of them revealing bloodstains.

I went outside into the backyard, through kitchen and service porch, and found a concrete incinerator.

I opened the steel door on the incinerator and put my hand inside. The ashes were cold in there, but not as wet as they should be. Unless George Manning was a fine housekeeper and only recently burned the last of his combustible rubbish. But having seen the inside of George Manning's bachelor quarters, I didn't think he was a fine housekeeper.

Inside the incinerator there was a smell of burned cloth. I reached my hand deep into the ashes, and pulled out the sole of a leather shoe. It was blackened, charred, and it smelled of gasoline.

I reached deeper and got out only ashes and some hard objects that were buttons. Everything was burned, charred. Everything had the smell of gasoline. A steel belt-buckle was almost warm.

I wiped my hands on my handkerchief, removing the blackness of the ashes, and I discovered that night had settled completely on the dunes.

I returned into the house through the service porch and kitchen. I flicked a switch and the electric lights came on. At the same instant there was a clap of thunder in the sky, and a downpour of rain.

In the living-room Mrs. Rufus La Farge still slept motionless on the sofa, under the fur coat. I found a towel in the bathroom, wet it under the cold-water tap, and returned to Mrs. La Farge and slapped it across her face. She rolled and groaned, turning the shape of her body away from me. But she didn't wake up.

"Come on," I said, "snap out of it...." And another voice came sharply from the noise of rain. "Take your hands off her, you son-of-a———!"

The last time I'd been called that was in the crypt at Valhalla.

HE WAS standing in the kitchen doorway with a Luger in his fist. He still wore the chauffeur's uniform, black boots, the tall-fronted cap with the stiff black visor. Behind him in the door, was a small worried little man carrying a doctor's satchel. His eyes blinked nervously through thick-lensed spectacles, and he didn't like the gun in the chauffeur's fist nor the way it pointed at me.

"If you'll excuse me a moment... my other case... I left it out in the car...."

Manning reached back with his free hand and clutched the little man by the collar. Take it easy, doc."

"But my other case?"

"Baloney," Manning said, "you didn't bring any other case. Just keep the ants out of your pants, doc. You won't get hurt. It's this other guy might get hurt."

I was standing beside the sofa and the sleeping woman. I had the wet towel in my hand, and against George Manning's Luger I felt about as capable of defense as a Boy Scout against the Dover artillery. My heart began to pound and my throat felt parched. I wanted to get away from Manning and the Luger as badly as the little doctor did. But it was the little doctor who acted first.

He swung up the satchel and hit Manning in the face with it. The Luger went off in one sharp explosion, like the hard slam of a door, and glass fell out of a window across the room from me.

The little doctor had a lot of guts—you had to hand him that. He almost hung suspended from the floor with Manning's firm grip still on his collar, but using that for a swinging pivot he kept slapping the satchel against Manning's face, against the Luger, against the fist that held it.

Mrs. Rufus La Farge sat up on the sofa and screamed thickly, like a person choking. She was trying to say something but the thickness of her tongue under the influence of drugs only allowed for choked screams and inhuman babblings.

I rushed across the room in a crouching run, tackled Manning, and went down under his kicking legs and the doctor's.

All three of us rolled and scrambled, and then the little doctor lurched to his feet, snatched up his satchel and his hat, and fled from the house like a rabbit.

That left me alone to fight Manning.

I had a grip on his wrist, and it took all my strength to keep the muzzle of the Luger away from me when it blasted again. The jerk of its firing, the jolt Manning gave me with his shoulder, almost tore my grip loose. Somehow we both struggled to our feet, and both of us were holding the Luger, as if it were some great weight which took both of us to lift.

We stood in the kitchen doorway then, chest to chest, and his face was sweating, inches from mine, his breath hot and panting. I suddenly let go of the wrist let him have the Luger all to himself for a split instant. But in that split instant I braced my legs and slugged him.

The Luger brought down several pounds of crumbling plaster from the ceiling, and George Manning went backwards in a stumbling, falling run. His outflung arm knocked a dozen empty gin bottles off the kitchen drain, and he went to the floor amid breaking glass.

I landed on his belly with both feet, in a running broad jump. The force of my landing threw me across the kitchen and against the stove, but the force of it also put the finish on Manning's fight.

He doubled up on the floor, holding his stomach, gasping for breath like a beached shark. His face turned green and he began to vomit. The Luger fell forgotten from his fingers—he was in too much agony to be bothered with it any more. I got the gun and stowed it on my hip.

I took down the length of clothesline from the service porch and tied his ankles together and his wrists behind his back.

I stepped cautiously into the living-room to see what had happened to Mrs. Rufus La Farge, but nothing at all had happened to her. She was asleep again, under the fur coat, and she still slept there long after the neighbors phoned for Law.

CAPTAIN HOLLISTER arrived in a squad car in time to prevent a pair of local radio officers from clamping steel bracelets on me.

"You been playing cop again, Steve?"

I told him, "I've done a pretty good job of it, at that," and pointed my chin toward the kitchen. "In there you'll find the guy who killed Lew Walgreen."

Hollister said: "Yeah?" He peeked briefly into the kitchen where an ambulance surgeon was using a pulmotor. "Who is he?"

"The name is George Manning."

He strolled across the living-room to the sofa and turned back the fur coat and frowned at the sleeping woman. "Who's this?"

"Mrs. Rufus La Farge. You've probably heard of her husband—the Silver Saint. Manning's the family chauffeur, but recently he's been spreading his duties over a wider area. This place is sort of a love nest."

"Oh. What's the matter with her?"

"Drugged. That's the whole story."

The captain flared a match to fire the soggy end of his cigar. "I'd like to hear it, Steve. If it's not too much trouble."
"Well, she uses dope. I don't know whether her husband knows it or not, but he knows she's always in a lot of trouble because he's been shelling out hush-money to blackmailers."

"You know that for a fact, Steve?"

"I know he tried to pay me five grand this afternoon—with no questions asked."

"Did you take it?" Then he grinned, "Forget that crack, Steve. So she used dope and she got it from that doctor in Playa del Rey—the one you called me about. Doctor Jelks. We found him lynched down there."

"She used to get the dope from Jelks," I said, "but recently she couldn't get enough. After July first there was a new federal law about doctors filling narcotic prescriptions. They couldn't use their old pads any more, they had to use certificates issued by the government. And of course if they filled too many prescriptions, the feds would want to know why, and how, and who. So that left Jelks in a tough spot. The patients that patronized his dope-concession couldn't get enough of it from him now, and the doctor was blackmailed into giving out too many prescriptions."

"Mrs. La Farge?"

I shook my head. "Not her. I don't think so. When Doctor Jelks began to fail her she had enough money to find somebody else. She found Lew Walgreen. Maybe Jelks himself steered her to Walgreen, because Jelks' nurse said she used to see Walgreen hanging around the office and Walgreen once served a federal narcotic rap—you told me that yourself."

"Correct," the captain said.

"And you told me Walgreen was financed into a night club. The answer is Mrs. La Farge. He was supplying the dope the doctor couldn't supply and more. And making it pay."

"Blackmail?"

"I think so. You don't get a night club and a nice car just peddling dope. Not when you've served a rap for it in the past and you're watched closely by parole officers and the feds. So he must've been getting all his financing just from Mrs. La Farge. He demanded too much from her. She decided to get rid of him."

"Shoved him under a freight train?"

I shook my head. "It's a little more complicated than that. She was having this treasure hunt party. You know what that is. Notes hidden at out-of-the-way spots. She wouldn't plant those notes herself—climbing in tombs to hide notes. The chauffeur is the logical one for that task. And Manning went around planting them.

"When he was down at Valhalla, the day before the party, he saw it was a good spot for a bump-off. He was the boyfriend of Mrs. La Farge, and he went back home and told her how nice it would be if Lew Walgreen happened to get killed on the treasure hunt. A lot of railroad bums use Valhalla as a hide-out from yard dicks, and it would be just swell if Walgreen met up with one of these bums and got polished off. With robbery as the motive. And very little police investigation. See what I mean?"

"I see," the captain said. "So they framed the party so Walgreen and his blonde would get the series of notes leading to Valhalla. And Manning hid out there, with gloves and a pick-handle. To finish Walgreen."

"Exactly," I said, "Manning propped a heavy statue, against the door of the tomb. That was to keep the blonde from coming in with Walgreen. One murder was all he wanted. He knew a blonde wouldn't climb in the tomb with Walgreen through a skylight.

"It was a nice scheme, except Walgreen got drunk, and the blonde hired a cab for the rest of the treasure hunt. It was me that climbed into the tomb instead of Walgreen.

Manning saw the mistake and robbed me. That was just to make it still look like some bum had been in the tomb.

"Then Manning left the tomb, and there was no blonde around. She had fled. He went down to the cab and found Walgreen. Passed out. Drunk. So Manning got a swell idea. The murder scheme hadn't soured after all. Walgreen would get robbed and shoved under a train down in the yards. He had to take Walgreen out of the cab in a hurry, because he didn't know when the blonde would come back to the cab. Or the driver would come back. So the train idea seemed fine."

"I get it. And he was already wearing gloves to conceal his prints."

"Sure. But he got blood all over him down there in the freight yards. He had to get rid of his clothes. I found where he burned them. In the incinerator back of this shack."

"How about Jelks? Did Manning lynch the doctor?"

"No," I said. "That was a real suicide, and it gummed up the works. Doctor Jelks was supposed to be on the party himself. Escorting his nurse. Dorothy Tyler. By the way, did you nab her?"

"The feds did," Hollister told me. "They had a tail on her and they picked her up as she was boarding the train. They want her on the same narcotic rap. So Jelks hanged himself, huh?"

"He did. He couldn't face federal prosecution, so he decided to die. Mrs. La Farge couldn't understand why Jelks didn't show up for the party. Either she, or Manning, or both of them, went to the office in Playa del Rey. There he was, dead. And they couldn't have two deaths on the same treasure hunt party, not without a lot of investigation.

So they decided to switch plans and wash their hands completely of both deaths...."

"It seemed easy with the doctor. Mrs. La Farge's name didn't appear on any of the prescriptions, of course. Any narcotics she bought would be under assumed names. But she and Manning searched the doctor's place anyhow, just to be sure, and they discovered a lot of hidden, dusty prescription copies, her name not on any of them. So they placed all the papers on the desk. They left them there so the police would be sure to see the motive for the suicide and not dig too deep on an investigation. And to wash their hands of any connection with Walgreen's death, they just called off the treasure hunt."

The captain frowned darkly. "It was too late for that. The party had started."

"Sure, but you can guess the kind of people who attended it. Probably persons who worked in her husband's racket, those could be bargained with. Any others, like the missing blonde and Dorothy Tyler, could be reached with the La Farge money. So as they filed back to the house from the hunt she made it clear to them that *there hadn't been any party*. She broke it up in a hurry. She even worked out a story whereby she was supposed to be in Palm Springs for the last couple of days—if the police happened to check. Maybe she was even really headed for Palm Springs when she and Manning stopped off here."

"The love nest, huh?"

"Yeah, but I don't think that's why they stopped. Mrs. La Farge needed a bang in the arm, and this is where she took it, along with some of Manning's gin. The combination knocked her cold. That scared Manning. He went out for a doctor, and brought back one."

"A quack," said the captain.

"Yeah, but don't malign him. If the little guy hadn't slapped Manning with a satchel, I wouldn't be here. And you wouldn't have to loan me eighteen bucks."

Hollister scowled. "What for?"

"Meter receipts," I said. "I took twelve dollars and my watch back from Manning. But I'm still shy the fare to Valhalla that the blonde and Lew Walgreen didn't pay me. You wouldn't want me to lose my job, would you, captain? After all I've done for you, what's a little matter of eighteen bucks? You can get it back as soon as you find that blonde."

"You're a funny kind of a blackmailer, Steve. In one afternoon you turn down five grand from a guy that can afford it, and you hook a poor police captain for eighteen fish." He reached for his wallet.

THE WAY it turned out, George Manning pleaded guilty to dodge the death penalty and get life at Folsom. The court handed Mrs. Rufus La Farge ten years in the State Women's Pen.

Saint Rufus sadly informed the press: "I shall fight on alone, without Sheila, and in my great loneliness I shall continue to preach the doctrine of the Unavoidable, Unalterable, Inescapable—Death."

So it worked out fine. Just the blonde on the treasure hunt was still missing—and the eighteen bucks I owed Hollister.

The blonde, Maybelle Knapp, former torch singer for Lew Walgreen's club, had dropped out of sight completely.

One afternoon in early spring I was covering Olie Greenberg's run and I picked up a fare at a swank apartment house in Westwood. The fare was a blonde, and dressed in about a thousand dollars' worth of fur. Diamonds sparkled on her fingers and the scent of high-priced perfume almost wafted me to sleep.

I said. "Hello, Maybelle. I see you won the mink coat after all."

Her red mouth sagged wide. Her lips trembled. "Come upstairs," she said.

So we went up to her apartment, a beautiful place with carpet like fine lawn and soft ivory walls and furnishings showing the touch of an expensive decorator. She slammed the door and faced me.

"All right. How much do you want?"

"Just the eighteen bucks you owe me."

"You mean only eighteen dollars?"

"That's all," I said.

She got a roll of bills out of her purse, peeled off a twenty, and said: "Keep the change. The rest is a tip."

"Thanks," I said.

"Are you sure that's all you want?"

I glanced down at a crystal glass ashtray on a carved walnut table. In it were the stubs of several cigars—cigars that had been long, thin, and costly, from Havana. And there were crumpled foil wrappings with bands bearing the name of Rufus La Farge.

I said to the blonde: "One other thing, lady. When you see the Silver Saint, tell him a sucker who refused five grand sends regards. And hopes he won't be too lonely in his womanless world of remorse."

ABOUT THE AUTHOR

BORN IN San Francisco, where I had an early ambition to be a gripman on a cable car. Later moved to a small town in the Sierra Nevada Mountains, the historic country of the California Gold Rush.

Next south to Los Angeles. And this is always the most traitorous move a native San Franciscan can make. Frisco, forgive me; I'm still fond of the Old Town. Started writing stories as a kid. Enthusiastically wrote my way through, and almost out of, several schools. My university experience was largely fall attendance at football games. Have been a mail clerk and an automobile salesman.

Once went to New York with the intention of taking magazine offices by storm; had an idea my services would be invaluable to some lucky editorial staff. But no storm darkened the Manhattan sky, no job opened, and magazines were published just as when Butler lived three thousand miles away.

Some Hollywood-earned gold sobbed in the Butler pockets, crying to be spent, and Europe was just a few thousand miles across the Atlantic. So Butler boarded a boat. And when he hit New York again, sometime later, no crying sounds emanated from the region of his pockets.

Somewhere along the line I started work in Hollywood movie studios—not acting, though I once picked up a few bucks that way. My work in the flicker-factories was with stories, both editorial and writing ends of the game, and mostly the former. Altogether I did about an eight-year stretch at this.

My first published magazine stories appeared in *Dime Detective*. I hope all the *Dime Detective* readers enjoy the yarns half as much as my wife does.